# The Spinster's Last Dance

## One Night in Blackhaven
## Book 7

# MARY LANCASTER

DRAGONBLADE PUBLISHING, INC.

## ARE YOU SIGNED UP FOR DRAGONBLADE'S BLOG?

You'll get the latest news and information on exclusive giveaways, exclusive excerpts, coming releases, sales, free books, cover reveals and more.

Check out our complete list of authors, too!

No spam, no junk. That's a promise!

### Sign Up Here

www.dragonbladepublishing.com

*Dearest Reader;*

*Thank you for your support of a small press. At Dragonblade Publishing, we strive to bring you the highest quality Historical Romance from some of the best authors in the business. Without your support, there is no 'us', so we sincerely hope you adore these stories and find some new favorite authors along the way.*

*Happy Reading!*

CEO, Dragonblade Publishing

# Additional Dragonblade books by Author Mary Lancaster

## One Night in Blackhaven Series
The Captain's Old Love (Book 1)
The Earl's Promised Bride (Book 2)
The Soldier's Impossible Love (Book 3)
The Gambler's Last Chance (Book 4)
The Poet's Stern Critic (Book 5)
The Rake's Mistake (Book 6)
The Spinster's Last Dance (Book 7)

## The Duel Series
Entangled (Book 1)
Captured (Book 2)
Deserted (Book 3)
Beloved (Book 4)
Haunted (Novella)

## Last Flame of Alba Series
Rebellion's Fire (Book 1)
A Constant Blaze (Book 2)
Burning Embers (Book 3)

## Gentlemen of Pleasure Series
The Devil and the Viscount (Book 1)
Temptation and the Artist (Book 2)
Sin and the Soldier (Book 3)
Debauchery and the Earl (Book 4)
Blue Skies (Novella)

## Pleasure Garden Series
Unmasking the Hero (Book 1)

Unmasking Deception (Book 2)
Unmasking Sin (Book 3)
Unmasking the Duke (Book 4)
Unmasking the Thief (Book 5)

### Crime & Passion Series
Mysterious Lover (Book 1)
Letters to a Lover (Book 2)
Dangerous Lover (Book 3)
Lost Lover (Book 4)
Merry Lover (Novella)
Ghostly Lover (Novella)

### The Husband Dilemma Series
How to Fool a Duke (Book 1)

### Season of Scandal Series
Pursued by the Rake (Book 1)
Abandoned to the Prodigal (Book 2)
Married to the Rogue (Book 3)
Unmasked by her Lover (Book 4)
Her Star from the East (Novella)

### Imperial Season Series
Vienna Waltz (Book 1)
Vienna Woods (Book 2)
Vienna Dawn (Book 3)

### Blackhaven Brides Series
The Wicked Baron (Book 1)
The Wicked Lady (Book 2)
The Wicked Rebel (Book 3)
The Wicked Husband (Book 4)
The Wicked Marquis (Book 5)
The Wicked Governess (Book 6)
The Wicked Spy (Book 7)
The Wicked Gypsy (Book 8)
The Wicked Wife (Book 9)
Wicked Christmas (Book 10)

The Wicked Waif (Book 11)
The Wicked Heir (Book 12)
The Wicked Captain (Book 13)
The Wicked Sister (Book 14)

**Unmarriageable Series**
The Deserted Heart (Book 1)
The Sinister Heart (Book 2)
The Vulgar Heart (Book 3)
The Broken Heart (Book 4)
The Weary Heart (Book 5)
The Secret Heart (Book 6)
Christmas Heart (Novella)

**The Lyon's Den Series**
Fed to the Lyon

**De Wolfe Pack: The Series**
The Wicked Wolfe
Vienna Wolfe

**Also from Mary Lancaster**
Madeleine (Novella)
The Others of Ochil (Novella)

# Prologue

WHEN THE VALE twins, Leona and Lawrence, called their first ever family meeting, their prime worry was Julius, their eldest brother, who, they reasoned, had no need to retire from life so completely. Reviving the estate and committing to charities were important, but surely there should be more to his life than this? He was not an old man! So, as a beginning, they needed their siblings' help to get him to attend the Blackhaven ball. They won that argument without much difficulty, for they all thought the world of Julius.

It was Leona who said to her twin later on that evening, "Delilah agreed too easily."

Delilah was their eldest sister, a little too sharp of mind and tongue and entirely formidable when she wished to be. She was also the nearest thing they had known to a mother, and they loved her to bits.

"Did she?" Lawrence raised one thoughtful eyebrow. "Perhaps she *wants* to go the ball. After all, she often attended such parties with Papa. Though I'm not sure the Blackhaven assembly rooms compare with embassy balls in the capitals of the world." He frowned. "You don't think she'll wriggle out of it, do you?"

Leona shook her head. "No. She wants to go for her own reasons."

"Well, as long as she *does* go, it suits our purposes. And it would be excellent if she met some kind and dashing man there."

"It would, but is it likely she would do anything about it? She has been telling us for years that she's happily on the shelf."

"Well, she *is* thirty," Lawrence pointed out.

"Why does that matter for a woman and not for a man? Julius is six and thirty, and we all agree he should have some romance and fun in his life. Why should Delilah not?"

"No reason except she doesn't seem to want it," Lawrence replied. He thought about it. "She is as beautiful as Felicia in her own way."

"And as clever. Yet she gets no chance to be herself, to *shine* as herself."

"That is true," Lawrence agreed. "Everything was for Papa or for us. She can be quite intimidating, though."

"So can Julius. And Roderick."

"Less expected in a woman."

"Hmm. Perhaps. It's her protection, though, in case people look down their noses at her for being illegitimate."

"No one looks down their noses at *us*."

"They will," Leona said ruefully. "So far, we put it off by telling everyone about us first. Nobody regards us as grown up. Delilah is, and she deserves respect and appreciation with her happiness."

"Then maybe she will find all of those at the ball. Or at least open the way to finding them. It will be an excellent beginning for the family."

"Agreed," said Leona. She grinned. "And it will be more fun for us."

# Chapter One

DELILAH VALE WANTED to waltz.

Just one final, enjoyable dance in farewell to her youth, and then she would step discreetly back onto the shelf and turn to face her new life. It was not so much a decision as an acknowledgment of reality. She had turned thirty, and her opportunities for marriage, always slim, were now nonexistent. She didn't mourn their passing—there was no point, and in any case, she had always been too independent in spirit to seek the subservience of matrimony. She merely wanted to mark the boundary in some way, an ending of the old, the beginning of the new.

For the first time ever, she and her siblings were all living together in their childhood home of Black Hill. There was both fun and security in that, but she knew very well it was a mere interlude, while everyone drew breath and found their own ways forward. Delilah had found hers, and she wanted to dance into it.

Her siblings all seemed to be dancing, even her brothers, those of them she could see, and her widowed sister Felicia, who regarded it as her prime duty to introduce prospective partners to everyone else. Delilah was no debutante. She would find her own partner in her own way.

Rising, she picked up her wine glass and strolled around the room, watching the dancers with an odd twinge of melancholy. Nostalgia, no doubt. She had frequently accompanied her diplomat father to important state events all over Europe, even played hostess at embassy receptions. That kind of company, that undercurrent of power and decision beneath the amiability, was what she missed most.

Well, soon she would be able to travel again. For now, there was this ball at the Blackhaven assembly rooms, where, surely, she would find her last dance with a partner of her own choosing. She was a diplomat's daughter and could arrange anything.

She spotted her little sister Lucy laughing happily as she twirled down the line with her enthusiastic companion. It made Delilah smile as she reached the pillar that had been her goal. From here, with only the musicians' gallery above and a curtained alcove behind her, she could watch the dancers more discreetly and identify just the right waltz partner.

It should be easier than she had once feared, for the ball was well attended, and by many distinguished people, such as the Earl of Braithwaite, who lived in the local castle with his family, and several town dandies who seemed to have accompanied ailing relatives to take the famous Blackhaven waters. There was a scattering of red-and-gold-coated army officers, presumably from the regiment stationed nearby, while the ladies were almost universally well dressed in expensive silks and jewels that sparkled under the chandeliers.

It could have been a ball in London, or Paris, Vienna or St. Petersburg, Madrid or Rome... A hundred different scenes merged in her mind, blurring the movement of the dancers so that she could no longer make out their faces or admire their grace. Suddenly, it was like a puzzle from which half the pieces were missing and the rest had been covered with disintegrating gauze.

*Oh, the devil!* It was happening again, and most inconveniently. She drew back fully behind the pillar and closed her eyes. Perhaps she could still will it away.

"Surely you cannot be hiding?" a light male voice speculated close by. The timbre seemed to soak through her skin in an oddly pleasing way, and it was several seconds before she realized he might be addressing her. "Or are the rest of us so gruesome you cannot bear to look?"

She opened her eyes. A tall man in smart evening dress stood before her, with parts of him missing. The parts she *could* see appeared to be handsome. She tilted her head in an effort to see the rest, but she could not catch the whole man at once.

"I would gladly look, sir, were I given the opportunity." She spoke her mind and generally did, though for once she had no real desire to be fully understood.

Too late. Something had changed in his posture. And in his voice, no longer so light or teasing. "Are you quite well, ma'am?"

"Perfectly," she replied. If he would get out of her way, she could retreat into the alcove until her sight returned to normal. "Excuse me. I believe I would like a moment's quiet."

Unexpectedly, he took her free hand and placed it on his arm. For a moment, she dug in her heels, reluctant to move when she could not see properly where she was going.

"There is an alcove, just here," he said, his voice oddly soothing. She advanced with him, saw the curtain swish dizzyingly, and made out two chairs and a small table between. The man handed her civilly into one chair and took the glass from her fingers, placing it on the table. "May I fetch a companion for you?"

"No!" The word erupted with unexpected force, taking both of them, she suspected, somewhat aback. "Um, I mean, I shall be right as rain in just a moment. My thanks, sir. I shall do better alone."

"You have a migraine?"

"Oh, no, nothing like that. There is no pain, and I shall not faint or have a fit of the vapors. You may leave me with a clear conscience."

"I find I don't wish to leave you at all."

"I don't believe you have a choice, sir, as a gentleman, since I have made my wishes plain."

"All true gentlemen are flexible," he said, sitting down in the other chair. "You may ignore me until you feel more the thing."

"And then?" she asked, allowing an irritable edge into her voice.

"Oh, then you may scold me at your leisure—or, if you prefer, whoever it was you were seeking with such assiduity."

She laughed. "And, of course, ladies of a certain age exist only to scold."

"Ladies of a…" He sounded both amused and flabbergasted. His voice turned light and quizzical once more. "Is the cause not character rather than age?"

"You wish to insult me further? Carry on."

"I meant the character of the scoldee as much as the scolder," he said mildly. "Who were you looking for, and what has he done? If you require a champion—"

She turned and stared at him. She could see most of him now, and he really was handsome, in a refined, understated sort of way—much like his evening clothes, which spoke of good taste and gentlemanly restraint.

"What, you'll rush over and threaten to run him through?" she said in contemptuous disbelief. "On my word alone?"

"Good heavens, no. Merely point him out and I'll give him a dashed good—er…scold."

"I don't know anymore which of us is making fun of the other."

"Oh, I'm not making fun of anyone, merely talking nonsense for the sake of distraction." He turned his head toward her and smiled. The effect was devastating. "Ah, there you are."

She gazed into steady, smiling gray eyes, and memory tugged.

"Have we met?" he asked.

"I cannot think where. I do not go out in Society." As she remembered where she was, heat seeped into her cheeks. "As a rule," she added.

"A rule I am very glad you broke." He rose to his feet and bowed. "And now I shall leave you in peace as you originally requested. Madam."

She inclined her head with a hint of mockery. "Sir."

DENZIL TALBOT, FIRST Baron Linfield, strolled out of the alcove with very mixed emotions. She was not at all what he had expected. Too beautiful and too vulnerable, she had struggled to see him, her eyes darting, unfocused, blinking as though to clear them. Of course, the excuse of taking her somewhere quiet until she recovered was a gift to him, and he had happily made use of it. But he hadn't expected to like her.

Nor could he shake off that odd feeling that they had met before.

Perhaps they had. He had encountered her father often enough. He should not have been surprised to discover Sir George Vale's daughter was a woman of character... Even if she was a traitor.

Well, with luck, he would also have made an impression on her, so that she would look forward to their next encounter, even if only to spar. He looked forward to it himself, and not just because it was duty. No wonder he was uneasy as he skirted the dancers.

He found his sister Elaine chatting to a couple from the hotel, though as they greeted someone else in passing, she whispered to him, "Antonia has met an old friend."

Antonia Macy was Elaine's companion who had traveled with them to Vienna and back, along with her young son. It was an odd arrangement by most standards, but it worked for all concerned.

"Is that good?" Denzil asked.

"It seems to have shaken her up," Elaine replied with odd complacence.

"And *that* is good?"

"She is too young to settle down as companion to a spinster."

A familiar twinge of guilt twisted through him. Elaine was only a spinster because she had given up a settled life in order to travel with him wherever the Foreign Office sent him, from the Americas to the Ottoman Empire. He was well aware she added to his comfort—and to his career—which had certainly left him free from the constraints of marriage.

He knew she had enjoyed herself in the process, but now she was no longer young, and her recent spell of exhaustion, which had provided the excuse for this visit to Blackhaven, was also a genuine worry to him. Elaine needed a settled home.

"Can I fetch you some wine?" he asked, including the hotel couple in his offer. When no one took him up on it, he left them to continue their comfortable gossip and sauntered off in search of his next prey.

He found her—at least, he supposed it was her—walking arm in arm with Blackhaven's acerbic physician, Nicholas Lampton. Denzil had made a point of consulting Dr. Lampton about Elaine, for two very good reasons. One, of course, was Elaine's health and the benefits of the local waters. The other was the doctor's wife.

"Ah, doctor," he greeted Lampton with a smile. "I'm very glad to see you do make the odd escape from the demands of your patients."

"Oh, I just neglect them," Lampton said.

"Nicholas!" exclaimed his companion. "You will have no practice if you keep saying such things!"

Denzil laughed. "Fear not, ma'am, I am in no danger of believing him."

"My love, I don't believe you are acquainted with Lord Linfield," Lampton said. "He is a distinguished diplomat, lately come home from Vienna. My lord, this is my wife, Princess Elizabeth, formerly of Rheinwald."

"Mrs. Lampton will do very well," the princess said dryly, offering her hand, which Denzil bowed over.

Somehow, it fitted with the character of Blackhaven that the local doctor was married to a princess.

"Delighted to make your acquaintance, Mrs. Lampton," he said, instinctively sensing which title pleased her more. "I believe I met your brother-in-law in Vienna."

Her eyes changed very subtly, enough to tell him she did not care for her brother-in-law, which was a relief to Denzil.

"He was certainly there."

"It did not seem fair to me that your son was disinherited."

"It suits me that he is away from the whole toxic situation in Rheinwald. When he is grown, he may make his own decisions."

"Quite."

"Join us, if you wish," Lampton said, pausing beside a table where a good-looking couple sat. "Do you know our vicar and his wife, Mr. and Mrs. Grant? Grants, Lord Linfield."

The Grants too were an interesting couple, he a one-time army officer turned country vicar, she a formerly scandalous leader of the London *ton*'s fast set. Denzil, always happy in unusual and charming company, found it easy to make friends and to find a moment to draw Mrs. Lampton into a deeper conversation about German politics.

"Perhaps you also know the Princess of Hazburg?"

"I did, and I like her," Mrs. Lampton said frankly. "The congress did the right thing in allowing her to keep the principality. She is the choice of her people and an excellent ally."

"It disappointed her half-brother, Prince Karl," Denzil pointed out. "Who is not without his own following."

"But too autocratic and likely to bring the country to the verge of revolution—or ruin. Prussia would then swallow Hazburg and upset the balance of power."

Denzil smiled. "You retain a firm grasp of the situation."

"I might have no influence, but I never lacked understanding." Her gaze went beyond him, and she smiled. "Mrs. Maitland, how do you do?"

She was greeting a rather beautiful young lady who, Denzil

knew, was the widowed sister of Delilah Vale. He rose to bow over her hand, and since Mrs. Lampton had turned aside to answer some remark of Kate Grant's, he invited Mrs. Maitland to dance.

She looked surprised. "Oh, why not? I have missed dancing, though I am really here to chaperone my sisters."

Mrs. Maitland danced with enthusiasm, like a child suddenly released out of doors on a previously wet Sunday afternoon. She conversed cheerfully and amusingly whenever they came together. It wasn't difficult to see her father in her. He was much too subtle to ask directly about her sister Delilah, although he gathered rather more from her chatter than she was probably aware.

The Vale siblings had come home to discover their family estate on the verge of ruin. Sir Julius, who had inherited it, was doing his best to repair the damage, with the aid of his brother Cornelius, a land steward by profession, while the other siblings contributed what money or skills they had in making Black Hill into a home. Denzil gathered that this was good for everyone in the family, leaving him with an impression that they were all healing in their own way from unspecified troubles—which might have been simply mourning for their larger-than-life parent, who had dragged them all around the world with him at some time or another.

This caused a faint bell to ring at the back of his memory, but before he could pursue it, the dance came to a close.

"Allow me to escort you back to your family," he said. "Or to Mrs. Lampton, if you prefer."

"It had better be to my family, who should be over *there*. I should make sure Lucy..."

Denzil missed the rest because he had just caught sight of Delilah Vale gliding across the room at some speed. He was about to steer Mrs. Maitland in that direction and increase their own pace in order to intercept Delilah when, rather to his surprise, Mrs. Maitland made the adjustments of her own accord.

As they met, a hunted look crossed Delilah's face. She did not look at him—quite deliberately, he suspected.

"Oh, Delly, have you been dancing?" Mrs. Maitland said as though surprised to run into her. "So have I. This is Lord Linfield, who is visiting the town with his sister for the benefits of the waters. My lord, my sister, Miss Vale."

Delilah responded with a distant curtsey, and yet a hint of color stained her cheeks. "How do you do, my lord?"

"How do *you* do, Miss Vale?"

"Ah, excuse me," Mrs. Maitland exclaimed, and shot off, leaving them alone together in the midst of the swarms milling across the dance floor.

"We are not supposed to have met?" he guessed.

Her chin lifted. "My sister is on duty, you might say, believing that she alone can ensure that the rest of us enjoy the ball, which involves making sure we all have dance partners—respectable ones, in Lucy's case. Since I am no Society debutante, Felicia and I have an agreement that she does not drag appalled young men over to dance with me."

"Is that your way of telling me you do not wish to dance? Before I embarrass myself by asking?"

"I'm not sure you ever embarrass yourself, Lord Linfield."

"It's the impression I like to create, but, sadly, a damnable lie."

Amusement crept into her eyes, which was something of a relief, for in truth he hadn't been sure what to make of her, or been able to tell if his charm was entirely wasted on her.

"How did you know?" she asked abruptly. "About my sight?"

"It was only a guess. I used to suffer migraines as a youth. Have you consulted a physician?"

"Goodness, no, it is hardly debilitating." She met his gaze. "But I would be grateful if you did not mention it to my family."

"I won't," he agreed, "though it puzzles me why *you* don't."

"Do you tell *your* siblings everything?"

Instinctively, he glanced toward Elaine, who once more had

Antonia Macy by her side. "No."

"The next dance is a waltz," she said casually. "You should hurry to secure the young lady of your choice."

Now that was interesting. She was providing him with an excuse to leave, and yet at the same time almost prompting him to ask *her*.

He felt his lips twitch of their own accord. "You are quite right. Would you do me the honor, Miss Vale?"

She smiled at him, and all the air seemed to leave his lungs. "Thank you, my lord. I believe I will."

And that was when the memory slid into place. He *had* seen her dancing, and smiling like *that*... Where?

# Chapter Two

D ENZIL LED HER out onto the floor, and the orchestra struck
up the introduction to the waltz. She was quite tall for a
woman and fitted perfectly into his arms. She felt unexpectedly
fragile, despite the delectable curves. And she waltzed divinely,
gracefully, giving herself to the music.

Memory slotted into place, and he smiled. "St. Petersburg.
The summer of 1806."

She blinked. "*That* is where we met? I was certainly there
with my father. Why do I not remember you better?"

"Oh, I was very junior then, and I don't believe we actually
met. I only attended the ball to pass an urgent message to your
father. I was not invited. I was only plain Denzil Talbot in those
days, a very minor functionary of the British Embassy."

"You inherited the title from your father?"

"Oh, no. It was conferred upon me after Vienna."

"Not such a minor functionary nowadays, then?"

"All things are relative."

"And yet you remember me."

He thought about it and stuck to the truth. "It was your poise
that impressed me. I thought someone so young and lovely, with
that much self-possession, must be royalty, or at least of the most
powerful aristocracy."

She laughed. "If only you knew how amusing that is. I was

merely used to the company of such people through my father. In those days, I knew my place was to help him."

"And now?"

"Everything changes," she said a little dreamily. The smile lingered on her lips, sweet and oddly sensual at the same time.

"How is it you remember me at all?" he asked, more in an effort to understand her than because he really wanted to know. In truth, he had always been able to make an impression when he chose to, and he had been young and ambitious ten years ago in St. Petersburg.

"Now that it's coming back to me... You were different," she said.

He blinked.

She smiled. "It was a long time ago. I remember you seemed...intense. And yet fun. I believe I hoped you would dance with me, so of course, I didn't look at you again after those first moments. And when I did look, you had gone. But I was right then—I like the way you dance. I'm glad I chose you tonight."

"I thought I chose you."

"Only because I gave you the opportunity."

"No," he said, "but let us not quarrel over it. Why *did* you choose me?"

She considered. "Perhaps because when I saw you before I wanted to dance with you. There seems a pleasing cycle to it now, a closing of the circle. It is a good way to end."

"End?" he repeated, startled. "Miss Vale, are you truly ill?"

"Oh, goodness, no. It is merely the end of an era for me. The ending of my old life and the beginning of the new. Rejoice, my lord. This is my last dance."

"Ever?" he said cautiously, for he distrusted the self-deprecation, the mockery in her voice.

"Ever," she confirmed.

"But why?"

"I am thirty years old. I am a confirmed spinster and I wish to stand on my own two feet."

"I am almost five and thirty and have no intention of giving up dancing."

"You are a man, not a spinster who wishes to earn her own living."

Was that what it was about? Payment? Money? It did not fit with the dreamy girl in his arms, her body swaying to the music, following his every step with grace and joy.

"It would be a crime against nature if you never danced again. Can you not do both? After all, the dancing would still be your choice, as is, presumably, whatever you choose to do to earn your living."

"At my age, if one dances, one is accused of pathetically hunting a husband. Rest easy, my lord, I am not. But I do not wish to be mistaken for any such thing when I have only my reputation to protect me."

"Then you plan to leave your family?" he said slowly, his waning suspicions re-aroused.

"Eventually. When my twin siblings no longer need me. The older ones will all marry or find their own way in the world. A spinster hanging around the house like a bad smell—"

"Miss Vale," he protested, only half laughing. "Trust me, no one would accuse you of that!"

"I would," she said.

"So what is your alternative? To take up a position in someone else's household? Perhaps as companion to a capricious old lady?"

She shook her head. "That would not do for me."

"Oh, I don't know. My sister has a companion who travels with us. In fact, she is with us tonight."

"Is your sister a capricious old lady?"

"No, she is the best of sisters," he said ruefully. "And very happy with her companion. So what is it you have in mind?"

"What I am good at."

His pulse had quickened. Perhaps it was the movement of the dance. Or it might have been her air of confessional. Was she about to admit her sins to him? Would it really be that easy? "Go on."

"Organization," she said, surprising him all over again. "I can organize people's lives, libraries, papers, according to whatever purpose is necessary. I am also fluent in several languages, so I can act as translator as well as secretary, and as interpreter at personal meetings."

"And there is call for such work? In a private capacity?"

"I have two clients already. One who sent me a huge parcel of haphazard notes to organize for a book he is writing. Another requires translation work in the short term, and in the long, he will need my organizational skills."

*Got you*, thought Denzil, although he felt no triumph. From her openness, she was a dupe rather than a deliberate traitor, but it would amount to the same thing. Something like disappointment churned in his innards. He rather liked this odd woman, and she was causing chaos, whether deliberately or not.

"What does your family think of your plans?"

"They do not yet know," she admitted.

"Something else you want me to keep from them?"

"I can't imagine the conversation will come up, should you ever meet."

"Then you are content with your arrangements?"

"So far."

"Hmm… And are these clients Blackhaven people?"

"Oh, no. I advertised my services. My clients send me work and instructions by post."

"You are very…enterprising," he observed.

"Perhaps you will remember me if your department has need of such skills."

"Oh, I will remember you," he promised.

Her lips twitched, as though she caught the irony in his words—under no circumstances could he allow her anywhere near Foreign Office documents—but she did not appear to be troubled. Instead, she seemed to lean into the music once more, and he spun her around and around just to make her smile and to feel the quickening of her warm, lithe body that never quite touched his. He had an urge to stroke the curve of her waist, to draw her so close she would rest against his chest, his hips...

He had been quite wrong about the girl he had glimpsed ten years ago. Although she retained the unique outward poise he had noticed then, she possessed no power at all. He had yet to make up his mind whether she was actively seeking it, or just blundering into it. Either way, she would have to be stopped, preferably in a manner that did not reflect badly on the great diplomat, Sir George Vale, her late father.

The music was coming to an end. He had no doubts that he could keep her by his side, inspire more confidences, even persuade her to dance again despite her insistence that this was the last.

She sighed, her breath whispering against his cheek as the dance ended. And yet her smile was dazzling as she curtseyed to him, depriving him of breath all over again.

"Thank you, Lord Linfield," she murmured. "That was perfect. Goodbye." And she slipped away from him into the crowd before he could even reply.

SHORTLY AFTER HIS dance with Miss Vale, Denzil enjoyed an amusing reunion with old friends from Vienna days. The Gaunt family had always been delightful. Its head, Lord Launceton, now played up his Russian connection, wearing his Cossack uniform and saber to annoy the more staid of his English critics. He was still a beguiling mixture of hedonism and family responsibility, while his wife was simply delightful, and her sister, fulfilling her early promise, was stunningly beautiful.

Denzil was not best pleased to be interrupted by a smiling matron claiming acquaintance with him.

"My lord, what an unexpected pleasure to discover you in Blackhaven! How do you do?"

"How do *you* do, ma'am?" he responded civilly, racking his brains in an effort to recall who the devil she was. Normally, he had an excellent memory for names and faces, so he suspected they had never been formally introduced. On the other hand, she did seem vaguely familiar, so they had possibly attended the same party in London.

Still smiling, the woman reached behind her and all but dragged a blushing young lady to her side.

"You remember my daughter, Marjorie, of course."

His instinct to crush the mother's pretensions withered in face of the daughter's clear misery. The girl had a pretty enough face, marred by excessive, nervous embarrassment, even fear.

He found himself smiling kindly and lying. "Of course. How do you do, Miss Marjorie?"

She fell into stammering disorder, which clearly infuriated her mother. Denzil, with the same foolish impulse that caused him to rescue abused dogs and donkeys, immediately asked the daughter to dance and knew he would regret it.

The girl looked both stunned and relieved, while the mother beamed with delight. Dutifully, Denzil led the girl into the country dance set beginning to form.

"I'm so sorry," Miss Marjorie whispered. "My mother believes you must remember us, but I can tell you do not."

"I meet so many people," Denzil explained. "And am happy to do so. And since we are now fellow conspirators, perhaps you could remind me of your name."

"Marjorie Match, my lord. My mother is Mrs. Match, and my brother—"

"Mr. Match?" he guessed.

A fugitive smile passed her lips and vanished into alarm. "I'm sorry. I have such a dull habit of stating the obvious!"

"Not at all. I did ask. Forgive my inappropriate sense of humor. Are you enjoying the ball?"

"Oh yes!" Her lie was obvious. Clearly she was hating it, not least her dance with him, which she imagined had been forced by her mother.

When the dance began, she looked unflatteringly relieved, since it meant she was not obliged to talk to him for most of the time. Denzil felt sorry for her, but since he so clearly terrified her, as soon as the dance ended, he thanked her, escorted her back to her mother, and effaced himself.

"At least he danced with you," Marjorie's mother said with a sniff. "But really, Marjorie, could you not have made an effort to keep him with you a little longer? He might have asked you again."

"Oh, no, he wouldn't. I am not nearly clever enough for him. I don't understand most of what he says."

"You are not meant to be clever, merely decorative, submissive, and capable of running his house."

"But Mama, I could not be *comfortable* in his house."

"You would learn to be. And you needn't look so terrified, because he is hardly ever *in* any of his houses. He is someone important in the Foreign Office and is constantly abroad. Rich and absent, he would be perfect for you."

Marjorie, who had not looked on either Lord Linfield or marriage in quite those terms before, wondered if she might survive the institution after all. Especially if it took her away from her mother. A peaceful home was suddenly very attractive.

Maybe the thing could be achieved, she decided some time later. She cast a glance around the room, seeking him out, and eventually found him sitting beside a very beautiful lady, older and much more elegant than Marjorie. He was smiling, though it made him no less intimidating.

"*She* is lovely," Marjorie murmured with just a shade of envy.

"I cannot compete with her. Unless she is already married to someone else?"

"Who?" her mother demanded, following her gaze. Somehow, Mama always knew who everyone was. "Oh, dear me, no. That is a person you will *never* encounter. My dear, she is only Delilah Vale, the illegitimate scion of a very ramshackle family, and if he is courting her, it is *not* for marriage! That is where *you* come in, and for his considerable fortune, you will kindly make the effort! We came all this way to secure him, and that is what you will do."

"Yes, Mama," Marjorie said, sighing.

THERE WAS SOMETHING about Lord Linfield, Delilah had acknowledged as she made her way away from him through the crowd of retreating dancers. Perhaps the contrast between the intensity of his eyes and the lightness of his easy manners. Or just that she liked the way he looked. And danced. Feelings and desires she had almost forgotten held her in their grip as they waltzed. He was perfect.

*How sad, how lonely, to say goodbye.*

And yet that was what she did, though with unexpectedly sharp regret.

She knew in her heart that nothing had changed. She was aware he had danced with her because she had given him little choice. If he wasn't laughing at her, he would have been bored with her. And when she saw him almost immediately with other ladies, it merely confirmed what she already knew.

It didn't matter. She had said farewell to her youth in style. And now she would embrace spinsterhood in her own way. She sat at the shadowy end of her family's table, making occasional forays to keep Lucy under her eye. Even before they lost her, she had been up to something. Delilah knew the signs.

Actually, they were all up to something. Julius fled before supper. Roderick was so tense he should have splintered. Felicia and Cornelius were both excited, while Aubrey, mischievous and predatory, appeared to be in pursuit of the most beautiful girl in the room.

For Delilah, the ball was over. Now, she merely sat it out, waiting for tomorrow, when her work could begin.

"Pardon me, are these seats taken?" drawled a grating female voice.

"I'm afraid so, ma'am," Delilah replied politely. "My family…" Words and thoughts both dried up as the woman smiled at her. Tall, slender and yet large-bosomed, she wore a low-cut gown of daring, vibrant scarlet with a black lace train. Her face was carefully painted, as ladies of the previous generation sometimes did—subtle but unmistakable in this case, enabling Delilah to recognize her right away.

"Well now, I count as family," the woman said with a trilling laugh. "Here we are—Reggie, put the champagne down here. Oh, did you bring a glass for my Lah-Lah?"

The "Lah-Lah" still made her cringe.

"You gave me the name Delilah, Mother," she pointed out. "Could you not bring yourself to use it?"

"Oh, hush, Lah-Lah. Call me Nell, or all your highborn friends will hear and cut the acquaintance with you. Here she is, Reggie—doesn't she look more beautiful than ever?"

"Charming, utterly charming," replied a beaming Reginald Miller, once the handsomest actor ever to tread the boards of a London theatre, now running a little to seed. But he was so talented and good-natured that everyone pretended not to notice, and he still got most of the leading roles he wanted.

Delilah had nothing against him, except that he was married—probably—to Nell. Even Nell herself had exhausted most of Delilah's hurt, tears, and anger long ago, leaving only weary, slightly irritable tolerance behind. Or so Delilah believed. Hardly the maternal type, Nell had dumped Delilah on her married father at the age of six months. Almost thirty years later, Delilah could acknowledge that she had enjoyed a much better life with George Vale. However, the realization that neither Julius and Roderick's nor Cornelius, Felicia, and Aubrey's mother was hers had hit her child self hard. As had Nell's neglect.

No, Nell was not maternal. But she still thought she had a right to buzz in and out of Delilah's life whenever she chose, which was, on average, every five years or so, usually when she wanted something from George. She had even turned up at the funeral, asking for a memento. Julius, generous by nature beneath his harsh exterior, had given her the gold tie pin that now adorned Reggie's cravat, and a bed for the night. She had gone again by morning, which meant that this evening's meeting was well within the customary five-year gap.

"What brings you to Blackhaven?" Delilah asked. "Are you ill?"

"Lord, no, never better," Nell assured her. "Just come to see my beautiful little Lah-Lah. And of course we're in a new traveling play, which opens at the Blackhaven Theatre next week. You must come and see it! I'll send you tickets for the first night. Reggie has the leading role, and he is wonderful—aren't you, darling?"

Delilah didn't ask how they had gained admission to the assembly rooms. Although the ball was strictly for the aristocracy and the gentry—with a small handful of the most respectably wealthy middling families—both Nell and Reggie were adept at accents and lies.

"Congratulations," Delilah said politely to Reggie. "I'm sure I shall enjoy it."

"Best not bring any of your nob family with you," Nell advised. "We don't want to show you up."

"Where are you staying?" Delilah asked, hoping she would not be left to pay her mother's hotel bill, which she could not afford under any circumstances.

"Oh, the theatre hired us lodgings nearby. Miserable little

place, not like Sir George's vast pile."

"Black Hill House is hardly a vast pile," Delilah said mildly. "And it is Julius's now."

"He doesn't begrudge you house room there, does he?"

"No," Delilah said.

"Ooh, look, there's a gentleman coming this way! Are you courting at last, Lah-Lah?"

"No," Delilah said again, and looked beyond her mother to discover with some horror that Lord Linfield was strolling in their direction, a glass of wine in each hand. *Why would he do that? I dismissed him!*

"Come on, Nell," Reggie said, standing decisively. "We've pushed our luck far enough here, and we don't want to spoil little Delilah's chances."

He smiled directly at Linfield as he said that. Linfield smiled distantly and inclined his head. There was very little chance he had not heard.

*Please don't let Nell wink at him...*

She winked.

"What an extraordinary couple," Linfield remarked. "Who are they?"

"You wouldn't believe me if I told you."

"You intrigue me. First, however, may I join you? I brought you wine by way of pleading my case."

"What case?"

"Joining you, of course," Linfield replied, setting down the glasses and sitting beside her. "I'm sure your chaperones will appear forthwith."

"I am beyond the age of needing chaperones," she said irritably.

"Why are you in such a hurry to be old?"

She blinked. "I assure you, it is something over which I have no control."

"What about those two characters who just left? Do you have control over them?"

*Characters.* A surge of anger clashed with her jangling nerves. "Such disdain for my parents! Considering they have done nothing to earn it."

For once, she had actually surprised him. He paused, his glass halfway to his lips, and set it down again. "Parents? Sir George—"

"Sir George neglected to marry my mother," she said. "She is, as you have so loftily pointed out, not quite the thing. I imagine you judge my stepfather similarly." There was no mistaking the startled shame in his expression. She doubted he was a man who put his foot in his mouth very often. "I am illegitimate, my lord. Born on the wrong side of the blanket. A *bas*—"

"I understand," he said mildly. "Please forgive my crass words."

"Already forgotten, I assure you." She sat back, unsure where all this fury was coming from, just as Felicia sat down opposite them.

Lord Linfield turned his gaze to her, smiling with pleasure or relief, or both. "Mrs. Maitland."

And abruptly, Delilah understood. She almost laughed aloud. Of course he had not sought *her* out. He had come for Felicia, with whom he had danced before. As suddenly as it had arrived, her anger vanished, leaving in its place a sense of shame and disappointment that pricked at her eyelids.

*Foolish. Foolish.* He was her last dance, not her first, and it was already over.

ONE OF DENZIL'S skills, which had been particularly useful in his diplomatic career, was his quick and accurate judgment of people. Even from a distance, he had seen that the couple who sat beside Delilah were *wrong*. Their mannerisms were too ostentatious, their dress just the wrong side of flamboyance, distracting, clearly, from the inferiority of the materials. To most they would have seemed like a slightly eccentric pair, a wealthy couple, perhaps from abroad, or merely *nouveaux riches*.

But that was not what Delilah Vale thought. There was tension as well as irritability in the stiffness of her posture. They had upset her poise, which both interested and annoyed Denzil. He wasn't quite sure which of those emotions propelled him across the room to investigate. He wasn't surprised that the couple scarpered, merely flabbergasted by Miss Vale's explanation.

He cursed himself for his stupidity. He had always known George Vale had illegitimate children whom he acknowledged and lived with, so why had he never thought that Delilah could be one? Why had he not been told?

*Because it doesn't matter.* He saw that quite clearly while he chatted with Mrs. Maitland. The sisters were comfortable together, and when one of the brothers appeared, a quick exchange of glances seemed enough to communicate the safety of the youngest sister, now dancing the final waltz of the evening with an elegant young man.

As he left the Vales and walked around the edge of the dance floor to his sister and her companion, Denzil found himself wishing he danced again with Delilah. Though stupidly touched to be her last dance partner of choice, he found her decision disappointing, not least because of her admission that it was to focus on her new career, a career he was there to sabotage at all costs.

She troubled him deeply. Not just because she was the daughter of a man he had liked and respected, but because there was an innate vulnerability in her that she hid from the world. Whatever she was doing, she was not a wicked person. And that was saddest of all.

# Chapter Three

THE FOLLOWING AFTERNOON, Denzil called casually on Dr. Lampton. Not entirely surprised to learn that the doctor was out on sick visits, he asked if Mrs. Lampton was, by chance, receiving.

It seemed she was. He was shown into a comfortable parlor, where the doctor's wife, the princess, sat on the floor playing jackstraws with a small boy who was clearly her son—the rightful Prince of Rheinwald, according to many.

"My lord, an unexpected pleasure," the lady greeted him. "Please, sit, and I shall join you immediately after this game."

"May I not join in?" he asked.

"Of course!" the young prince said generously, casting him a singularly sweet smile. "Mama is bound to bring the whole pile down, but we can begin a new—"

"I shall not," the princess insisted, carefully drawing a straw free without calamity. "Ha!" she taunted her son, who merely grinned.

Denzil sat on the floor and watched the boy choose his straw.

"I'm sorry, Nicholas is out," the princess said. "He is unlikely to be back before tea."

"Oh, that's no problem," Denzil said. "It is only a social call, since I was passing. Though in fact I was wondering... We spoke last night about the Princess of Hazburg. Do you know her well?"

"Not really. But I liked her—quite aside from agreeing with her on political matters."

"Then you would know her if you saw her again?"

"Oh yes. Well done!" She applauded her son, flexing her fingers before reaching for another straw.

"Then I'm very glad I called upon you. The thing is, in my Foreign Office capacity, I have been asked to make sure that the princess might safely visit Blackhaven incognito. May we rely on your discretion, should you run into her?"

"Of course." She glanced up at him in surprise. "I did not even know she was in the country."

"It is a private visit, to do with negotiating the return of her brother to Hazburg. A meeting on neutral soil, as it were."

"I wonder why they did not choose some closer-to-home soil?"

"Because the princess wished to visit on both unofficial state and private business. She included Blackhaven on her itinerary to take in the waters, whose fame appears to have spread far and wide. And it means she might meet with her brother's representatives away from prying eyes in London. I tell you this in confidence, of course."

"Of course." She met his gaze. "Between ourselves, Lord Linfield, I am mightily glad to leave German politics behind me. I shall not appear to notice the princess." She extracted a straw at apparent random.

"Ha!" exclaimed the young prince with an unfilial show of jubilation. "You brought it all down!"

"Only in the game," his mother murmured. "Tea, my lord?"

DELILAH FOUND THAT her new life of independence would have to be postponed for the day at least. Not only did she have her mother to worry about—why would she and Reggie be playing such a small theatre as Blackhaven's?—but also her brother Julius.

At breakfast that morning, while Julius was out apparently looking for wild horses who'd careered across Black Hill last night, Delilah's private thoughts were interrupted by her youngest sister Leona saying innocently, "Who is Mrs. Macy?"

*Macy...* How did Delilah know that name, and why did she not like it?

"Julius danced with her," Leona explained, looking around the siblings. "You must have noticed."

"I saw him talking to a Mrs. Macy," Lucy said. "She was rather beautiful, actually, if slightly...tense. But I've no idea who she is. I didn't see him dancing with anyone."

"He did," Felicia said. "But he left early. I'm not sure we achieved anything by getting him to the ball."

They all turned back to eating, drinking tea, and reading.

Except Delilah, who suddenly recalled that Antonia Temple, once Julius's betrothed, had jilted him in order to marry a wealthy landowner called Macy. *Oh no, it couldn't be...*

Leona said, "*One* of you must have heard of her. Antonia Macy?"

The others shrugged. But Leona's gaze found Delilah's and remained.

Delilah drew in a breath. "I would not go near that particular lady."

"Because she is married?" Leona said, disappointed. "I was hoping she was a widow."

"Poor Mr. Macy," Felicia murmured.

"Antonia is the past," Delilah said firmly, setting down her teacup and rising to her feet. "*Not* the future."

"How do you know?" Lawrence demanded. "Perhaps there are lots of Antonias!"

"Let us hope so," Delilah said, walking out of the room to hide her agitation.

So Julius had met *her* again—Antonia Temple, who, ten years ago, had broken his heart. Delilah remembered only too well the sick, empty look on her brother's face. Never before or since had she seen him so distraught.

She and her father and her younger siblings had stopped off in Portsmouth on their way to Russia, in order to welcome Julius's betrothed to the family, and even attend the wedding if there was time. And then, before they had even met her, Antonia had heartlessly jilted Julius for a landowning gentleman. Now the woman was apparently widowed and somehow had her claws in him again.

The twins had achieved their wish to wake him up, but what cruel fate had thrown Antonia in his path to do so? Delilah could not allow Julius to be hurt again by this poisonous female. Another reason to go to Blackhaven.

She drove herself in the gig, leaving the carriages for Julius, who apparently had business in the town that day, and Aubrey, who had promised to take his daily dose of the waters.

Studiedly casual, Lucy refused to accompany Delilah— probably because she had made a conquest the previous evening and was hoping he would call. Felicia would be there if he did. They were all agreed Lucy should not be held to her loathed childhood betrothal to a man none of them had met, and it was time she spread her wings. Without getting into mischief, of course.

Abandoning the pony and gig at the town's livery stable for a couple of hours, Delilah took the quieter back streets toward the theatre, where she discovered the address of the visiting company's lodgings.

Here, the door was opened by a harassed-looking maid. Hidden from a view, a vocal argument was in full flood. Since the maid ignored it, so did Delilah.

"I'm looking for Mrs. Hampshire," Delilah said.

"Come in," the maid said with a sniff. "If you want to with this racket going on. What name shall I say?"

"Miss Vale," Delilah replied. It wasn't her but her mother who insisted on keeping their relationship secret. Nell pretended it was to protect Delilah from the slights of her own class, but truly it was to prevent anyone realizing that Nell was old enough to have a thirty-year-old daughter. Delilah didn't mind. The theatre was notoriously unkind to aging women.

In a very few moments—much to Delilah's relief, for the argument had reached screaming point—the maid leaned over the banister and beckoned her upstairs.

"Oh, thank God!" Nell exclaimed as soon as Delilah walked through the door. "I'm so glad you've come, Lah-Lah. I'm at my wits' end."

Nell didn't exactly fall on her neck, but she did embrace her and kiss the air over her cheek.

"What's the matter?" Delilah asked prosaically, sitting down on the edge of the unmade bed to await the inevitable request for money, which she could not fulfill until she at least received her fee for work not yet completed.

Nell wilted onto the bed beside her and shaded her eyes with her hand. "My life is over. Reggie is unfaithful."

Delilah sighed with genuine sympathy. In her experience, very few husbands were faithful. Look at her own father. Look at Felicia's late husband, Nick. "I'm sorry. Do you know that, or are you just guessing?"

"I know," Nell said tragically. "A wife always knows."

"Who is the woman?"

"Elsie Manners—calls herself *Elise*, but mark my words, she was born Elsie. First, she takes my leading role, even though she will never have more talent than I have in my little finger. Now she is after my husband too. Oh, Delilah, what can I do?"

Relieved not to be Lah-Lah, Delilah tried her best. "Tell him he must stop or he has to find alternative lodgings, along with alternative care for his person, clothes, and meals."

Nell dropped her arm. "But what if he goes?"

"Then he is not worth having in the first place. I understand men of a certain age tend to stray, in order to confirm their virility, but it is quite obvious that it is you Reggie loves."

"Do you think so?" Nell asked wistfully.

"I do." Delilah crossed her fingers around the fabric of her gown.

"The thing is, I am too proud to play the nagging wife, Lah-Lah. *You* speak to him."

Delilah widened her eyes in horror. "I can't possibly! Besides, he'll know you sent me, so what's the difference?"

"All the difference in the world, foolish child. Besides, of course he won't know. He's with her now."

Delilah's jaw dropped. "And you expect *me* to interrupt them?"

Nell curled her lip. "They're supposed to be rehearsing. Which means he has to teach her how to act. But you're bound to see some sign of affection or possessiveness between them, so use that as an excuse to tell Reggie how worried you are. Hint at your influence among the *ton* and the theatre-going public throughout the country."

"I don't have any influence whatsoever...!"

"They don't know that. Reggie is impressed by titles. Throw your brother's around. And that lord's."

"What lord's?" Delilah asked in bewilderment.

"The one who's courting you."

"No one's courting me. I've been on the shelf for years."

"Nonsense," Nell said bracingly. "You're rather lovely, you know. You're just so...*severe* that you scare off all but the bravest."

"You don't need to flatter me. I'll try to see Reggie on my way out."

"Go now," Nell urged. "You'll definitely find him. And insist on privacy. Don't say anything in front of that—"

"You know so clearly what you want that you'd be better doing it yourself. You also have a much better right to speak alone to your own husband."

"No, Delilah. It has to be you."

"Knowing, as I do, so much about marriage," Delilah muttered.

"You are calm and talk sense, which is so hard to do when one is married."

Delilah gave in and rose to her feet. "Where is he?"

Nell hung out of her bedchamber door, flapping her hands to guide Delilah along the passage to the correct door. When she reached the second-last one, she glanced back at Nell, who silently clapped her hands and vanished back inside her room.

Delilah sighed and knocked on the door.

There was an immediate rustle, accompanied by a loud male voice declaiming. He paused long enough to command, "Enter!"

Delilah lifted the latch and went in. It appeared to be a sitting room, with chairs and sofas around the walls and a large, empty floor space at the center.

Reggie sat on a sofa, a play script on his lap, his arm stretched casually along the sofa back. A young woman, pretty and commanding in appearance, stood in front of the window, smoothing her hair. Like someone who wanted to be caught with someone else's husband.

"Delilah! Miss Vale!" Reggie jumped up, hurrying toward her with his hand held out. "What an unexpected pleasure!"

Delilah gave him her hand, which he bowed over with perfect grace.

"Come," he said, beaming, "let me take you to Nell, who will be overjoyed—"

"I've just come from Nell," Delilah interrupted. "She is about to join us. Perhaps this young lady would excuse us?"

"Oh. Yes, of course, run along, Elise, there's a good girl. We'll get back to it in an hour."

Elise, displaying all the irritation any adult might feel being told to "run along," snatched up a script from the windowsill and stalked out. Delilah wondered if she listened at doors.

"Sit, my dear, sit. I imagine Nell is ordering refreshment—"

"Reggie, what are you about?" Delilah interrupted once more. "How far has this relationship gone?"

"How far? Relationship?" spluttered Reggie. "What on earth—"

"You and that girl who is young enough to be your grand-daughter. Are you trying to humiliate Nell, or have you just not thought about her at all?"

"My dear Delilah—"

"The latter, I gather. I don't know if that is in your favor or not. Look, I know you are a great actor, but bearing in mind that you are two generations that girl's senior, have you wondered what she gets out of flirting with you? Aside from further humiliating Nell, whose role, I understand, she has already taken over."

Reggie flushed hotly. "You must understand, my dear, that darling Nell is of an age and stage in life when playing a young girl can lack conviction!"

"So is a grandfather playing a young man," Delilah said ruth-lessly. "Do you really want to end your illustrious career as a laughingstock? Worse, tied to a shrewish and ambitious young woman who cares nothing for your comfort and everything for her own career? Think of yourself, Reggie, if you cannot think of Nell. Who would you miss more?"

He hung his head. "Nell," he said a small voice. "Of course, Nell."

"Then don't hurt her." She met his apologetic gaze and nar-rowed her eyes. "Don't dare. Good afternoon, Reggie."

Leaving the house without seeing her mother again, Delilah was very glad to step out into the damp, salty air. She inhaled with relief.

What now?

Should she call upon Antonia Macy? Or would that immedi-ately make more of last night's reunion than there necessarily was? Whatever else Julius was, he wasn't a fool. Perhaps it was even no bad thing for them to have met again and cleared the air. Probably, Julius was wondering what he had ever seen in her...

No, she should not interfere. Instead, she would walk round

to Dr. Lampton's house and make an appointment to consult him about her occasionally erratic eyesight. Aubrey liked him, said he was a man of sense, which was a rare compliment from her brother about a doctor. He had seen far too many of them in his young life.

The maid who opened the door invited her inside immediately. "Dr. Lampton is out, but Mrs. Lampton will arrange an appointment for you."

Delilah followed her across the hall of the modest but pleasant house. Laughter rang out from the open door of the room the maid entered. Delilah caught a glimpse of a lady and a small boy sitting on the floor playing jackstraws. A gentleman in smart morning dress sprawled carelessly on his stomach, clearly about to take his turn.

"You'll bring it all down!" the boy cried gleefully. "Especially if I make you laugh."

The maid murmured in the lady's ear, and Delilah recognized her as having attended the ball the previous evening. The jackstraws collapsed, to the gleeful shout of the child and the laughter of the man who rose fluidly to his feet and turned to face the door.

Lord Linfield.

ELISE MANNERS WAS irritated to be ejected in favor of the strange woman, not least because the woman was beautiful. A man who strayed from his wife once would stray again, and she needed Reggie's favor to stay in Blackhaven. Without it, she would be dismissed. His wife, the raddled old hag, was feeble competition, but this new woman in the worn cloak and unfashionable gown had an air of class that worried Elise far more.

Pacing the floor of her own room, which was next door to the parlor they used for rehearsals, she waited for the stranger to leave. She even tried pressing her ear to the wall—with the aid of an old teacup—but the voices were too low. Still, at least the woman didn't stay long. Elise heard her footsteps in the passage and rushed to the door. She waited to see if the visitor would stop anywhere else. She didn't and went straight downstairs.

Elise opened the door and came face to face with Reggie leaving the rehearsal room.

"Who was that?" she demanded.

"Oh, just a friend of Nell's," he replied, smiling.

He was lying, which troubled her further. "What did she want?"

"Just to greet me. She lives in Blackhaven, you know."

Elise sniffed, in a jealous kind of a way. "Then I suppose you can look forward to more of her company."

"Not if I can help it," Reggie said, and that at least was honest. "Excuse me, I'll just look in on Nell. You'll be fine for the evening performance."

She wouldn't, of course. Although she could act—and frequently did—she had the stage presence of a small, annoying fly. The whole troupe knew she was only there because Reggie fancied her and was prepared to coach her in the necessary stage techniques.

In fact, she was there because in a theatre company, she could hide in plain sight.

# Chapter Four

D ELILAH'S HEART GAVE a peculiar lurch. It was just so unexpected, so incongruous, to come across Lord Linfield here in this intimate scene with the doctor's wife and child. His eyes alight with fun, the smile lingering on his lips, he was beguiling.

*What a wonderful father he would make...* The thought came out of nowhere as their eyes met and held in mutual surprise while the boy chattered away. Then the lady was walking between them.

"So sorry to keep you waiting. I'm Elizabeth Lampton. If you'd follow me in here, where I attempt to keep track of my husband's consultations..."

Far from the comfortable chaos of the other apartment she had glimpsed, the doctor's consulting room was spotlessly clean and uncluttered. Medical books lined the wall behind the desk, and a tall cabinet of drawers stood against the far wall. The doctor's wife—a princess by a previous marriage, according to Aubrey, who was making a study of the town—closed the door and opened a large book on the table behind it.

"When would you like the doctor to call?" Mrs. Lampton asked.

"Is it not possible to see him here?" Delilah asked uneasily. "I don't want to worry my family for nothing."

"Of course. In fact, it is simpler here, and saves him traveling time. What about tomorrow afternoon? Or Monday morning?"

They settled on Monday morning, and Mrs. Lampton wrote her name in the book. "Ah, you are one of the Vales of Black Hill!" She smiled. "I'm very glad to make your acquaintance. I think I saw you at the ball last night, although we were not introduced. I have met a few of your siblings, though I really only know Sir Julius because of his involvement with the hospital. Would you care to join me for tea?"

"Oh, no, thank you. I would not disturb you further."

"Please do," Mrs. Lampton urged. "A doctor's wife leads a lonely life without friends! Are you acquainted with Lord Linfield?"

For some reason, the open way she mentioned him gave Delilah a sense of relief. "Slightly," she managed.

Mrs. Lampton smiled mischievously as she led the way back across the hall. "He is quite unexpected, is he not?"

"I suppose diplomats adapt to whatever situation they find themselves in."

"Of course, your father was also distinguished in such service, was he not? Did you travel with him?"

And somehow it seemed rude not to follow her hostess back to the parlor. Lord Linfield now sat more conventionally in a chair, although he rose as they entered, and bowed to Delilah.

"Miss Vale."

"My lord."

Tea almost followed them in. The boy bowed to Delilah too, with a beguiling grin. He hung around only long enough to be allowed a sandwich and a biscuit, which he took in each hand.

"I'm off to play in the garden," he announced, and shot off.

"He has too much energy," Mrs. Lampton said. "But I feel he is not yet old enough to go out and about with the other children."

"He must be about the same age as Edward Macy," Lord Linfield observed.

Delilah's gaze flew to his face, but he was not looking at her. His attention was all on Mrs. Lampton.

"Mrs. Macy is my sister's friend who travels with us," Linfield continued, dismaying Delilah considerably. "Her son is similarly lively. Perhaps you have met?"

"No, but if you are attending the garden party at the castle on Saturday, I shall look to you to introduce us. The children are always invited, too. Are there not children in your household, too, Miss Vale?"

"Well, there are the twins," Delilah said, pulling herself together, "but they are fifteen years old."

"I look forward to making their acquaintance." Mrs. Lampton frowned. "Actually... Twins, you say? I might have seen them around the town."

"I wouldn't be surprised. I'm sure they are here more often than they tell us about. Since there are two of them, we tend not to worry about them. In fact, I suspect they worry more about the rest of us!"

Delilah found herself rather liking Mrs. Lampton, although Lord Linfield's presence—and his connection to Antonia Macy—unsettled her too much to relax into the company. She determined not to stay long, though she was perversely glad when she rose to take her leave and Linfield left at the same time.

"Allow me to walk to your carriage," he said civilly.

"There is no need. My gig is at the livery stable, which is bound to be out of your way."

"Not in the slightest." He offered her his arm, and after an instant's hesitation, she laid her hand on his sleeve. It would have been rude not to. "I hope you enjoyed the ball last night."

"Of course I did."

"Then you must definitely attend another. I believe there is to be a masquerade ball at the castle in a couple of weeks. I hope you will be there."

"My sister Felicia keeps track of the family's invitations," Delilah replied indifferently.

"Mrs. Maitland?" he guessed.

"Indeed. She is the most sociable of my family." And would therefore make an excellent ambassador's wife. The thought did not please her somehow. Although Felicia needed a new husband, a kind one, even if she did not know it. Was Linfield kind? He seemed so, but he was so much the diplomat that she could not read the character beneath.

*He dances like a friend. Like someone to be trusted.*

*Delilah Vale, your brains are addled.*

"What brought you to Blackhaven, my lord?" she asked.

"The waters," he replied. "My sister was ill after we returned from Vienna, and she has never fully recovered. She believes the waters are helping."

"We believe they help my brother Aubrey too. He has been sickly since childhood, and yet here, he thrives. Dr. Lampton says it is the fresh air—we have usually lived in large cities until now—but Aubrey keeps drinking the water, just in case."

"Perhaps you should try them, too."

She had almost forgotten he had seen her semi-blinded and vulnerable. Instinctively, she attacked. "So it was your sister's idea to come to Blackhaven? Or Mrs. Macy's, perhaps?"

His eyebrows flew up. "Mine, as I recall. Why should you imagine it was Mrs. Macy's?"

"Her position appears to be ambiguous. Is she your sister's companion? Or merely her friend?"

"You must allow her to be both." His voice was cool.

No doubt the woman had him fooled, too. No doubt she would reject Julius again for this man if no one better offered.

"Must I? I have no interest in her at all."

"Well that's a whopper," he observed, and unexpected laughter caught at her breath. "It was you who mentioned her."

"So I did. I merely recognized the name. I have never met her. Is your sister satisfied with her companion?"

"Ah. You are after her position."

Delilah turned on him, narrowing her eyes with indignation.

"I am not." Too late, she saw the teasing glint in his eyes, and added, "My work is quite other."

"Organizing and translating. Which is not so very different from Mrs. Macy's in some ways. You must let me see examples of your work some time, so that I can recommend you. I might even have my own use for such services."

"Really?" she asked.

"You sound doubtful. Is that of my worth or yours?"

"Neither," she said, flustered.

As though letting her off the hook, he changed the subject. "Tell me about your family. I have met Sir Julius and Mrs. Maitland, and I know of a younger sister, a brother Aubrey, and a set of twins. Who else lives with you at Black Hill?"

"My brother Roderick—Major Vale. And Cornelius, who looks after the land. Lucy was at the ball, too. And the twins are Lawrence and Leona. Why?"

"Curiosity—my besetting sin. Large families intrigue me, probably because I only have the one sibling. And, of course, the fact that you are all Sir George's children fascinates me even more. I liked your father very much."

From nowhere, emotion sprang up, clogging her throat. She couldn't speak.

"I'm sorry," he said with unbearable gentleness. "I didn't mean to upset you."

"You didn't," she managed, speeding up as if she could outrun both the emotion and him, but he simply lengthened his stride.

"Do you know about this hospital that Mrs. Lampton mentioned?" he asked.

Glad of the subject change, Delilah said, "I am not involved. Julius became so because there are so many sailors and soldiers among the patients. He employs them when he can. Once they are better, of course." Mercifully, they had reached the livery stable gates. She removed her hand from his arm and turned resolutely to face him. "Goodbye, my lord."

A rueful smile flickered across his face and was gone. She could almost imagine he was disappointed. At the last moment, probably to prove she could, she stretched out her hand to him, and he took it. His grip was firm, drawing her attention to his ungloved hand—strong, capable, warm. His thumb glided over her knuckles like a caress, surely by accident, and yet her skin tingled under his touch.

"Until we meet again," he said lightly.

"Of course." She slid her hand free and walked through the gate without looking back. She almost collided with an emerging horse and rider and swerved at the last moment. She hoped his lordship didn't see that either.

WHEN SHE RETURNED to Black Hill, absorbed in her own problems, she found her siblings planning the capture of whoever was, apparently, driving wild horses over their land for some unknown purpose. It certainly provided a distraction from Antonia Macy and Julius, Lord Linfield, and her mother's marital problems, so she found herself entering into the spirit of the adventure—which, however, ended in Julius injuring himself further and Aubrey capturing a horse who was far from wild but suffering from some neglect.

Delilah cared for the horse as best she could—as yet, they had few servants—and was rather touched by its surprise at her gentleness. Someone had neglected and mistreated the animal, probably all the animals she had seen from the window being driven across the hills.

In the morning, Julius, his limp more pronounced, insisted on going into Blackhaven about his charitable duties at the hospital. Delilah was hopeful that between the hospital and the horses' mystery, he would be distracted from Antonia.

As everyone else scattered about their own business, Delilah divided her time between the captured horse and her own work. She was excited to receive a parcel of papers in the post from Mr. Charles, her promising new client, who wanted everything translated into German, apart from a few letters in German that he wanted translated into English, and everything ordered according to date.

There was a pleasant morning room at the corner of Black Hill House that caught the best of whatever sunlight managed to pierce the perpetual cloud of this northern summer. Since no one else used it and visitors were rare, Delilah set up her office there, arranging the documents into their required order.

They were in several different languages—French, Italian, Polish, and Russian, as well as English. Delilah sharpened her pen and drew a fresh sheet of paper toward her before reaching for the document at the top of her pile.

She didn't know how long she was working before the door opened, distracting her from a very convoluted sentence.

"Oh, there you are, Miss Vale," said Betsy the parlor maid. "There's a gentleman to see Mrs. Maitland—Lord Linfield."

"What?" Delilah sprang up from her chair, very conscious suddenly of the ink stains on her fingers, the darned patches on her old gown, and her unruly hair escaping from its pins. "Well, run and find Mrs. Maitland. Where have you put him?"

"Nowhere," said the man looming behind Betsy in the doorway. "I'm afraid I just followed the maid."

"Mrs. Maitland went out, ma'am," Betsy said, standing aside and blushing furiously for her mistake. Delilah and Felicia had taken her on because they liked her rather than because she had any experience of domestic service.

Linfield sauntered into the room. "I seem to have called at a bad time. Shall I just leave my card?"

Delilah had no idea what the time was, but she would not deprive her sister of so distinguished a caller if she could help it. "I'm sure Felicia won't be long. Betsy, would you bring tea? Shall we repair to the drawing room, my lord?"

"Only if you wish to. I am quite charmed to find you au naturelle, as it were."

"Don't be so diplomatic," Delilah said wryly. "I am at work, as you see. Won't you sit down? I'm sure several of my siblings will be along momentarily."

"Carry on working if you wish," he said mildly, taking one the upholstered chairs. "I shall even bring you a cup of tea when it arrives."

"Oh, no, the break will do me good." She sat in the chair opposite, nearest the tea table, and tried not to think of how attractive he looked in riding dress, his short hair pleasingly windswept, the glow of fresh air about his skin. He wore a dark green riding coat with a casually knotted cravat, and his breeches fitted close to his muscular legs. Heat seeped through her body, and she hastily raised her eyes to his face.

"Perhaps it is even working with close-written papers that upsets your eyes," he said.

She blinked, somehow surprised that he even remembered the incident. But then, he had seen her at Dr. Lampton's house. She said hurriedly, "I wondered that, but I didn't read anything at all at the ball."

A large fellow Delilah didn't recognize carried in a heavy tea tray at Betsy's instructions. He looked more like a groom or one of the farm laborers, and the maid shooed him out again as soon as he set the tray down on the table. He went meekly enough, though Delilah made a mental note to discover who the devil he was—perhaps someone Julius had recruited straight from the hospital.

She busied herself pouring tea, and he reached over to accept his cup and a proffered sandwich.

"Did your sister not care to ride out with you?" Delilah inquired.

"I believe she has gone to investigate some charitable opportunity. And then to the pump room. Though she does enjoy making calls. I shall bring her next time, if you permit."

*Next time...*

"What a beautiful view you have from this room," he said, setting down his cup and wandering toward the window.

"It will be better once we have fully tamed the garden. Since it's merely for show, we have neglected the formal gardens in favor of necessities like making the house habitable and reviving the kitchen garden. But we are each taking a turn now, so it might be beautiful before the end of the summer."

"I can see why you all came home," he murmured. "It is beautiful here."

"Julius and Cornelius are working very hard to make the estate viable again. My father neglected it for too long."

He moved toward the other window, glancing at her desk beside it. "Is it enjoyable work?"

"Not as much as I had hoped," she confessed. "I prefer to learn something that keeps my interest. These reports and letters are frankly dull."

"They must be riveting to someone," he observed, his gaze returning to the desk.

"Presumably. Forgive me, my lord, although I was not so instructed, I believe I owe my clients some duty of confidence."

His lips curved, but when he looked up, there was no warmth in his eyes. Had she offended him? And why did she care when he had come for Felicia?

*And when I have had my last dance,* she told herself severely.

"Forgive me," he said easily, moving away from the desk. "From old habit, I glance at every document and discard from my mind anything irrelevant. Do you have to risk sending your translations overseas?"

"Not in this case, but sometimes."

"If I can help by using diplomatic bags, do let me know."

"Thank you," she said in surprise. "I will. More tea? A honey cake?"

"Perhaps just half a cup." He sat back down and for the next quarter of an hour made pleasant, amusing conversation. The time flew by for Delilah, and yet even before he rose to leave she felt uneasy, even hurt. For the first time since she had met him, she sensed he was merely making small talk without any interest or care for her replies.

*He* has *no care or interest in me. He came to see Felicia. And that is as it should be.*

To show she did not care either, she escorted him personally to the front door to bid him a distant farewell.

At that, he suddenly smiled and took her hand, although she had not offered it. "Thank you for your kindness. I'll call again if I may."

"Please do," she managed. "My brothers and sisters will be sorry to have missed you."

He bowed over her hand. For a startled moment, she thought he was going to kiss her fingers and stopped breathing.

He straightened and released her. "Good day, Miss Vale."

"Good day, my lord." *And of course I am not disappointed. I am not that foolish.*

DENZIL FELT UNACCOUNTABLY weary as he mounted his hired horse and trotted out of the stable yard toward the drive. Delilah Vale was still working for the enemy. He should have been glad to identify her, for it made the rest of his task much simpler. But he didn't feel glad at all. He felt disappointed and grim and as if something delightful and innocent had slipped through his fingers…

At the top of the drive, two figures stepped out of the undergrowth and halted in front of him, grinning. For a moment, he thought he was seeing double and blinked rapidly to clear his eyes. No, they were definitely two different people, for one was a girl, the other a boy. At least from their dress.

"Greetings!" said the boy. "Have you been calling at the

house?"

"I have," Denzil replied.

"We're the twins," the girl informed him.

"I don't believe you."

They laughed with clear delight and turned to walk on either side of his horse.

"You're funny," the girl said. "Did you see Delilah?"

"I did. Everyone else appears to be away from home."

The boy looked up at him, clear-eyed. He had old eyes for fourteen or fifteen or however young he was. "Wasn't Delilah enough?"

"More than enough."

The warmth came back to the boy's eyes. "I'm Lawrence. This is Leona. We both think Delilah works too much."

"On her papers?" Denzil asked lightly.

"On everything," Leona said. "She did everything for Papa, you know. And now she's trying to do everything for the rest of us, when she should be dancing and enjoying herself. Are you her friend?"

"I would like to be."

"Perhaps there is hope for you, then," Lawrence said with a grin. "People don't always *see* Delilah. They just see a managing female, a sharp-tongued spinster-in-waiting, when she is actually funny and kind and motherly."

"She is a lady of many parts, I am sure."

"You *should* be sure before you make her your friend," Leona observed, causing him to peer down at her. She was looking straight ahead, though she turned quite suddenly to meet his gaze. "She's like us, you know."

"Impudent and overtalkative?"

"Illegitimate," Lawrence said.

Denzil had the measure of them now and didn't even blink. "Some of my best friends are illegitimate."

"Really?" Leona asked, narrowing her eyes in a shrewd kind of way.

"Really. It's hardly the first thing I notice about them, though. Do you find it a barrier to friendship?"

"No," Lawrence said cautiously.

"Well, I would like to be your sister's friend. I might even like to be yours, but I'm reserving judgment."

"So are we," Leona said cheekily, and they ran off again, their movements perfectly aligned with each other.

# Chapter Five

"**Y**OU'VE *WHAT?*" DELILAH stared at Felicia as they met in the hallway before dinner.

"I've invited Antonia Macy to dine with us on Tuesday."

"But why?" Delilah didn't know whether to wail or stamp her foot.

"Lucy asked me to. She thinks it will be good for Julius."

"It won't," Delilah said between her teeth. "The woman is poison."

"I rather liked her. More to the point, so did Lucy."

Delilah closed her mouth. It was true Lucy had a knack that amounted to a gift of being able to gauge someone's character almost instantaneously. No one was infallible, of course, but it did mean Delilah should probably give Antonia a chance. People did silly things when they were young. It didn't make them monsters. Necessarily.

"Her friends, Miss Talbot and Lord Linfield, are invited, too."

"Linfield," she said aloud without meaning to.

Felicia raised her eyebrow. "Another objection, Delly?"

"No, no," Delilah said, willing away the heat rising to her face. "It's just that he called this afternoon asking for you."

"Did he?" Felicia's mind seemed to have already moved on. "I wonder why?"

LEAVING THE HOTEL the following morning to escort Elaine and her companion to church, Denzil witnessed the arrival of a modest lady and gentleman. They stepped out of their uncrested carriage and sailed through the front door of the hotel, which Denzil held open for him.

The lady, who was undoubtedly the Princess of Hazburg, inclined her head by way of thanks, and Denzil wished he had not agreed to take Elaine to church. She and Antonia could just as easily go without him. However, the aim had always been to preserve the princess's anonymity, so he merely offered his own ladies his arms and strolled around to St. Andrew's.

The Vales, he saw at once, were out in force, including the twins, scrubbed much cleaner than the last time he had seen them. They grinned at him by way of acknowledgment. So did Mrs. Maitland and Miss Lucy Vale, and Aubrey. Delilah did not appear to notice him.

Elaine had already accepted an invitation for all three of them to dine at Black Hill on Tuesday, so he would have to make a plan before then. Especially now that the Princess of Hazburg had arrived in Blackhaven.

Mr. Grant, the vicar, led an uplifting service, his sermon apparently light and yet thought-provoking. He was worth listening to, and Denzil did just that, until he became distracted by Delilah, several rows in front, on the other side of the aisle. Her attention turned toward the clergyman, and still, her beauty hit Denzil like a blow in the chest.

Gentle, vulnerable, and oddly prickly, she touched him in some way he could not grasp. She was also fiercely intelligent and clever with languages. The translations he had glimpsed yesterday had been incisive, some from Russian script, some from English, all into German. But surely there was no *pretense* in her?

She could not be the real sinner here. She was being used.

And yet if he warned her, and he was wrong, she could warn *them* and provoke catastrophe.

Something ached in him—a lost chance, a profound regret, though he didn't even know for what. Sir George Vale had been proud of his eldest daughter. And of all his children—the hardworking, the heroic, the charming, the clever...

And none of that mattered. Denzil had a task to perform to keep the world safe, and his own feelings did not matter beside that. There would be time afterward to...

To what? To know her better? Court her? The idea excited him. He had paid court to many women over the years, but never with serious intent. Delilah Vale was no pleasure-seeking lady of power or influence waiting to be seduced. No merry courtesan. She was doing her best to retire into spinsterhood, as though she did not deserve even the innocent pleasure of dancing.

A sharp nudge in his ribs dragged his attention back to his sister.

"Shall we go?" she suggested.

The service was over. People were leaving the church, gossiping with friends as they went. Delilah Vale walked past him, her head bent toward Leona, who was chattering at her side. Her skirts brushed against him. He caught the faintest whiff of perfume, light and yet arousing.

*What the devil's the matter with you, Talbot?* he asked himself severely as he stood aside to usher out his sister and Mrs. Macy.

IT WAS LATER in the afternoon before he sent his card to the princess's apartments and was invited to join her and her husband for tea in their sitting room.

Princess Irena of Hazburg was in her thirties, the mother of two young daughters who did not accompany her on this occasion. Neither regal nor particularly beautiful, she could have been any country gentlewoman—until one looked into her bright, intelligent eyes. Her people loved her for her care and her compassion. Her fellow rulers in Europe admired her ruthless acumen. One underestimated Princess Irena at one's peril.

Her husband, also a great admirer, beamed as Denzil entered and bowed first to the princess and then to him.

"Lord Linfield, a pleasure to see you again," Irena said in her perfect English, giving him her hand.

He bowed over it. "The pleasure is all mine, Your Highness. I trust your travels have not fatigued you too greatly?"

"We find being incognito quite liberating, do we not, Friedrich?"

"Much more fun," Prince Friedrich said, his eyes gleaming mischief. He offered Denzil his hand. "How do you do, Linfield?"

"Please sit and tell me how arrangements progress," Irena said, pouring tea into the hotel's porcelain cups. "Is my brother in England?"

"I believe he is in York, Highness, still gathering intelligence."

"About what?"

"Everything. The political situation in Hazburg and throughout Europe. He has no intention of coming to you in ignorance."

"Do we have any idea what he wants? Apart from to come home."

"A position in your government. Which position is unclear, but it is bound to be one of influence and opportunity. And I presume he will want some estates. Obviously these are matters for you to discuss."

"And have you found any indication that he means me harm?"

"Only the whispers we warned you of earlier. But..." He hesitated, wondering why this felt like betrayal. "He is using a new and previously unknown translator. In time, this should give us access to his true intentions before he or his representative reach Blackhaven."

"My brother could save himself a lot of trouble if he simply bothered to learn other languages."

"He never saw the need," Friedrich said with a flash of contempt. "He expected to inherit a large staff to do all the work for him. He never expected to be deposed and replaced. To be frank, he brings nothing to Hazburg except dissent. Irena knows my views. I do not wish to see him back in any capacity."

"He might have changed," Irena said. "People do, sometimes, when faced with reality. And...he is my brother."

Friedrich patted her hand. "I know. We shall see in the fullness of time."

"There is one other thing," Denzil said. "Elizabeth, the widowed Princess of Rheinwald, also lives in Blackhaven with her new husband. I believe you have met, but she has promised to betray no recognition should you encounter each other during your visit."

"I should like to see her again," Irena said. "Perhaps you could arrange something discreet, Lord Linfield?"

"I'll see what I can do." Denzil finished his tea and set down the cup. "In the meantime, although I have discovered no hint of danger, you should be vigilant and wary of strangers. Is there anything else I might do for you to make your stay pleasurable as well as safe?"

Prince Friedrich asked, "Is there a theatre here? We love the theatre."

"There is a small theatre here in Blackhaven, a larger one in Whalen. I believe there is a new play opening next week with Helena Hampshire."

Irena laughed. "How fortunate, Friedrich! Your favorite actress."

"I saw her in Paris," Friedrich said. "Such emotion, such depth. She brought tears to my eyes."

Denzil rather suspected Hampshire made her daughter weep, too, though for entirely different reasons.

RIDICULOUSLY, AS THE dinner party at Black Hill approached, Delilah felt butterflies in her stomach. She assumed they were caused by anxiety over Antonia's return into Julius's orbit and distracted herself with work. A consultation with Dr. Lampton over the odd lapses in her eyesight proved to be comforting.

"I have come across such symptoms before," he assured her. "Similar to migraines but accompanied by little or no pain and suffered for relatively short periods at a time. My guess is that it occurs when you concentrate too hard on close-written documents, perhaps accompanied by anxiety of some kind. I can prescribe a tonic that may help with the anxiety, though in such matters there are no guarantees. Either way, unless you notice some kind of change, I would just sit down, close your eyes, and wait for it to stop."

"Thank you," Delilah said happily, "that is just what I thought."

Leaving the doctor, she thought of calling on her mother, who had sent her theatre tickets for the following Monday. She wondered if there was something wrong with her that she was still so pathetically grateful for such notice, even when she had long since given up on her mother's affections. She should probably scowl at Reggie again too, to be sure he was staying away from Nell's rival.

Or perhaps she would just wait and go to the theatre—though with whom? Aubrey, perhaps, the least judgmental of her brothers. She hesitated to take her sisters into the company of an actress.

Still considering her options, she ran into Lucy and took her to the hotel for tea instead. Lucy was up to something, though she didn't reveal what.

The following day, while juggling translation work with preparing the house for its first formal visitors, Delilah sustained an unexpected visit. Lady Alice Conway, the Earl of Braithwaite's sister, had come, Delilah suspected, on account of Cornelius, which was intriguing. She liked Lady Alice, not least because of the young woman's interest in her hardworking brother.

The twins had been right. Going to the ball seemed to have added new dimensions to everyone's lives...although they could have done without Antonia Macy. Still, Delilah acknowledged that she did not know the woman. Lord Linfield seemed perfectly happy with her company for his sister, and they had traveled across Europe together. Antonia must be given the benefit of the doubt. At least until the end of tonight's dinner party.

Delilah had picked out her newest, most matronly evening gown. However, Leona surprised her by following her into her bedchamber and scowling at the dress with clear disapproval.

"Frumpy," she pronounced. "And designed to be worn with one of those horrid caps middle-aged women wear."

"Since when did you even notice fashion?" Delilah demanded.

But Leona, already raking through Delilah's wardrobe, merely shrugged. "We notice lots of things. Here, this one." She drew out an older lilac evening gown that had once been a favorite. "It always suits you."

"It is several years out of fashion," said Delilah, who refused to be manipulated.

"Oh, well, if you wish to outshine everyone..."

"Give it to me," Delilah said resignedly. If it was out of fashion, then she was clearly *not* trying to impress Lord Linfield.

Leona handed it over with a radiant smile and skipped off.

*Damn*, thought Delilah, torn between amusement and annoyance. *I have been manipulated.*

Even so, she caught herself pinning her hair high on her head in a soft style that Papa and Felicia had both said suited her best and peering into the looking glass for signs of imperfections.

*What is the matter with me?* she thought irritably, and strode out of the room to join their guests.

On the way, however, she suddenly decided she should send

what translation she had done by tomorrow's post. By doing so, she hoped to receive a fee more quickly, and therefore be able to help her mother if it turned out to be necessary. So, she went into the morning room, wrapped up her work with the original documents, tied the parcel with string, and addressed the whole to Mr. Charles in York.

It made her uneasy that she was putting off her drawing room entrance when the event was important to Felicia and Lucy, whatever it was to Julius. Accordingly, she placed her parcel on the hall table with the rest of the post, which would be taken to Blackhaven first thing in the morning, then walked straight into the drawing room.

Although her mind was fixed on Antonia and Julius, it was Lord Linfield she saw first. In perfect evening attire, he was handsome enough to take anyone's breath away. Somehow, he was utterly, overwhelmingly distinguished, and she, who had greeted emperors and princes with equanimity, felt the world tilt dizzyingly.

No migraine. Merely powerful physical reaction to his presence. She appeared to have offered her hand, for he held her fingers in a light but firm grip and bowed.

"My sister, Miss Talbot," he murmured, and Delilah was both relieved and disappointed to be forced to turn her attention elsewhere.

"How do you do, Miss Talbot?" she managed.

Linfield's sister was tall like him, past her first flush of youth, perhaps, but attractive for all that. Her eyes smiled and her words of greeting sounded genuine, which was, Delilah knew, an art form in itself. But then, as Delilah had assisted her father, Miss Talbot had assisted Linfield.

*One of the world's formidable spinsters. It is what I should aspire to, if on a lesser scale.*

"My friend, Mrs. Macy," Miss Talbot said, and Delilah rather liked that she avoided the belittling inherent in the term *companion* by introducing Antonia as her friend.

Delilah curtsied to the woman who had so devastated her brother's happiness ten years ago, and knew at once that here was a completely different kettle of fish. She recognized her from the ball, but up close, Antonia was lovely. Keeping the smile on her face, Delilah felt her heart sink.

The twins had openly cajoled them all into the ball for Julius's sake, but it struck Delilah now that they were in the midst of several more plans. Especially when they attached themselves to Antonia as everyone strolled in the half-finished formal garden before dinner.

*Oh no.* They weren't trying to promote a rekindling of Julius's old engagement, were they? They knew nothing of the damage they could cause...

Delilah had already seen the shy smile in Antonia's eyes when she looked at him. Worse, she had seen Julius watching Antonia when he thought he was unobserved. It all added to Delilah's unease. Her good intentions to leave well alone, at least for tonight, flew out of the window.

Walking with Miss Talbot, she gave the twins a few more minutes with their prey. Then, leaving Miss Talbot to answer some question of Cornelius's about plants, she strolled on and made sure she came upon Antonia and the twins at the end of the path.

"Don't monopolize Mrs. Macy," she told her siblings. "Surely it is Lord Linfield's turn?"

The twins took the hint and ran off, although Leona glanced back over her shoulder, her face troubled. Delilah ignored her.

"Sorry," she said lightly to Antonia. "I'm afraid you have been 'twinned.'"

Antonia smiled. "Don't apologize for them. They are delightful."

"And ruthlessly inquisitive. Especially about Julius, since he is the brother they know least and admire most."

"I suppose that must be true of all of you, since he spent so long at sea. You must be very glad to have him home at last."

"Yes. It is good to be together. To support each other," Delilah added significantly.

Antonia met her frank gaze with a spark of understanding. She knew Delilah did not want her here, but rather than cringe or melt into the background like a good companion, she tilted her chin. "If you wish me to go, of course I shall. Only, I wish you had not invited me in the first place."

"I didn't," Delilah said bluntly. "Lucy invited you. But, of course, I am not so rude or inhospitable as to ask you to leave. I ask you only to leave *him* alone."

Antonia's eyes widened, but interestingly, she didn't back down. "Make the same request of your brother. If you dare."

Spirited. Unafraid. In other circumstances, Delilah would have admired that. But she had already seen Julius destroyed by this woman. She would not stand back and let it happen again if she could prevent it.

"It isn't a question of daring, Mrs. Macy," she said. "We are all here to pick up the pieces. But I don't want to do it again. Come, let us catch up with the others. It is almost time for dinner."

Antonia walked beside her in silence, and that suited Delilah perfectly.

On the other hand, dinner was an oddly tense affair, and not just because Delilah had been unforgivably rude to one of their guests. The tension came from Julius and Antonia. They were so unsure of each other that it struck Delilah she had had no need to warn the woman off. Besides which, she had made the party awkward for Felicia.

Yet somehow the informality seemed to make the meal not only bearable but pleasant. Felicia was an excellent hostess, the twins were their bright, amusing selves, and both Linfield and his sister, no doubt with experience of defusing fraught diplomatic dinners, were entertaining guests.

Until Linfield spoke of Papa.

His stories were amusing, showing Sir George's humor and

quick thinking, and yet they were told with such clear respect that Delilah found her eyes filled with tears. Missing Papa was an ache that never truly went away. More than any of her siblings', her life had been wrapped up in her father's.

Slowly, trying to block out the conversation, she blinked to be rid of the tears before they betrayed her. When she heard laughter around the table, she forced a smile, glancing warily about. Linfield's gaze met hers for an instant, then he turned to Lucy.

It was something of a relief when Felicia rose from her place at the foot of the table, and the ladies left the gentlemen to their port. Delilah found herself beside Miss Talbot, with whom she discovered she had much in common. The woman had a dry wit, a quick mind and appeared to be interested in Delilah's opinions. So it was some time before Delilah realized Antonia was not among them.

"Do you suppose Mrs. Macy is quite well?" she said.

"I expect she went to the cloakroom," Miss Talbot said, beginning to rise. "I'll make sure she has not been taken ill."

"No, let me," Delilah said, suddenly suspecting that Antonia had managed to detach Julius from his guests. "I would hate her to be unwell..."

Only when she was out of the room did she realize that she had already done everything she could to keep Antonia from Julius. Interrupting them would change nothing. In fact, warning her off achieved nothing either. She had merely been horribly rude.

Antonia was not in the cloakroom. A twinge of guilt smote her. She began to cross the hall toward the garden door when some faint sound from the morning room distracted her. Who would be in there at this hour?

She changed direction and pushed open the morning room door.

Lord Linfield walked toward her.

# Chapter Six

S HE CAME TO an abrupt halt. "My lord? Might I help you?"

"Actually, yes. I hoped I might run into you if I skulked here for a few minutes."

"You do not enjoy the conversation of my brothers?" she said coldly.

"I do, very much. But I wanted to speak to you alone."

Her heart lurched. "Why?"

"To apologize. I think I upset you, speaking of your father at dinner." He stood in front of her, his head bent solicitously toward her. She could smell his soap, the hint of wine on his breath, make out the texture of his smooth, recently shaved skin...

"I was not upset," she managed. "To hear him spoken of in such terms is a pleasure to all of us."

"Pleasure and pain," he said. "I am sorry for the latter. You were very close to him, I think. I know, when we worked together, he missed you very badly."

"That must have been while I went with Aubrey and the twins to visit Felicia in London." She blinked rapidly. "His passing has left a black, empty hole," she blurted, and was appalled.

"Is that why your work"—he waved a hand toward her almost-cleared desk—"is so important to you?"

"Partly, perhaps. Everyone needs...purpose."

His gaze dropped to the region of her mouth. Nervously, fearing she had left crumbs there, she flicked her tongue over her lips, and heard his breath hitch. He raised his hand and touched her cheek with the very tips of his fingers—such a brief, butterfly-like caress, and yet her blood seemed to sizzle.

He bent nearer, his gaze curiously intent. Was he going to *kiss* her? Heat surged beneath her skin, and yet she did not step back.

What did she want? What did *he* want? For an instant he held perfectly still, almost like a painting, a living, breathing portrait. And then his lips quirked, drawing her helpless gaze to their fine texture and curiously sensual shape. How would they feel against hers?

"You don't know, do you?" he said softly. "You have no idea how extraordinarily beautiful you are."

"Fustian, my lord," she said, swinging away from him. "There is no point in flattering me. I was looking for Mrs. Macy."

He straightened. "I think she is with Sir Julius. They have old business to discuss."

*Damn the woman.* And yet… "You like her," Delilah said, frowning. "Your sister likes her."

"Yes. Does that mean you do not?"

"She caused him pain. I have never seen—" She broke off, shrugging impatiently. "I cannot wish him such anguish again."

His steady eyes caught hers. "That is not up to you or me. Pain and anguish are part of life. One has to feel to live."

For no obvious reason, she sensed threat and attacked first. "What do *you* feel, then, my lord? What pain or anguish gives you the right to wish it on my brother, who has suffered so much already?"

"I don't wish it on him. But we cannot prevent it either. Not for him or her."

She curled her lip. "*Laissez faire?* Was that what your diplomatic missions amounted to also? You will excuse me, sir. I'm sure you can find your own way back to the dining room."

She needed to escape from him, from the emotions and desires churning in her stomach. Yet as soon as she left him, she felt his loss. Had he really been about to kiss her? Why? And why had he not?

*An impulse born of kindness, but I am too ill-tempered and too old. And a bastard, besides…*

Antonia had returned to the drawing room when Delilah slipped back inside. Lucy sat beside her, deep in animated conversation. For some reason, that made Delilah feel very alone.

The gentlemen joined them shortly afterward. The twins played a clowning duet on the pianoforte that was really very funny. The next time Delilah noticed, Lucy had moved seats, and Julius now sat beside Antonia.

She wasn't entirely surprised when he escorted her out of the French window to the terrace. Everyone else spilled out too, enjoying the fresh evening air, for once without rain to dampen the spirits and the paths underfoot.

Julius and Antonia were nowhere in sight. Delilah tried not to care. He was older and wiser than he had been ten years ago. And perhaps Linfield was right that *feeling* made one truly alive. Was that not at the heart of the twins' scheme to send him to the ball?

"Shall we have tea?" Felicia said as the servants wheeled the trolley into the drawing room. "Oh, tell the others, will you, Delly?"

This time, Delilah was reluctant to track them down. She wasn't surprised to find them in a close embrace. What astonished her was the fact that she felt not anxiety or anger but envy.

She whisked herself away. "I think they're just coming," she called to Felicia.

"You look flustered," Linfield said. He stood in the shadowy part of the terrace some distance from the lights shining through the glass doors.

It struck her suddenly that if she told Linfield what she had seen, Antonia might well be dismissed from his sister's service. *That would teach her… And what have I become that I could even consider such small-minded tale-bearing?*

Disgusted with herself, she shook her head and muttered, "Not in the slightest. I am looking forward to tea."

She walked quickly inside and accepted a cup of tea from Felicia. The place next to her sister was free, but, leaving it for Linfield, she moved on.

Unexpectedly, he stayed with her. "Am I correct in guessing that your mother is Helena Hampshire?"

Delilah blinked. "You recognized her?"

"Not until I saw the bill advertising her play outside the theatre. She is quite famous, is she not? Illustrious, even."

"I have tickets for the opening night of her play, if you would like to go."

"I would very much like that. Especially in your company."

"Don't be silly. The tickets are yours. Go with a friend or take your sister."

"I would rather take you."

She frowned. "Are you trying to make my sister jealous? It won't work."

"Your sisters are all very charming, as is mine, but I am at a loss where they fit in this conversation. May I not escort you to the theatre?"

"No," she said automatically, for it was hardly proper for an unmarried lady. Then she remembered that she was thirty years old and a confirmed spinster. Was this not the independence and the freedom she had craved? And his presence might well prevent any further confidences from Nell about her marital problems. It was even possible Linfield's titled presence would scare Reggie back into line where her own threats probably bounced off him.

And why on earth would her mother want to be married to someone who had to be threatened into staying with her? The pride and status of being the wife of so admired an actor?

Her gaze refocused on Linfield. "I'll give you the tickets before you go."

"You can give me them on the night. The theatre is more fun

with friends. And I promise to be the perfect gentleman."

She frowned at him. Why did he press her? Was it possible she had got everything wrong and he was not pursuing Felicia? Or...did he imagine that because she was the daughter of an actress she was some lightskirt? But then again, why would that make any difference to him? Linfield, distinguished, refined, and handsome, could surely have his pick of the most beautiful women of whatever degree.

"I shall think about it," she said, and he smiled, which did very odd things to her insides.

The evening drew to a close. Lord Linfield's carriage was sent for, and the whole family prepared to escort their guests to the front step.

Delilah, melting into the background as she struggled to understand Lord Linfield and her own foolish feelings, followed the others from the drawing room and found the man himself holding the door for her.

"What is it?" he asked.

"I don't know what you mean."

"You have been on edge all evening. If you are troubled, I would like to help."

Heat seeped under her skin. "You are mistaken. I have nothing to be troubled about. But I thank you for your concern."

He still stood in front of her, gazing down at her, a faint frown between his brows. "Nothing at all? About your family? Or the path you have chosen? Your work?"

"Nothing," she repeated, relieved he had not guessed. "Or not beyond my concern for Julius."

A few moments longer, he waited. And then he stood aside to let her pass.

DENZIL HAD GIVEN her every opportunity to confide. He could

not believe she *knew* the harm she was doing. But he had seen the parcel in the hall addressed to Mr. Charles in York. And he had seen that her desk in the morning room still bore about half the documents he had seen there before. She was sending her work early. Because it was urgent, or because it troubled her?

Either way, she did not tell. And so he picked up her parcel in passing and hid it beneath the folds of his traveling cloak. An ungracious act toward gracious hosts, though in fact he was doing her a favor. "Mr. Charles" would be searched soon enough, and the less connection to Delilah and her family, the better.

All the same, he spent the carriage ride back to Blackhaven trying to throw off his guilt. He remembered he had almost kissed her in the morning room. He had been distracting her, of course, from the fact that he was where he should not have been, but somehow he had forgotten that when he stood so close to her, inhaling her heady scent. She was all allure and vulnerability, and the combination was irresistible.

And yet he *had* resisted, because even he was not that big a scoundrel. He wanted her to trust him, not take him to bed. He shifted position, staring out of the window at nothing. He hardly knew her, and yet he was sure she would never give her body without her heart. He doubted her heart had ever been won. And suddenly, he wanted to be the one to win it. He wanted to win *her*.

Perhaps he should have begun with honesty. Not deceit and now theft, dishonorable by any standards. But while his heart seemed to trust her, his head could not.

Both Elaine and Antonia were largely silent on the journey to the hotel, so it was not difficult to wish them both goodnight at their respective bedchambers and enter the sitting room.

There, he lit the lamp and several more candles, and untied the parcel he had purloined.

It didn't take him too long to find what he searched for. And it stunned him, because now he had a date and a place for assassination. And it was all to do with the Blackhaven theatre, and the visiting company that included Delilah's mother.

DELILAH, DISCOVERING HERSELF alone in the drawing room with guttering candles, rose and blew them out. She only vaguely remembered the others retiring, all pleased with the way the dinner party had gone. Despite Antonia, Delilah was conscious of a novel excitement building in her stomach, like the fluttering of butterfly wings.

She had believed Lord Linfield's calls, his attention to her, were part of his attraction to Felicia. But what if that were not so? What if he only asked for Felicia because she was the nominal lady of the house, being the only one who was married?

Delilah had been admired in her youth. She remembered bold young men flirting with her. Some had been princes. It had been so common she had stopped noticing, because no one ever intrigued her enough for her to allow any relationship to develop. No one had ever asked for her hand, and she had not expected them to, because although she often moved in her father's important circles, she was still illegitimate.

Papa had said the right man would not care about her irregular birth, though her various stepmothers had disagreed. But Linfield... Even that glimpse of him years ago had stayed with her. And he had remembered her.

Had he really almost kissed her this evening? Why? Why did he want to take her to the theatre unless he liked her? And he must agree that she was at an age when no one would consider it improper. Perhaps she should give him the tickets and buy more for herself and whoever else in the family would like to come, make it a large party. Although the thought of being alone with him was intoxicating...

Taking the last candle with her, she crossed the hall toward the staircase and saw the light shining under the library door. The servants must have forgotten to put them out. She changed direction and opened the library door.

Julius stood gazing out of the open window toward the sea. He often did that. The sea had been his life for so long that he missed it. He had borrowed a vessel from a neighbor and longed to buy it—only until the land was profitable again, there was no money for such luxuries.

"I didn't realize you were in here," she said as he turned toward her. "I came to douse the candles, since I sent the servants to bed."

"I'll put them out when I go." He met her gaze, and a frown twitched his brow. "Is everything well?"

"Yes, of course." Her fingers twisted on the door handle, then she came into the room. "It *is* her, isn't it? *That* Mrs. Macy?"

"The lady I was engaged to, yes."

"Is she pursuing you again now that her first choice of husband is dead?"

He winced, then let out a short breath of laughter. "I think, rather, she was in pursuit of the truth. We had a conversation this evening that we should have had ten years ago. She never sent me away. In fact, she was at least as hurt as me and pushed into what I think was an unpleasant marriage, besides. It was her parents who lied to me, and to her, and hid our letters so that she would marry Macy."

Delilah stared at him in disbelief. "Is that what she told you?"

"It is what we deduced," he retorted.

"Oh, Julius, don't fall for the lies again," Delilah pleaded. "She has Linfield and his sister eating out of her hand, *their* servants caring for *her* son while she still receives a salary and, through them, access to the best Society. Now she has seen that you have a fine estate here. Macy left her with nothing, you know."

He scowled. "Of course I know. And you are misinterpreting everything."

"Am I?" she challenged.

"Yes. You don't know her, Delly."

"I know what she did to you ten years ago."

"What was done to both of us."

She went up to him, scowling with worry and fear for him. "Don't be foolish, Julius. She married Macy a bare three weeks after she dismissed you. One does not find oneself married accidentally. She snared him and his wealth as easily as she caught you. Only he at least protected his family from her machinations."

"By leaving her dependent on a brother whose face would curdle the milk?"

"Exactly! Why would he have done that unless he had reason not to trust her?"

"Don't, Del," he said between his teeth. "You don't know her at all."

"I know enough. Ten years ago, you had me frightened to let you sail away. Even Papa was anxious."

"And you imagine this is history repeating itself?" he said.

"It does, you know."

"Perhaps. But not consistently." He gave her his crooked half-smile. "Believe it or not, I was never a fool. I am used to reading people's characters. Instead of hating her, consider why I loved her in the first place." He bent and kissed her cheek. "Goodnight, Delilah."

DELILAH TRIED. BUT everything around her felt suddenly unsettled. Her siblings all seemed to be harboring secrets and went about with an air of excitement that contrasted too vividly with the peace of their early months at Black Hill. Change was in the air. And Delilah, for so long the mother figure of the family, could not protect them.

Julius was different. Six years her senior, he had always been her admired and adored big brother, and she could not bear to see him brought low, as he had been ten years ago. And yet he had a point. He really was no fool. He had been a Royal Navy captain, about to be promoted to commodore when he chose retirement instead. He understood men in all their best and worst characteristics. And while it was possible he had a blind spot where women were concerned, she should not assume it.

And there had been no excuse for her behavior last night. She had been unforgivably rude to a guest.

She could not concentrate on her work. Linfield and his theatre invitation kept intruding. If she forced herself to stop thinking about him, she instead saw her brother's face when he spoke of Antonia. And Antonia herself, a flash of hurt in her eyes at Delilah's attack, yet refusing to be intimidated.

Guilt niggled at her.

She had no right to interfere in Julius's life and undoubtedly owed Antonia an apology. And if she were to see Lord Linfield again while she was with Antonia...

Abruptly, she pushed the papers away from her and jumped to her feet. She would not think of Linfield. She very much doubted he was thinking of her. He flirted to pass the time, and really, he was much more suited to Felicia, who deserved a kind, loyal, and loving husband after the unspeakable Nick Maitland. When Linfield was her brother-in-law, she would feel much more comfortable around him.

She strode away, as though she could leave her sillier self behind. She was behaving like a sad, twittering old maid convinced the young man courting a beautiful young family member really came to see her.

She could not keep dwelling upon Lord Linfield. She would think about mending the bedroom curtains instead, and perhaps call on Antonia to clear the air.

Both the old carriage and the decent one had already been taken by her siblings, so Delilah was reduced once more to driving herself in the gig. She was just climbing into it when the twins appeared in the stable yard.

"Are you going to Miss Talbot's 'at home'?" Leona asked cheerfully.

Delilah frowned, reaching for the vague memory of a conversation last night. "Did I say I would?" she asked cautiously.

"She didn't require a response, just said she would be receiving in her hotel sitting room this afternoon. Julius is going. And Felicia and Lucy. At least."

"Oh." Then there would be few opportunities for private speech with Antonia. Was that a good thing? "I'm not sure," she said. "I'll see if there is time. Don't get up to too much mischief while I'm gone."

On reaching Blackhaven, she devoted herself to finding thread of just the right shades. She found a couple at a market stall near the harbor, and then some better ones at the draper's shop in the high street. After that, in need of refreshment, she went to the hotel tearoom, a respectable enough place for a mature lady to sit alone.

Here, she tried to decide whether to call on Miss Talbot. Antonia would undoubtedly be there, but what Delilah had to say should not really be overheard. Besides, Lord Linfield would be present too, and her desire to see him again should not be pandered to.

As she poured a second cup from the pot, she saw Roderick, Cornelius, and Aubrey leave the hotel without noticing her. Perhaps Antonia would have more time now if the guests were thinning out.

But before she had finished her second cup of tea, Delilah glimpsed Antonia herself crossing the foyer to the front door, and with her was Julius.

Her lips tightened before she forced herself to relax. Nothing had changed, and she could speak to Antonia another day. Doubtless she would be at the castle garden party.

What was the matter with her? She had wasted a whole day vacillating, when she should have been working, and all she had to show for her efforts was a few reels of cotton.

She left the tearoom and was crossing the foyer to the front door when a stranger approached her. He appeared to be a gentleman and bowed to her in a respectful manner.

"Excuse me, ma'am. We have not been introduced, but am I correct in believing you to be Miss Vale?"

"I am."

"My name is Macy. Timothy Macy."

That got her attention.

Macy smiled apologetically. "My brother was married to the lady who left the hotel with your brother Captain Vale only five minutes ago. Forgive me, but I could not help noticing that the sight appeared to distress you."

"You are mistaken," Delilah replied, for that was no one else's business, and she most definitely did not care to be observed. "You will excuse me."

"Of course." He stood aside at once. "I merely hoped you and I might be allies in a common cause. Are you sure you cannot spare me a moment of your time?"

He spread his arm, indicating the sofa he had just risen from. Another man sat there, though he rose when she turned to him. She recognized him as Mr. Dunnett from the charitable hospital, a man whom Julius disliked.

Delilah knew she should walk away. But she wanted to know the truth about Antonia, and as usual, curiosity won. "A moment only, sir, for I am expected elsewhere."

"Allow me to be frank, Miss Vale," Macy said as he sat down opposite her. "My poor brother made a bad choice in his bride. You might say he was driven to his early grave by his disappointment. In short, the woman is a menace, and it grieves me to see her dig her claws into such a great man as Sir Julius. I think it grieves you also."

Delilah's instinct urged her to walk away. Instead, she chose to defend Julius and, by implication, Antonia. "You are aware that my brother and your sister-in-law are old friends?"

"They were engaged," Macy said wryly, "before she decided

my brother was richer."

It was so much what Delilah had always believed that all her old anger returned.

"Then she needs another distraction," she snapped.

"I have one in mind," Macy said blandly, glancing significantly at Mr. Dunnett, who beamed at her. "But I might need your help in deflecting her from the captain."

Delilah gazed at him. She did not trust him or like him. But she had to agree that Julius's relationship with Antonia must be nipped in the bud. "What is it you want me to do?"

"Merely inform your brother of Antonia's betrothal to Mr. Dunnett, who is, contrary to the general belief in Blackhaven, an extremely wealthy man. She has been flirting with Sir Julius only to inspire Mr. Dunnett to make her an offer."

Delilah looked again at Mr. Dunnett. Julius was right. The man was a weasel, and no woman in her right mind would prefer him over her gallant brother. Even one eyed and lame, Julius outshone him in every way. Except wealth. Was Antonia really so mercenary? She had jilted Julius before for a richer man, although he now believed they had been lied to by others—probably, in fact, by Mr. Macy, who sat smiling at her now.

This man had the guardianship of Antonia's child, which gave him a huge hold over her. What motivated him to interfere? Mere spite?

"And Mrs. Macy is willing to marry Mr. Dunnett?" she asked.

Macy smiled. "Not only willing but eager, as you will see."

It didn't make a great deal of sense. Why would Dunnett want to marry this mercenary and awful creature that they were making Antonia out to be? She was a lady by birth, of course, and Dunnett did not appear to have much claim to gentility of his own. However, Macy's attitude to a family member he was supposed to protect turned Delilah's stomach. Against the odds, all her sympathies were with the victim of this nastiness.

She rose and coldly inclined her head. "Most illuminating, gentlemen. Goodbye."

She walked regally out of the hotel, nodding to the doorman, while inwardly she felt grubby for even listening to Antonia's brother-in-law.

She would have nothing else to do with him.

# Chapter Seven

T HE FOLLOWING DAY, Delilah forced herself to translate all the remaining documents on her desk. However, since her mind had been wandering again, she left them to be read over again later, and took herself for a brisk walk to the beach.

It did her good. Since she was alone, she even picked up her skirts and ran for some of the way in her bare feet, and that was even better. Everything had got out of proportion for her, and the exercise seemed to clear her mind of confusion, particularly about Lord Linfield.

She should enjoy his friendship—which was all there would ever be between them—for as long as he remained in Blackhaven. The decision made her feel human again.

As for Antonia Macy... Delilah would indeed apologize for her rudeness and would tell Julius about Timothy Macy's machinations. Then she would step back from what was decidedly not her business.

With both decisions made to her satisfaction, she sat on a rock to replace her stockings and shoes. To her surprise, the sky had darkened alarmingly. The first spots of rain were already pattering gently on her hat. The wind had got up too, riling the sea to quick, choppy anger with dashes of white froth. Seabirds played in the air currents as they made their way to shelter. She was about to be deluged.

A glance at the shore showed her she was within sight of Blackhaven, which meant she was more than halfway to the town. She would shelter there until the storm had passed.

By the time she had fastened her shoes back on, the rain was coming harder and she had to hold her hat on to prevents the wind whipping it off. She hurried onward, fighting the growing gale, and then racing the tide that was suddenly speeding in. On this part of the beach, there was no easy way up onto the road. The cliff was too high and too sheer. But she was sure there was a cave close by. She remembered playing there with Julius and Roderick when they were children. They had clambered over rocks—surely *those* rocks—and the cave had been high enough up to avoid the high tides of spring and autumn. Surely she would be safe there from a summer storm.

Since the sea was rushing over her shoes, she began to climb over the wet, slippery rocks. It took her feet and her skirts out of the water for now at least, but she had to hold on with both hands, buffeted by the wind and soaked by the relentless downpour.

She was no longer a ten-year-old child in short skirts, playing in the sunshine with two big brothers to help her. Her clothes hindered her almost as much as the weather. She could barely make out the cliffs through the driving rain, never mind spot the cave opening. The sea itself vanished into mist.

But something was moving through it—a horse, splashing through sea that was up to its knees, its rider in a large, dark overcoat, urging it on. He would make it to Blackhaven easily before the tide cut him off. Whereas if Delilah could not find the remembered cave, she would have to perch on the highest rock she could find and pray hard.

Resting, and deciding on her next direction, she saw the rider suddenly pull his horse to a halt. His head was turned toward her. Even with his hair plastered to his head, he looked familiar.

*Linfield?* Or was her mind playing tricks on her, making her imagine every man she glimpsed was *him?* Perhaps she had a secret yearning to be a damsel in distress rescued by her hero.

Snorting with sudden mirth, she waved to him, gesturing him to ride on while she negotiated the treacherous, rocky journey to the cliff face.

When she glanced back, the horse was riderless, galloping on through the sea and vanishing into the mist. She knew a moment of fear for the rider. Then she saw him, climbing over the rocks toward her.

*Oh the devil, now we are both cut off!* She did not want him to see her as silly or helpless, though the craven part of her was glad of the company because she had begun to suspect she could not reach the cave alone. She couldn't even find the wretched thing.

"Delly!" he shouted above the wind. "Wait!"

Even blasted by the storm, something in her warmed. Because it was Linfield. Because he had called her by the name only her family ever used. He must have heard and remembered.

*At least he didn't call me Lah-Lah.*

Clearly, she was on the verge of hysteria.

He made much better time over the rocks than her, and the soles of his boots must have gripped better, too, for he reached her in no time, flinging one strong arm about her waist.

"Are you hurt?" he shouted over the combined roar of wind, rain, and sea.

"No, just wet! You should have gone on with the horse."

"I couldn't leave you stranded. What are you doing here?"

"Looking for a cave where I played with my brothers. It's high enough to avoid the tide and will get us out of the rain and the wind. If I can only find it."

He helped her over the rocks, catching her when she slipped. The sophisticated diplomat appeared more like a mountain goat, albeit a very wet one. He had lost his hat somewhere.

"Is that it?" he said suddenly in her ear, and in spite of the situation, awareness thrilled though her.

She followed his pointing finger to the cliff face, saw the higher rocks rising toward the darker ridge of stone. "Yes, that's it!"

Climbing up was a lot more frightening as an adult. And once she reached the highest point of rock, the toeholds in the cliff looked impossible. Linfield took her by surprise, gripping her around the waist and swinging her upward as though she weighed no more than that ten-year-old child who had last been here.

Some instinct brought her knees up to the cave opening; she grasped the stone on either side and pulled herself in, quickly pushing herself aside and reaching down to help him. However, he landed beside her in a rush, filling the space that she remembered as much less cramped.

"Bliss," he pronounced. "No wind, no rain." He peered out. "The tide will never rise this high. God, you must be soaked to the skin."

"I am," she said shakily. "So are you."

"You're shivering," he said, beginning to strip off his coat. "Come, sit down over here."

She sat with considerable relief on the cave floor, her back against the wall. Crouched in front of her, he deftly unfastened her soggy cloak and cast it aside, before he sat down beside her and spread his overcoat over them both. Though the outside of it was horribly damp, the inside felt dry and warm from his body heat. She pulled it higher, and he pressed closer, throwing his arm around her and holding her to him for warmth. It felt dangerously natural.

"Where on earth were you going in such weather?" he asked.

"Nowhere, really. I was just walking and didn't notice the storm in time. I decided Blackhaven was closer for shelter and kept on, only then the tide came in so fast and I knew it was cutting me off. I could see I would never reach the town before I was up to my neck in sea, so I started looking for the cave." She shivered and burrowed closer into his warmth. "What about you? It's not great weather for a leisurely ride."

"I hacked out to Black Hill by the road and chose to come

back this way."

"Oh. Did you see Felicia?"

"No, I saw the twins before I even got to the house, and they told me you were on the beach. By then, I could see the storm approaching, so I came to find you. I almost didn't see you."

"I find I'm quite glad you did," she admitted.

"So am I." He hugged her, grinning with a boyishness she had never seen in him before. With his free hand, he shoved his clinging hair off his face, and then removed her sodden bonnet, his fingers struggling with the wet knots of the ribbons, pulled tight by the wind.

Shivering cold and dripping as she was, awareness sizzled beneath her skin. She had never been so close to a man who was not her father or her brothers. And *this* man... Like no one else she had ever met, his arm warm and strong around her, his fingers gentle against her throat, his hard body pressed against her side, his chest, his hips, his thigh...

The inside of her mouth was dry as he finally untangled the ribbons, plucked off her hat, and tossed it onto the cave floor beside her cloak. His gaze returned to her face, dropped to her lips.

"Better?" he asked softly.

She nodded. It was. She had never been so happy in her life than huddled with him beneath his coat, her clothes clinging uncomfortably to her skin. Because his fine gray eyes were warm and exciting and entirely focused on her. She must have resembled a drowned rat, and yet he did not look remotely disgusted. He looked...

Her stomach dived.

His lips parted and the flame inside curled lower.

She hurried into speech. "Why were you looking for me?"

"I like you."

The heat deep in her belly seemed to surge through her whole being. She tore her gaze free, but somehow it didn't make her any less aware. She wanted to laugh at him, or at least challenge him, but the words eluded her. There was only his closeness, his distinctive scent, heady amongst the freshness of rain and sea, and the smell of wet wool.

He said, "You must have been very lost in your own thoughts not to see the storm coming."

"I suppose I was."

"What troubles you, Delilah?"

She had not given him leave to use her name. Here, it hardly mattered. "Many things," she said, aiming for lightness. "Changes in the air, my siblings…"

"I have rarely met a more charming and capable set of people than you and your siblings."

"They are capable," she said, trying to ignore the fluttering of her heart. "But they are vulnerable, too, because they *care.*"

"Who in particular cares? Sir Julius?"

She nodded. It must have been the strange, unique intimacy of the situation, but the urge to confide grew too strong. "She hurt him very badly ten years ago. Antonia Macy."

For several moments, he was silent, although his gaze remained on hers. "As long as I have known her," he said at last, "she has carried some deep sadness. I do not think he was the only one who was hurt. She is kind, funny, fiercely devoted to her son, and my sister loves her. If she and your brother have let go of the past, perhaps you should too."

"Do you know her brother-in-law?" she asked.

His lip curled. "He is trying to wrest control of her son from her. I don't know why, because he has no affection for the boy."

"He wants her to marry Mr. Dunnett. I think he has some means of forcing her. If I didn't distrust her, I would feel sorry for her. As it is, I am glad she has you and Miss Talbot. Only…"

Without warning, he bent and brushed his lips against hers. "How can you be so sweet and so prickly at the same time?"

"I am not *sweet,*" she said, revolted. Her lips tingled and she had to look away, staring out of the cave mouth at the angry sea.

"Yes, you are. You can't look after everyone, you know.

Sometimes you have to let them solve their own problems. Trust them. But then, I think trusting is *your* problem."

Her gaze flew back to him. She opened her mouth to protest.

"Do you trust me, Delilah?"

She closed her mouth again, unsure what to say, unsure of the truth. "I suppose I must, since I am here with you, sharing your coat so improperly."

His eyes glinted. "Clever. Now I am bound to remain the perfect gentleman or lose that trust. What a pity."

"You'll cope," she said wryly.

"I might. Just." His hand on her shoulder slid upward to her neck, caressing just beneath her ear.

She caught her breath, but otherwise pretended not to notice. He couldn't know how his touch moved her. Such a casual, almost distracted stroking, and yet it played havoc with her pulse. He appeared to be lost in his own thoughts, while she could think of nothing but those tender, relentless fingertips, spreading heat and weakness and something far beyond mere awareness. Desire.

She reached up and grasped his hand. "What will you do next, Lord Linfield?" she asked desperately. "Where will you be posted?"

His fingers stilled in her grip, though he made no effort to withdraw. "I have been granted a long leave of absence. But I must return to London next month. I suppose I will learn then."

"Do you wish to go abroad again?"

"Probably. Do you?"

She didn't need to think about it. "If I can be useful. I like being abroad, meeting new people."

"Being the power behind the power. I think that is how Sir George saw you."

"Did he?" she said wistfully.

"Undoubtedly. He was proud of all his children—he spoke of you often. If you were a man, he said you would be an ambassador before you were thirty. As it was, he appreciated all your advice, and all you did to smooth his path."

She blinked. "Did he really say that?"

"Yes. You seem surprised."

She shook her head. "I have to watch my tongue. I can be too blunt for diplomacy. Besides, for such an eloquent man, my father rarely spoke of feelings. Or praise."

"Yet he was a man of deep passion."

She nodded, emotion blocking her throat.

"You are like him."

Heat flooded her. Right now, she felt like her rakish father. For the first time, she truly understood temptation rather than the mere frustration of vague, impersonal desires. She wanted to touch Linfield's face, trace the outline of his sculpted lips, run her fingers though his damp hair...

"Which has been your favorite posting?" she asked quickly.

The question served its purpose. She could enjoy his stories and relate to the people involved, some of whom she knew. They conversed like old friends, exchanging opinions of places and politics, of art and literature. In fact, it was some time before she realized that she was still holding his hand. She released it, and it fell lightly to her shoulder. The closeness beguiled her, surely an intimacy that would never be repeated.

She wanted both his arms around her. She wanted to hold him, just once...

Madness. He was being kind to her, no more. And the time flew past too quickly.

"The storm is not letting up," he said at last. "We can't stay here much longer or your family will call out search parties."

"The tide will be going out again."

"Then we can at least get to Blackhaven and root out my coachman."

"You cannot make the poor man drive in this! Think of the horses, too!"

"I see no other solution, do you? Much as I would love to hide away with you until after dark, your brothers would kill me, and by then they might well have cause. The road is safe enough, and I'll pay poor old Alf a good bonus."

He rose as he spoke, moving toward the cave mouth. Delilah shivered, drawing the coat up over her suddenly cold side. The loss of him felt like an ache, and he had only gone a step away.

A flash of thunder lit up the sky, illuminating his tall figure, the shadows and angles of his face. Her heart skipped a beat. *What is happening to me?*

"The tide is pulling away from the rocks. We should be safe to leave in another few minutes."

*I don't want to leave. This is all I will ever have, and it's so much more than a dance. And so much less than—*

"Delilah?"

She blinked and rose, lifting the coat with her and shaking it out. "Yes?"

His lips quirked. "Nothing." He came toward her, but only to pick up her cloak, still unpleasantly wet, and yet it would have to do. "I hope you won't take a chill from today."

"I'm healthy as a horse," she said lightly. "I hope you don't either, especially as you could have been warm and dry in your hotel all this time."

"Where is the fun in that? One needs a little adventure in life. Can you bear this?"

He laid the damp cloak about her shoulders. She could bear anything if he touched her.

He picked up her hat and waved it about. "Better than nothing, but a little the worse for the weather."

She reached for it, but he set it on her head and tied the ribbons. His fingers stilled, and she looked up at him, her heart beating and beating. He released the ribbons and lifted one hand to her cheek. He smiled as though the touch pleased him. She wanted to lean into his hand, only she could not move.

His hand fell away. Slowly, he took the coat from her. "What was I thinking? You should have this."

"It's ridiculously large for me. I'd only fall over it on the rocks. We can run once we reach the sand."

"True." He shrugged into the coat, then returned to the cave mouth, peering outside as though planning his route over the rocks. "Are you ready? I'll climb down first and catch you."

She nodded, going to stand beside him. She wanted to take his hand, lay her head against his shoulder. Her arms ached to hold him. Just once.

*I've already had my last dance.*

And yet he seemed to be waiting for something. He was looking at her now, not at the beach below, but she would not meet his gaze.

He crouched down, turned, and half slid, half climbed down to the rocks below. Then, planting his feet firmly, he reached up for her. Rain battered down on him, and on her as she held on to the cave floor and dropped into his arms.

There was no time to treasure the moment, although inevitably she would later on. For now, they merely clambered over the rocks toward the narrow strip of sand no longer bombarded by the sea.

In no time, it seemed, they were clear of the rocks, and running, hand in hand across the sand, blown on by the wind at their backs while the rain beat down. She smiled at the sight they must present, like playing children. Sheer joy in the moment, so different from her earlier scramble for safety, swept her up, and she ran faster, all but tripping over her sodden skirts as he held her up and pulled her onward.

Forked lightning flashed across the sky, followed almost at once by a crack of thunder like cannon fire.

He spun her around, and she fell hard against him, laughing. His mouth came down on hers, as electric as the angry sky. Something magical ignited inside her, making her gasp and throw her arms around his neck, grasping the dripping hair at his nape.

Never had she imagined a kiss like this, invasive and devouring and all she had never known she wanted. The wind ripped at her hat; the rain poured down over her upturned face and into her mouth. She could taste it on his lips. She could taste *happiness.*

As the storm lit up the sky, passion burned within her, absorbing everything. She caressed his face as she had longed to, the corner of his devastating mouth where it joined to hers. She reveled shamelessly in the hard masculinity of his body, arching into him.

"Oh, Delilah," he whispered. *"There* you are..." And then he was kissing her again, and she could have stood there forever. Or fallen into the sand with him, his weight upon her as this tempest of *feeling* raged.

At last, he tore his mouth free with a groan. She went after it, taking it back, and that was delicious too. But he had begun to shift, dragging her with him, and they had to separate enough to run.

# Chapter Eight

*S*HE IS EVERYTHING *I ever wanted*. And, in truth, never expected to find. But the intimacy of the cave had been too sweet, and *this*—holding Delilah in the rain and kissing her breathless—was as if the storm outside had swept into his heart. He felt all her shock, all her wonder, and then there was sheer delight as her passion was aroused to match his, elemental and utterly over-whelming.

But dear God, what was he thinking? This was neither the time nor the place to indulge. When he finally forced himself to break the astounding kiss and she claimed his mouth again, he could have taken her right there on the sand, pounded by wind and rain and rampaging need. It took a heroic effort to stop, but he had to care for her.

Still, he felt like a schoolboy with his first infatuation as he took her hand and ran with her, so aware of her every movement at his side, her firm grip on his fingers. She trusted him. She desired him.

He wanted to laugh and sing into the wind, but he needed all his energy for speeding along the beach to shelter.

They were both utterly soaked through—again—by the time they reached the town. Fortunately, the streets were deserted, but still he dropped her hand, dragging her arm through his instead. He guided her into the hotel stable yard, where the grooms and ostlers, including Alf, his coachman, were playing cards under cover.

They leapt to their feet as he appeared.

Alf said, "Sir?"

"I'm sorry, Alf, but I need you and the coach," Denzil said. "The lady needs to go home. Quickly as you can." He bent toward Delilah, and she gave a little shiver at the caress of his breath on her ear. "Wait here," he murmured, "and go straight into the carriage when it's readied..."

Although he hesitated to leave her alone with the stable staff, it would do her reputation less harm than trailing through the hotel with him, soaked to the skin, her clothes clinging all too revealingly to her every curve.

Glancing over his shoulder from the back door of the hotel, he saw Alf and a couple of stable lads bustling about, fetching horses and harnesses. The rest had already returned to their game, ignoring Delilah, who stood shivering just inside the open door, self-possessed as ever. At least on the outside.

He could not help smiling as he raced along the passage and up the staff stairs to his bedchamber, seeing no one but a maid carrying a tray of hot chocolate.

He was already shrugging off his wet coat as he entered his room. He changed with furious speed, abandoning his sodden garments on the floor and throwing on the first replacements he could find. Then, seizing a dry overcoat, he went to Elaine's rooms.

She was alone and pacing her sitting room floor. "Denzil! Have you seen Antonia?"

"No. Lend me a gown and cloak and stockings. And a shawl, perhaps."

To her credit, Elaine went immediately to her wardrobe, hauling things out apparently at random and shoving them at him as she spoke. "She took Edward with her to go on some expedition with Sir Julius. I think he meant to take them sailing. In this, Denzil!"

"There can't be a more experienced sailor in the country than Julius Vale," Denzil said, reaching for the carpetbag at the bottom of the wardrobe and shoving her garments inside. "They will be quite safe."

"You are right, of course," she admitted, though still anxiously. "Who are the clothes for?"

"Delilah Vale. We got caught in the storm. I'm taking her home."

"Oh," said Elaine, smiling.

At any other time, he would have challenged that particular *Oh*. Right now, he couldn't spare the time. "With luck, I'll be back in an hour or so."

"Take care, Denzil. Alf won't love you for this."

Denzil only raised a hand in response. He was already striding from the room.

A couple of minutes later, he ran across the stable yard to where the carriage awaited. The horses were snorting and stamping with annoyance, but at least the thunder had moved on to a mere distant rumble.

As Denzil climbed into the coach from one side, Alf, wrapped up against the storm, ushered Delilah in from the other. She was dripping wet and shivering again, strands of hair escaping her wrecked hat and clinging to her face, and yet his heart lifted at the sight of her. She was as beautiful as this semi-drowned waif as she was as an elegant lady in a ball gown.

He sat on the back-facing seat, the carpetbag on his knees. Delilah stepped inside and paused, her eyes widening to see him there.

"Oh!" She sat opposite with a bump. "You don't need to come, too. I am only grateful for the—"

"Hush," he interrupted, and leaned over to place the bag beside her. The carriage lurched as Alf mounted the box, and then the horses set off at a reluctant trot. "Take off your wet things and change into these."

Her jaw dropped. "I most certainly will not!"

"Pull down the blinds if you're so modest, but no one else will be foolish enough to be out in this."

"You are," she retorted.

"Being a gentleman," he said, "I shall gaze at the window until you are comfortable. The clothes are Elaine's, and she is happy to lend them to you."

She blushed, much to his delight.

"Please," he said more seriously. "You will be much more comfortable, and I would hate you to take ill from our adventure."

She hesitated, then nodded with odd abruptness. He pulled down all the blinds, then turned his head and stared at the blank window beside him. He tried not to think about the rustling and squelching as the wet clothes were dropped on the carriage floor.

What would she look like in nothing but her chemise? Without the chemise...

He shifted position and searched rather wildly for a distraction. "Elaine was worried about Antonia. Apparently she and Edward went sailing with Sir Julius."

"They will be safe. But Julius never minds the weather," she added with some satisfaction, "so she'll be as wet as I am and thoroughly outraged."

She underestimated Antonia, he suspected. "You might fight find her and Edward at Black Hill."

More rustling. The gown must be on, he thought with mingled relief and regret.

"I shan't be unkind," she said quietly. "You are right. I should not judge before I know her."

Her trust in his advice warmed him so much, he turned to smile at her, and all the breath left his body.

The gown was on, but it was not fastened at the back, allowing him a tantalizing glimpse of bare back and shoulders. More, she had drawn up the skirts at one side to pull on a stocking, and only a powerful effort of will prevented him reaching for her.

With a gasp, she flicked the skirts back over her leg.

"Sorry," he muttered, averting his eyes again. "I thought you were finished."

"I'm sure it is nothing you have not seen before," she said with deliberate lightness.

"If I have, it has not affected me so before."

"I find that hard to believe."

"Why? Do you really not know you are beautiful?"

"I do not need flattery, my lord. You may turn now if you wish."

"I do wish."

She was drawing a warm shawl from the bag, about to place it around her shoulders. Without thought he said, "Allow me to help with the fastenings."

Her breath hitched. Her gaze flew to his.

"I kissed you," he said softly. "I liked it very much. But you may trust me not to ravish you just yet."

"I'm sorry," she whispered, turning her back.

He moved across to the seat beside her. With some difficulty, because the carriage was lurching so much, he began to hook the fastenings of her gown. Her skin was soft and cool as his fingers brushed against it. A little shiver of awareness ran through her.

"Sorry for what?" he asked.

She shook her head. He couldn't resist brushing his lips against her nape. She gasped, arching her neck as though she couldn't help it.

"I hope you don't regret this day," he said, reaching around her to draw the shawl from her lap. "Because I do not. Can we see it as a beginning, Delilah?"

She glanced over her shoulder, searching his eyes. He placed the shawl around her, letting his hands linger on her shoulders. He kissed her mouth, softly, and then more deeply, savoring her, rejoicing in her instant response.

"The beginning of what?" she asked hoarsely.

"I don't know. Isn't that the exciting part?"

She swallowed. "I cannot tell. I have never been...here before."

"Neither have I."

"Please," she said, with a hint of pain, straightening and reaching for the dry cloak, which she whisked around her with no help from him. "I am not the first woman you have kissed."

"I am almost five and thirty," he said. "And I confess I have had my share of kisses, love affairs, and liaisons, each of them charming in their way. I know that, but right now, I can't remember them because there is only you."

"Carpe diem," she said, so softly that he almost didn't hear. "Seize the day."

"I want more than today," he confessed.

Color seeped into her pale face. "So do I," she whispered.

He took her hands in his and kissed her. To his delight, she laid her head on his shoulder, and he put his arms around her and simply held her. His heart was full.

"I will come to the theatre with you," she said.

It jolted him back to reality. To why he had sought her out in the first place. "We have much to talk about," he said, tightening his grip. "But perhaps not today."

DELILAH HURRIED FROM the bottom of the drive, where she had made Lord Linfield leave her, and up to the house alone. Fortunately, the rain had lessened, so she hoped his return to Blackhaven would be untroubled. Cornelius had worked wonders with the new drainage ditches. When they first came home, the roads and fields had flooded all the time...

She entered the house by the side door and fled unseen to her bedchamber to change. From somewhere in the house, she could hear the laughter of the twins, and a higher-pitched, more childish voice joining in. Antonia's son, no doubt, which meant she was here.

Because of today, because of *him*, she had more understanding of the powerful emotions of love. Vulnerability could so easily lead to mistakes... And so she would be kind to Antonia and her child. She was so happy, she would be kind to the whole world.

Dressed in her own clothes, she carefully hung up Miss Talbot's borrowed garments. As she smoothed down the gown, something rustled. Like her, Elaine must have pockets sewn into her everyday dresses. She smiled as she located the pocket and drew out the scrap of brown paper inside. It was screwed up, so she assumed it to be rubbish—until, as she walked to the wastepaper basket by her desk, something about it caught her eye.

A glimpse of ink, of a clear, familiarly shaped letter *C*. She smoothed the scrap out. Only a few letters were visible.

*r. Charl*

It could have been anything with any meaning, except that the handwriting was undoubtedly Delilah's, and the brown paper it was written on looked very like that she had used to wrap up the documents for her client, Mr. Charles of York.

"How the devil did you get into Miss Talbot's pocket?" she asked aloud.

She could think of only one solution, and a highly unlikely one at that. Miss Talbot, for whatever reason, was masquerading as Mr. Charles.

IT WAS VERY strange, joining her family for dinner. She felt changed by what had happened between her and Linfield, a pleasant knot of excitement in her stomach, happiness thrumming through her veins.

She looked with fresh eyes on Antonia, prepared to be convinced that the woman was as innocent as Julius in the events of ten years ago. Her delightful, lively son helped, of course. He already appeared devoted to Julius, with whom he seemed to be playing an ongoing game of pirates, and Antonia was clearly a loving mother, keeping him in line with a gentle word or two, but never damping his spirit with excessive strictness.

They too had been soaked in the storm, which sprang up faster than even Julius had anticipated, and Antonia was anxious for little Edward. Remembering her own terrible fears over Aubrey's asthma, Delilah had considerable sympathy for her in that too. She could even be glad they had chosen to stay the night.

It was a surprisingly pleasant evening, and yet Delilah was glad to say goodnight. She wanted to be alone, to savor her time with Linfield, to remember every moment of his kisses, every word he had said to her. And yet as soon as her head touched the pillow, she slept.

She woke to sunshine, outside and in.

She didn't even mind that at breakfast Julius was looking just a little too pleased with himself. Matters had progressed, she suspected, with Antonia.

Antonia and Edward left early, escorted by Aubrey *en route* to the pump room. Immediately, Julius went off to inspect the storm damage around the estate and, no doubt, to confer with Cornelius.

Delilah went happily about her own duties. It was her turn in the garden today, which meant a lot of clearing up after the storm. The ground was soggy, stray tree branches had fallen into new flowerbeds, and some saplings had been bent or uprooted by the wind.

She did what she could and then went inside to begin the hemming of the bedroom curtains. Her thoughts were still full of Lord Linfield, whom she would see tomorrow at the castle garden party.

At some point in the afternoon, she heard Julius's voice, and his distinctive, quick yet uneven footfall on the stairs. It was time that she told him about Timothy Macy's approach to her the other day.

She set aside her sewing and went quickly along the passage to Julius's door.

"Enter!" he called at once, and Delilah walked in.

She blinked, for he had already changed into evening clothes. It must be later than she had noticed. "Oh, you are dressed to go out. And very smartly, too. What event are you gracing with your presence tonight?"

"I don't know yet," he confessed. "I was hoping to dine with Linfield, but I may be too late."

It felt like a splash of cold water when she had been expecting warm. Perhaps mere jealousy because he would be with Linfield and she would not.

"By Linfield I gather you mean Mrs. Macy," she said, more waspishly than she had intended.

"She is usually present with Miss Talbot."

"You only saw her this morning," Delilah pointed out, uneasiness creeping in despite her good intentions. "Do you have to pursue her quite so assiduously?"

"I don't *have* to, no."

There was a warning in his voice, but she chose to ignore it. "Julius, you are making a spectacle of the woman and harming her reputation into the bargain. For goodness' sake, leave her alone for a few days."

He held her gaze. "Disingenuous, Delly. Don't pretend you give a fig for Mrs. Macy's reputation. Though I hope you will come to."

Heat crept into her face, but she refused to back down. "I care for yours. I don't want you making a fool of yourself. More than that, I don't want her ruining your life a second time."

Although it came out too harshly, it had to be said. Julius sighed, but he did not look entirely surprised by her outburst.

"There is no question of that," he said. "We understand the

lies told to each of us ten years ago. And you should know, I have asked Mrs. Macy to marry me—and she has accepted."

Delilah's blood ran cold. *Dear God, so soon?* That was sheer idiocy after what had happened before. Appalled, she clenched her fists at her side, then slowly unclenched them. She was giving Antonia a chance—really, she was—but for her brother's sake, she could not allow things to progress at this heedless speed.

"I'm afraid you must be told that she will not marry you," Delilah blurted. "She is already engaged to another, much richer man. She must be stringing you along for reasons of her own. Revenge, no doubt, because you sailed away from her before. Remember, she did not see your agony then."

"You make her sound like a monster," he said, scowling as he strode past her to the door. "Stop being ridiculous."

She caught his arm. "Can't you see it is *you* being ridiculous? Julius, she is going to marry Mr. Dunnett!"

He blinked and then laughed with what appeared to be genuine amusement. She had not even dented his confidence. "Dunnett is not rich, and she barely knows him."

"Oh, he is a lot richer than you think." Her cheeks burned with anger. "I had a very enlightening conversation with Mr. Timothy Macy just the other day. She used your interest in her to inspire Dunnett to propose. But I suppose she couldn't tell you that while she was at your mercy in a boat in a storm and then a guest in your house!"

Julius's eyes were freezing. If she had been under his command at sea, she would have withered.

"I did not constrain her to come with me," he snapped, "and you have gone beyond ridiculous to offensive on so many points that I don't know where to begin. Just *never* imagine I shall tolerate it. Goodnight."

As though struck, she snatched her fingers back, and he walked away.

AFTER DINNER, THE Vales dispersed quickly. Roderick had gone to Carlisle to promote the guarding business he and an old army friend were setting up. Julius had not returned.

Alone, Delilah paced the drawing room floor, her stomach knotted. Despite the urgings of Mr. Macy and Mr. Dunnett, despite her distrust of Antonia, she'd had no intention of spreading their lies in whatever cause. The very idea had made her feel grubby and treacherous.

And yet as soon as Julius had told her about his proposal of marriage, she had blurted it out, her one aim being to remove his blindness where Antonia was concerned, to slow the runaway horse of his courtship. But it had not worked. She had been prepared for his disappointment, grief, even anger. Instead, any disappointment had been with her.

He had been quite right not to believe the story. He could he be right about Antonia, too. Macy had shown he was quite happy to intervene in Antonia's affairs. Perhaps he had done so ten years ago to secure her for his brother. In which case, Antonia *was* as much a victim as Julius, and she, Delilah, was playing into the hands of their enemies.

At the sound of horses' hooves trotting into the yard, she hurried to the drawing room door, waiting impatiently for Julius to appear. One of the stable lads must have dealt with his horse, for he didn't take long.

She knew his leg was paining him by his halting advance across the hall and his slow ascent of the stairs. Even in the dim candlelight, she could see the lines and shadows of exhaustion on his face.

Impulsively, she went to him. "What is it?"

His eyes widened as though he were surprised to see her. "You were right. She is determined to marry Dunnett, and I don't know why. Do you? Beyond the grudge you bear her for ten years ago."

"No," she said honestly. "I did not ask. I just wanted her away from you."

"Something is going on between him and Macy. And she is the victim. She and Edward. That isn't right."

"No," Delilah whispered. "It isn't."

"She would not tell me."

Delilah swallowed. "She might. I believe she will be at the garden party at Braithwaite Castle tomorrow. I'll speak to her."

# Chapter Nine

S HE SAW LORD Linfield almost at once. He stood in a blink of
sunshine with the dramatic Lord Launceton and a group of
children who appeared to be entertaining him. Her heart turned
over.

He glanced up suddenly, and their eyes met. She forgot to
breathe, for there was no hesitation in his smile, and the sun
caught his glinting eyes.

*He remembers.*

Her chief fear had been that he would have forgotten all
about her, or, even worse, regret their unexpected intimacy in the
storm. She had therefore steeled herself to be ignored or treated
with polite distance. But in that one brief glance, the warmth of
relief flooded through her, before she was distracted by Lady
Braithwaite's welcome and the demands of civility.

She reminded herself that her main task today was to support
Julius—and Antonia, if she truly needed help.

Walking by Julius's side, it took a surprising amount of time
to reach the great hall where Lady Braithwaite had told them
they would find refreshment, art, poetry, and music. Many people
greeted them and paused to talk—Mrs. Grant, Dr. Lampton and
his wife, Miss Muir and her nephew, Mr. Winslow, the squire and
magistrate, and his daughter Lady Sylvester, and others who
looked familiar but whose names she had forgotten.

At the entrance to the great hall, the Earl of Braithwaite himself greeted them cordially, and right behind him, as though on their way outside, stood Antonia on the arm of Mr. Dunnett. Lord Braithwaite even turned and introduced them.

"My betrothed," Mr. Dunnett said as soon as Mrs. Macy's name was pronounced. He looked squarely at Julius as he said it, too, a smug smirk on his face.

Antonia's smile, on the other hand, was fixed and brittle. Tension radiated from her—unsurprising, perhaps, when she was faced with the man whom she had jilted twice, while in the company of her new betrothed. But this time, regarding her without the prejudice of the past, Delilah saw more. The woman was held together by a very fine thread. Delilah needed to talk to her very badly.

She squeezed Julius's arm to show she understood. As he handed her a glass of wine, Miss Talbot appeared, greeting them with apparent pleasure.

"I saw your twins with the Launceton children, being very kind to little Edward Macy," she said. "You must be very proud of them."

"We are," Delilah said, "though not very many people agree with us! They run a little wild."

"It is good for their self-confidence," Miss Talbot said, linking arms with Delilah. "Have you seen Lord Tamar's pictures?"

"Not yet."

As they walked together toward the stairs leading up to the gallery, Delilah wondered if she was about to be warned off. What had Linfield told his sister about her? Did she even know to whom her clothes had been lent? Should she bring the subject up? Or was Linfield keeping it secret?

"Have you recovered from your adventure in the storm?" Miss Talbot asked.

Delilah willed herself not to blush, though she wasn't sure she was entirely successful. "Oh, yes, thank you. I was most grateful to Lord Linfield for rescuing me."

Miss Talbot looked intrigued. "Did he? He never told me that part."

So Delilah told her briefly about her difficult clamber over the rocks to avoid the encroaching tide and his help in finding the shelter of the cave.

Miss Talbot looked pleased rather than shocked. "I am very glad to know he was of such use. It is like him, of course, but he rarely tells such things."

"I have to thank you also for the loan of your clothes," Delilah said quickly. "Without them, I fear I might not have avoided a severe chill. I did not send a servant to return them in case it caused any unwelcome speculation."

"Oh, there is no hurry. I'll tell you what, call on me on Monday and bring them with you. Then we may have a comfortable chat at the same time."

Talk of the clothes brought back the other niggling mystery. "May I ask you something, Miss Talbot?"

"Of course." She looked intrigued.

"Do you perhaps help your brother in his duties?"

She blinked. "I make him comfortable on his travels and act as his hostess or companion when he has need."

"No, I mean more practical help, such as with documents in need of translation or organization."

"Oh, no," Miss Talbot said, clearly shocked. "That would be most improper. Denzil is most careful of Foreign Office documents. They are entirely confidential. Besides, he has mastered several languages and has little need of translators. What on earth gave you such an idea?"

They had reached the gallery, but instead of moving toward the pictures on display, Delilah led the way to a group of chairs in the other direction and opened her reticule.

"This," she said as they sat down in as much privacy as possible and she passed over the scrap of brown paper.

Miss Talbot took it, frowning at it with clear incomprehension.

"I heard it rustling in the gown I borrowed," Delilah explained. "I was about to throw it away when I recognized the writing."

Miss Talbot looked at her blankly.

"It is mine," Delilah said. "I undertake such work for a client in York. He is a merchant, nothing to do with the Foreign Office, but still. I could not understand how the wrapping of my parcel came to be in your possession."

"I don't understand it myself," Miss Talbot said. "The gown is old and comfortable, and I do not normally wear it in company, only for—" She broke off. "In public places like hotels, I have a habit of tidying as I notice things out of place or fallen on the floor. If it is rubbish or something I don't know what to do with immediately, I stuff it in my pocket. If I have one."

Miss Talbot smiled triumphantly, clearly grasping a memory. *"That's* what I did with that paper. It was on the sitting room floor under the table, and I picked it up. My brother and I share the sitting room, have meals there and entertain guests." Her frown came back. "Mind you, I still can't understand how it came to be there."

"Perhaps you had a visitor? A Mr. Charles?"

Miss Talbot shook her head. "No, it's not a name I recall at all. You should ask Denzil."

"I will." Delilah shrugged. "It scarcely matters. It could have been walked in on the sole of someone's shoe."

"Or it came to grief being loaded onto the mail coach."

"Most likely of all," Delilah said, hoping the package had managed to reach Mr. Charles in the end. She hesitated, wondering how to ask about Antonia.

"Shall we look at the pictures?" Miss Talbot suggested, rising to her feet.

A QUARTER OF an hour later, Delilah strolled outside alone. Lucy walked right past her as though she didn't see her, which was another concern. Lucy was up to something, and Roderick thought she had met a man at the assembly room ball. Perhaps Delilah had not been paying enough attention to Lucy. After all, her gift for assessing character could only be trusted so far when she was still so young.

Almost immediately, Delilah was distracted again, this time by a little scene in the distance. Antonia was with Dunnett while Edward tugged at the man's hand. Dunnett shook the boy off like a rat, his whole stance one of angry distaste. Antonia stepped between them, but Edward suddenly ran off, hurling himself at Julius, whom he had clearly just spotted.

Julius hugged the boy briefly, glancing over his head toward Antonia and Dunnett. A moment later, he walked off with Edward and a group of older children.

Delilah shifted her attention back to Antonia, who abruptly dropped Dunnett's arm and strode after Edward and Julius. Then, abruptly, she halted, and Delilah soon saw why. Dunnett was walking away from her back toward the great hall, but Timothy Macy was striding from her left with the clear intention of intercepting her.

Antonia was like trapped prey, a prisoner, unable to do anything or go anywhere, even to her son, without either Dunnett or Macy at her side. Anger swamped Delilah. Julius was right. Something very nasty was happening here, and Antonia was undoubtedly the victim. Well, Delilah would not allow it.

She got to Antonia first. "What can I do?"

Antonia's head jerked around, startlement clear in her face. "Do?" she repeated, as though confused by Delilah's unexpected offer.

"I am not blind," Delilah said, "though perhaps I have been. Someone is coercing you."

Antonia inhaled sharply, a fleeting surge of desperation in her eyes.

"Julius will help," Delilah said intensely. "Tell him the truth. And tell me what I can do."

Antonia stared at her, searching her face. "Help him," she said in little more than a whisper. "Whatever happens, I know it is over, but I would spare him whatever pain—" She broke off, swallowing convulsively. "Excuse me."

Antonia fled to catch up with the waiting Dunnett. Delilah looked after her with serious concern.

"A penny for them," said a light voice beside her, causing every nerve in her body to thrill.

"We have to get Mrs. Macy away from him."

"I'm glad you agree." Lord Linfield's gaze was warm, not distant at all. "What changed your mind about her?"

"She cares for Julius. She trusts him with her son as much as she does not trust Mr. Dunnett. He is coercing her, somehow, and her brother-in-law is part of it."

He offered her his arm. "Then let us play our part in protecting her."

"You already do that, don't you?" she asked shrewdly.

"She is my sister's friend."

"What can we do?"

"In the short term, prevent him tormenting her. In the longer term, I believe Sir Julius may take matters into his own hands."

The twins raced past her, pausing only to grin over their shoulders at her.

A noisy game of pall-mall was taking place on the lawn, and in the marquee, some children were dancing to the music of a trio of musicians. One of the earl's sisters was joining in.

"I believe Lady Braithwaite has engaged a wonderful pianist to play for us. Would you care to listen?"

"I would," she said, her heart singing because he was choosing to spend time with her.

In the hall, Antonia and Dunnett were together, talking to a group of people near the refreshment tables. Lucy dashed by with a glass of wine in one hand and an extremely rakish-looking young man on the other, a feverish glint in her eyes.

"Daxton," Linfield murmured. "She is safe enough with him. These days he is devoted to his estates and to his wife."

"She is upset." And not in the mood to let anyone near her. A worry for another day.

Some chairs had been set up in rows near the very grand pianoforte. Linfield handed Delilah into a seat at the front and went off to fetch refreshment. When he returned, he handed her a glass of punch and sat next to her. Her worries seemed to disintegrate, leaving only happiness.

Frederick Baird, the young pianist, was indeed excellent. His music soared, seizing Delilah's excited emotions and tying them in knots. At one point, she had to stare straight ahead of her in case a tear squeezed out of her eye. To her amazement, Linfield's warm, strong fingers closed around hers, just for an instant, as though he understood.

Delilah joined in the rapturous applause and spilled out her thoughts to her companion, who shared a few of his own before the next performer sat down at the instrument—Lady Alice Conway, the earl's sister. After the delight of Baird, Delilah was in no mood to listen to a young lady's so-called accomplishment, which more often than not turned out to be sadly lacking. But Lady Alice surprised her. While she might have lacked Baird's technical polish, she had an undeniable talent that went far beyond accomplishment, her music touching Delilah's heart.

"I feel I have been wrung out," Delilah confessed as they finally stood up.

"Clearly, you need fortifying. I believe we are to be supplied with tea before an informal dance. And there go the young people."

The twins and Edward Macy were among those leaping up-stairs to where, no doubt, a less civilized tea would be served by the earl's busy servants.

To her surprise and secret delight, Linfield stayed with her, perhaps as an excuse to keep his eye on Antonia and Dunnett.

While the little orchestra moved from the marquee to the great hall, Lady Braithwaite welcomed new arrivals—a very dignified lady only just on the right side of forty and her amiable-looking husband.

Feeling Linfield's eyes upon her, she glanced up at him.

His lips quirked. "Come," he said, setting down his teacup. "There is someone I'd like you to meet."

He led her over to the newcomers, who were now greeting Mrs. Lampton, the one-time Princess of Rheinwald.

"Lord Linfield," the strange lady said, smiling and offering her hand to Linfield, who bowed over it and then shook hands with the husband.

"Allow me to present Miss Vale. Miss Vale, Mr. and Mrs. Harris, who are also staying at the hotel."

Delilah curtseyed. "How do you do?"

Mrs. Harris smiled very graciously. "Delighted to meet you, Miss Vale. My husband and I are so enjoying your pretty town, and already the waters improve my health." She spoke with a very slight foreign accent that Delilah, for all her travels, could not quite place.

"I'm very glad to hear it," Delilah replied. "My brother has also noticed the benefits."

She felt Linfield's gaze upon her and glanced up at him to see why this introduction was so important. But Mrs. Lampton was already whisking the couple off to find them seats and refreshment.

"Who are they?" Delilah murmured.

"Oh, just travelers. I thought you might like them."

"I do, as far as I can tell from such a brief exchange." She noticed that Antonia was still being towed about the room by Dunnett. Her shoulders were so tense, they almost touched her ears. Miss Talbot intercepted her.

"Good for your sister," Delilah approved, and suddenly remembered her last conversation with the lady. "Oh, I wanted to ask you something."

"Shall we take a stroll before the rain comes on again?"

"Why not?" She was not being discreet spending so much time with him, but who would notice or care? Only the match-making mamas out to attract his attention, and they would hardly consider her a threat. It was a lowering thought, but she refused to let it trouble her. The present was intoxicating.

"What did you want to ask me?" He drew her hand into the crook of his arm as they strolled past the marquee.

The ground was damp, and most people were inside, giving the illusion of privacy. Lord Linfield was on leave from his main duties, but it had struck her that he might well have a mountain of minor documents to deal with that were neither important nor sensitive. Much like those she had been working on.

"Are you Mr. Charles?" she blurted.

DENZIL, IN DANGER of falling completely under Delilah's unique spell, had forced himself to introduce her to the Princess of Hazburg, just to gauge her reaction. The name Harris had been in the documents she had translated, but she never batted an eyelid at the introduction.

In truth, he hadn't expected her to. Delilah was undoubtedly involved but in all innocence. She had no notion what the translated documents signified, and she was no more the assassin than he was. This he knew beyond doubt.

And then, out of the blue, she asked if *he* was Mr. Charles.

Surprise and guilt hit him with a thud. And then a tiny shoot of suspicion returned.

"Not the last time I spoke to my parents," he said lightly. "Who is Mr. Charles?"

"My employer. The man I have been translating and arrang-ing documents for." She released his arm and delved into her reticule. A moment later, she produced a tiny, crumpled piece of brown paper. "I found this in the pocket of Miss Talbot's dress."

Puzzled, he took it from her. Only when he saw the few letters did he recognize it. Part of the wrapping of the parcel he had intercepted. He had opened it in his hotel sitting room. The string had torn off a piece of the paper. He must have missed a bit when he cleared up and Elaine had found it instead. Careless... But what were the odds of Delilah herself discovering it?

"But this could be anything," he pointed out.

"No, it's in my hand."

"I don't see how you can be so sure. It's such a tiny fragment of writing."

She frowned. "Then you are not Mr. Charles. It is very odd. I'm beginning to wonder if my work ever reached him. Try as I might, I cannot believe this was walked back all the way from York to your hotel sitting room. I shall have to ask at the mail office—"

"You and I need to talk," he interrupted. "About many things. But not today."

He took her hand, drawing her behind the marquee. No one was in sight, not even children.

"Why not today?" she asked.

A pulse beat at the base of her throat, and he brushed his fingertips over it before sliding his palm around to cup her cheek.

"Because today I want to kiss you," he said with perfect honesty.

Her eyes darkened. Her lips quivered, parting for him, and he lowered his mouth to hers.

God, she was sweet and trusting... Her need thrilled through him, matching his own. There was a strange recognition in kissing Delilah, a knowledge that this was *right*. She moved him as no one ever had. Desire growled, and he deepened the kiss. Her tongue tangled with his, seeking, learning as he slid his hand down the front of her dress, hearing her soft moan of pleasure. She would be such a sweet, passionate lover... He yearned for that day.

But it was not today.

He released her mouth, gazing down into her beautiful face. Her eyes were closed, her lips still parted.

*I love you,* he thought in wonder as her eyelids fluttered open. *After all these cynical years, I am finally caught. And you are the one.*

Madness. He had known her little more than a week.

Music drifted to his ears. Dancing was beginning in the great hall.

He swallowed, drowning in her eyes. "We should go back." Was he trying to convince her? Or himself?

"Antonia," she said determinedly, giving herself a little shake. She drew back from him, and his arms felt empty.

But this was not the right place to talk, let alone to court or to plan. He searched wildly around for the next time to see her. "Your theatre tickets—what evening are they for?"

"Monday. It is the opening night of the play. Oh dear, is it raining again?" She took his arm without his offering, which made him ridiculously proud, and they hurried around the marquee to the covered walkway that joined it to the doors into the great hall.

"We can dine before we go," he suggested. "In private, perhaps, though Elaine and Mrs. Macy will be present, of course."

"I need to return Miss Talbot's clothes," she replied.

"Should I ask Sir Julius's permission?"

"I am hardly of an age where I need my brother's permission to attend the theatre."

"Then it is settled." It felt wonderful to have their next meeting agreed.

Until he remembered. According to the documents he had taken from Delilah, Monday was the day scheduled for the assassination of the Princess of Hazburg.

THE FACT THAT Lord Linfield had accorded her no more than a

pleasant smile and a bow was something of a relief to Miss Marjorie Match. She felt proud to have his genuine smile without any of his difficult conversation.

Mama, however, was furious with her for not insisting on greater attention. She only let up in her angry litany of complaints when the wandered into the great hall to hear the music. The earl's sister, Lady Alice—who, like Marjorie, had been one of the Season's debutantes—was playing on the pianoforte, and Mama was suddenly rendered speechless by the sight of Lord Linfield seated beside the lovely Miss Delilah Vale. Afterward, the pair even went outside together.

Marjorie was just thinking rather wistfully what a striking couple they made, when Mama exploded in her ear once more.

"Well! I call that shabby! Very shabby indeed!"

"I thought she played beautifully," Marjorie ventured.

Her mother blinked uncomprehendingly, then uttered in withering tones, "Not Lady Alice, you silly goose! Lord Linfield! To pass you over for that... I cannot believe that Lady Braithwaite would even invite her!"

"Well, she obviously has," Marjorie pointed out, greatly daring. "In fact, I saw the Vale twins playing with the earl's own children."

To Marjorie's surprise, this observation seemed to choke off her mother's anger. She merely sniffed. "I suppose the aristocracy needs to pay less attention to the rules of respectability followed by the rest of us lesser mortals. Unless..."

Mama's eyes began to gleam, and Marjorie's heart sank. "Unless?" she asked doubtfully.

"Unless the girl has some other flaw in her virtue."

"But she doesn't, does she?"

"By the determined way she is setting her cap at your Linfield, you may wager your best gown that she does!"

"He is not *my* Linfield!" Marjorie whispered, glancing around her to be sure no one else had heard.

"Only because you have not tried to fix his interest. Well, I shall do it for you."

"Oh, no, Mama—"

"By detaching him," Mama continued ruthlessly, "from that hoyden. A word or two in the right ears, a scene before the right eyes… Go and fetch your brother."

Marjorie obeyed, trailing her heels and finding the idea of a home of her own—perhaps even abroad, anywhere well away from Mama—increasingly appealing.

Gerald was discovered drinking and making silly wagers with Lord Tranmere and his friends. For a moment, Marjorie wondered why Mama should not have made efforts fix Tranmere's interest, but she had always dismissed him as too young and unsteady and destined for the devil. In some ways, it was a pity, because he was very handsome, never talked down to her, and wasn't remotely frightening to Marjorie.

The young men all rose as she approached, obliging Gerald to stand up too.

"Mama wants you," Marjorie said morosely.

"Am I in for a scold?" Gerald cast an apologetic smile at his friends and ambled beside her back toward the hall.

"No," Marjorie said with a sigh. "She just wants you to do something despicable. You couldn't see your way clear to not doing it, could you?"

"Depends if it's amusing," Gerald replied. "If it's boring, I'll forget."

The trouble was, he didn't find the idea boring at all.

# Chapter Ten

A FTER THE GARDEN party, events around Delilah seemed to move very quickly. Lucy, Felicia, and Roderick all seemed unhappy but uncommunicative, while Julius was merely determined. Having linked the business of the horse thieves last week to the discovery of a cache of guns this week—and the whole to the unpleasant Dunnett, his supposed rival in love—he suddenly saw his way clear and sailed off in his borrowed ship to capture the lot and save Antonia.

Delilah, dazed, restless, and afraid to hope—though exactly what she might hope for remained unclear to her confused mind—found herself in Blackhaven with the twins. She wondered if she should worry about how well known the twins appeared to be among market stall holders, doormen, maids sweeping front steps...

"Perhaps you should have a new coat," Delilah said to Lawrence, eyeing his worn, old hand-me-down that had once been Aubrey's. "And Leona, you definitely need a new gown."

"Oh, we're in no hurry," Lawrence said carelessly. "Shall we meet you later at the ice parlor?"

Delilah gave in. "Why not?"

Having seen some pretty muslin, she was gazing in the modiste's window for ideas for Leona when she was accosted by Miss Talbot, in company with a middle-aged couple.

"Miss Vale, how delightful to see you. Are you acquainted with Mr. and Mrs. Temple? Antonia's parents, you know. Perhaps you would join us for tea?"

"You're very kind, but I have promised to meet the twins for an ice."

"Then let us do that instead."

Accordingly, they all trooped off to the ice parlor. The Temples—who, according to Julius, had lied and hidden letters in order to separate him from Antonia—were somewhat overwhelming, and Delilah suspected Elaine Talbot had seized upon her to dilute them as far as possible. Although the twins would have been valuable in this respect, there was no sign of them, even by the time they had finished their ices.

Miss Talbot, claiming another engagement, left as soon as she laid down her spoon, mouthing "Sorry," behind the Temples' backs.

"Such a charming lady," Mrs. Temple said. "Don't you agree, Miss Vale?"

"Indeed I do," replied Delilah, who had been more charmed before being abandoned with the lady's unwanted hangers-on.

"She has been a great friend to our daughter. As has her brother, Lord Linfield. In fact..." Mrs. Temple leaned forward in order to confide in a lowered voice, "I believe there is an understanding between them."

"Between whom?" Delilah asked, bewildered.

"Lord Linfield and Antonia, of course."

Just for a moment, it felt like a blow to her stomach.

*Could* Antonia really be holding out for the best offer? Delilah thought of the woman's genuine misery yesterday, her plea for Julius to be helped, and her surprised delight in being preserved as far as possible from Dunnett's attentions. Julius and Linfield had danced with Antonia; Miss Talbot and Delilah had whisked her off to join conversations and to meet people. Antonia was certainly comfortable with Linfield, but it was Julius her eyes constantly sought.

No, the Temples were merely ambitious and indulging in a little wishful thinking. They wanted their daughter to be a baroness. And Linfield himself...

Was Delilah a fool to fall for such a confirmed bachelor? Men kissed easily—and more than kissed—without love or fear of retribution.

*Lord Linfield is not such a man...*

But in truth, she did not know that. She did not know *him*. There was an air of experience and sophistication about him that somehow was part of his attraction. But he had no reason to cozen her. Was it so hard to believe that she was sought after by such a man? That to him, she was as unique as he was to her?

She yearned suddenly to see him now, to feel the reassurance of his steady eyes and his gentle touch.

She blinked, for the Temples were saying goodbye to her and returning to the hotel to wait for their daughter. "Though I hate to leave you alone," Mrs. Temple added without obvious regret.

"There is no cause for concern here," Delilah assured her. "And my siblings will be here momentarily."

Although when one of the twins did finally appear, it was only Lawrence, who all but dragged her outside the shop.

"Where is Leona?" Delilah demanded.

"By the shore watching. Dunnett abducted Mrs. Macy and Julius has captured the ship, stopping a huge cache of arms going to Ireland. Hurry!"

At the shore she discovered most of her family—including Leona—and half the town watching the approach of a rowing boat that contained a waving, smiling Julius and Antonia.

A tall man stood aside to allow her a better view.

"I wondered where you were," Lord Linfield murmured.

"Abandoned in the ice parlor by your sister and my twins. What are you doing here?"

"Summoned by your twins, of course. No wonder Mrs. Macy was late for luncheon. They look well."

They did. Julius and Antonia came ashore hand in hand,

laughing at some private joke, and so clearly in love that all Delilah's foolish doubts fell away. This was Julius as he used to be, not just capable and determined, but glad to be so. He was happy.

Her feelings for Linfield seemed to have imparted some greater empathy. Even though he stood some distance from her now, she was aware of his every movement, every word and gesture. Which was odd when her heart was full for Julius and she was smiling at her new sister-in-law with genuine welcome and gratitude.

THE ENTIRE FAMILY ended up in the hotel for an impromptu tea party celebrating Julius's engagement to Antonia. Several people who had helped in the retrieval of the guns and the arrest of Dunnett and his accomplices joined them. Relief and pride in Julius, as well as pleasure in his obvious joy, banished the troubles of his siblings, and the party was a merry one, taking up the largest part of the hotel's spacious tearoom. The Vales, it seemed, had become part of Blackhaven.

Miss Talbot and Lord Linfield joined them, bringing little Edward. Antonia's parents appeared a little later, looking both bewildered and affronted, although they soon succumbed to the general good cheer. The happy couple was toasted many times in both tea and champagne.

Delilah, part of it all and yet curiously separate, seemed to be in her own little bubble of happiness. It was to do with Julius and Antonia, with being surrounded by family and new friends, the whole atmosphere of uncomplicated joy in the present and the future. And with the man not even sitting beside her, but somehow, for her, central to everything.

Denzil Talbot, Baron Linfield.

Her eyes sought him without permission and found him on

the other side of the table, laughing with the twins and the squire, Mr. Winslow. He rested one wrist on the table, idly playing with the stem of his wine glass, a smile lingering on his lips. Lips of such devastating passion. Her stomach dived.

He raised his gaze quite suddenly, meeting hers over Lawrence's head. His eyes warmed excitingly, and he lifted his glass very slightly in acknowledgment. Delilah felt her happiness complete.

EARLY ON MONDAY afternoon, Denzil called on the Princess of Hazburg, alias Mrs. Harris.

"Ah, Lord Linfield," the princess greeted him. "I have heard directly from my brother than he plans to be in Blackhaven next week. He does not hurry himself, so there is no reason we should not go to the theatre! Did you obtain tickets for the opening night of the new play? Helena Hampshire and Reginald Miller are a big attraction to us both."

"Ah." Denzil bowed his apology. "I'm afraid I did not. The intelligence we have is of an attack on you at the theatre. And the best date we have is today. Until we know more, it would be extremely unwise for either you or the prince to attend."

The princess's face fell. "But who could hurt me in a theatre full of people? The perpetrator would be bound to be caught. This intelligence of yours seems terribly vague. Where does it come from?"

"From documents sent directly to and from your brother Prince Karl," Linfield said. "There is no longer any doubt about that."

The princess sighed. "Then he does not negotiate in good faith. Why do I always fall for his lies?"

"Because he is your brother and you want to believe the best of him. I'm afraid in his case there is no best."

For a moment, her expression was distant and sad, then she pulled herself together. "But you are certain about the date for this supposed attempt upon my life?"

"No, not certain, Your Highness, but it is the latest word we have."

"Then we are safe tonight if Karl does not come until next week."

"He *says* he comes next week," Denzil corrected her. "And in any case, I'm sure he would rather be some distance away, were anything to happen, so that no blame attaches to him."

"Then I am safe nowhere," she said restlessly.

"Not entirely true, Highness. We know it is the theatre—the place names are disguised, but easily recognizable in any language, when one knows what to look for. I will go myself tonight and see what I can discover among the visiting players and theatre staff."

The princess tapped her foot. "We are bored, Lord Linfield. My husband is worse than bored."

"I believe the prince enjoys a flutter, Your Highness. There is a gaming club tonight here in the hotel. Security is always high, and I believe he will enjoy it. I shall report to you again in the morning."

Exactly what he would report was, of course, another matter. It all depended on tonight, on Delilah's understanding and cooperation. For him, it would be unspeakable relief to tell her everything, to receive her forgiveness and her help.

Returning to the sitting room he shared with Elaine, he found his sister with Antonia.

"I'm surprised to see you here," he teased Antonia. "I thought you would have fled to Black Hill." The wedding banns had been called at church yesterday, and Antonia had spent the rest of the day with the Vales. Denzil had found himself ridiculously jealous because he wanted to be there too, with Delilah.

Antonia smiled, all the underlying sadness of years, and the tension of the last couple of weeks, entirely vanished. Julius Vale really was a lucky fellow—almost as lucky as Denzil hoped to be by the end of the day.

"Ah well," Elaine said. "In effect, Black Hill is coming to us. Sir Julius, Miss Vale, and Miss Lucy will join us for tea. You will be here, Denzil, will you not?"

"Try to keep me away."

Elaine peered at him as though picking up the sincerity of his apparently flippant response. She was a very perceptive sister, and he was very glad she seemed to like Delilah.

"I suppose you are going to this horrid gaming club in the hotel this evening," Elaine said with a sniff. "Apparently, all sorts of riffraff are admitted, although the manager assures me staying guests will be perfectly safe and the gamblers kept strictly to the back hall."

"There will be more than the hoi polloi and card sharps," Denzil said. "Braithwaite will be there, along with Lord Wick-enden, Daxton, Bernard Muir. I might look in later on in the evening, but I shall be at the theatre first."

"Without us?" Elaine said, then threw up her hands, adding hastily, "No, don't tell me—I don't want to know."

"It is a very respectable theatre party to which I have been invited."

Antonia laughed. "While you yourself, ma'am, never go anywhere without Lord Linfield, do you? I'll just go and order tea, shall I?"

As soon as she had closed the door behind her, Elaine said, "You are up to something."

"I am not. Merely, I am escorting Miss Vale to the theatre."

Elaine blinked. "Then Julius or one of the other siblings is going too?"

"No, it will be just Miss Vale and myself."

Elaine frowned. "Is that wise? Blackhaven is a small town. There will be talk. In London, there would be talk!"

"Miss Vale is convinced she is of such mature years that such conventions do not apply to her."

She gazed at him in some consternation. "And you are in agreement? Denzil, she is several years younger than I, and you have always insisted I take a female companion while junketing about the world with you, who are my brother! Do you not owe Miss Vale at least the same consideration?"

"In this particular case, there is no cause for concern."

Her eyes widened. "Denzil! You do not mean because of her birth!"

He scowled. "Of course I do not."

"Then I presume Sir Julius is happy about this excursion?"

"I have not discussed it with him. Miss Vale did not wish it. She is of an independent spirit." He frowned. "Don't look at me like that. I have every respect for the lady and care nothing for her irregular birth. I would never harm her."

"I see." And perhaps she did, for she sat back in her chair, a fleeting smile visible on her lips.

Denzil, feeling heat rise traitorously to his face, turned and went to his desk, shuffling papers as though looking for something in particular. *Delilah, Delilah...*

"I like her," Elaine pronounced.

IT WAS NOT quite the tea party Denzil had planned, where detaching Delilah from the crowd should have been simple. Lucy Vale was late in arriving, but the three slightly older women were natural friends, while Edward had clearly attached himself to Sir Julius, leaving Denzil unexpectedly hurt.

For nearly two years he had been the most constant adult male in Edward's young life, and he had grown fond of the boy, taking him on occasional excursions when he had the time, and even giving him odd lessons in Latin or whatever else occurred. Edward liked Denzil, but clearly he did not compare with the heroic Captain Vale.

Which was as it should be. But Denzil would miss the boy. And Antonia. He spared a thought for Elaine, whose friend Antonia had become.

Elaine's future had been on his mind even before they came to Blackhaven. He sensed her unspoken yearning for a more settled home than he had provided over the last ten years, but the companion he had vaguely imagined being with her, in whatever home she chose, was about to marry and leave her. And Denzil...

His sister would always have a home, with him or apart from him, whichever she wished. But when this irritating Hazburg business was dealt with, they must talk seriously, for Denzil's own status, his whole life, was about to change.

As the conversation flowed around him, amusing and friendly, he gazed at Delilah, who was smiling at Edward while she set her teacup in its saucer and answered some of his nonsense. Denzil's heart swelled, not just with acknowledged love, but a recognition of the loneliness within himself that she smoothed away. It was as if he had missed her forever, loved her forever, and now everything he did, in his own service, or in that of his country or his family, had a new purpose—to be worthy of this sweet, big-hearted lady, so fiercely loyal and passionate. He yearned for her to be truly happy, to be the one to make her so...

She glanced up suddenly and caught his steady gaze. He didn't look away. He wasn't sure he could, even when color seeped into her cheeks.

"Denzil?" Elaine said, and he realized from her voice that it was not the first time she had said his name.

Dragging his gaze back to his sister, he said, "Sorry. I was miles away, woolgathering."

Where he wanted to be was alone with Delilah. He had so much to tell her, so much to learn about her, and over everything hung this Hazburg business. He needed to confess and clear the air before anything else. And yet his sister and friends seemed to conspire to keep them apart.

"Where on earth is Lucy?" Sir Julius demanded of Delilah as

tea came to a close. "She should have met us here before this. I apologize for her rudeness, Miss Talbot."

"Scatterbrained is not rude," Elaine said. "I know it was unintentional."

"She has a friend staying at the hotel," Delilah said, rising to her feet. "A Miss Poole. I'll see if she is there."

"No need," Sir Julius said with a hint of grimness. "I have a better idea where she might be. You take the carriage home, Delly, and Lucy and I will follow in a hackney—when I find her!"

"No, I shall stay on in Blackhaven for the evening," Delilah said calmly. "You take the carriage, Julius. And Jules? She might be upset, but she is not foolish."

Sir Julius hesitated, clearly torn between his sisters' needs.

"I will make sure Miss Vale returns home safely," Denzil said.

Sir Julius met his gaze with his one fierce eye, then nodded curtly and departed with no more than a bow to Elaine and a kiss to Antonia's hand.

After which, Elaine blithely sent Denzil away. "I know you have work to do, and Miss Vale and I have matters to discuss."

Denzil, who felt more like stamping his foot, actually laughed, recognizing there would be no time alone until the theatre. But he was a seasoned diplomat, not the impatient schoolboy he seemed to have turned into.

He dined early with Elaine, Antonia, and Delilah in the sitting room. By this time Delilah had changed into evening dress and looked both beautiful and subtly magnificent. Every nerve in his body screamed its awareness.

And yet there was a simple pleasure in it, too. A casual intimacy that drew her into his family as if she fitted there perfectly.

She showed no embarrassment, no consciousness of impropriety as she thanked Elaine for her hospitality and bade a cheerful goodnight to Antonia and Edward. And then he had the pleasure of walking with her on his arm. Alone at last.

But the walk to the theatre was too short to say all he needed to, the streets too busy to explain what he had done and why.

In the foyer of Blackhaven's little theatre, he recognized several people, including Dr. and Mrs. Lampton, Mrs. Match and her daughter, and, in one noisy corner, young Mr. Match with a few other young bucks, clearly already three sheets to the wind.

"Why, Lord Linfield, what a delightful surprise," Mrs. Match exclaimed as Denzil and Delilah made their way to the staircase.

Courtesy forced them to stop. "Ma'am. Miss Match." Denzil bowed. Miss Match gazed up at him with her somewhat pitiable mix of hope and embarrassment, barely remembering to curtsey, though she did, after a nudge from her mother, extend her hand, which Denzil politely took with another bow.

However, from the corner of his eye, he saw Mrs. Match's flash of outrage. Before he could even begin to introduce Delilah, the matron seized her daughter by the arm as though to protect her.

"My lord," she said glacially, and walked off, dragging her bewildered offspring with her.

Denzil was not slow in social situations, but for an instant this rude behavior mystified him, until he turned his amused gaze upon Delilah to share the joke. And understood with a sickening jolt.

Mrs. Match had basically refused to be introduced, hurrying her daughter away before she could be contaminated by Delilah's presence. His sudden fury must have shown in his face, for Delilah smiled ruefully. Her color had risen a little, but her expression was resigned, and that angered him even more.

"Ignore it," she said lightly. "I do. Papa said it betrayed their lack of breeding, not mine, and he has a point. But if you would prefer to leave…"

"I would not," Denzil said, controlling his outrage for her sake.

Dr. and Mrs. Lampton met them at the stairs, their natural, friendly greetings like a balm to Mrs. Match's nastiness.

"I thought Mrs. Harris was coming tonight," Mrs. Lampton said as they mounted the stairs together. "But I don't see her."

"I believe she decided to attend on a different evening instead," Denzil replied. "Mr. Harris had a notion to go to the gaming club."

"I expect she could do with the restful evening," Mrs. Lampton said. "Our box is this way. Would you care to join us at the interval?"

Denzil found their reserved box, where they discovered a letter on one of the seats addressed to Miss Vale.

"It's from my mother," Delilah said, picking it up. When they were comfortably seated, she read the note. "She asks me to call on her after the show. Backstage. I shall see her another time."

But this was just what Denzil needed—a view behind the stage, of the actors and the staff. "I should be charmed to meet your mother again."

Delilah regarded him doubtfully.

He smiled. "Truly."

"I have had little time to see her," Delilah admitted. "Life seems to have been so busy, but she did ask for my help…"

He could not help the sickening jolt of his stomach. "Help in what?"

"A personal matter," Delilah said uncomfortably. "For one thing, she is a little upset that the leading role went to Elise Manners and not to her. She feels it as an insult."

It wasn't the whole truth, only the part she was prepared to tell him. Oh yes, decidedly, he needed to go behind the stage with her. The cerebral part of him was looking for information. But all of him was concerned for her, for her feelings and for her safety. And he made an interesting discovery.

"You love your mother. You would do anything for her."

She flushed, more brightly than when Mrs. Match had cut her. "I believe it is a normal emotion. In my case, of course, I barely know her." She cast him a quick, almost-embarrassed glance. "In my loneliest moments, I make believe that, in her own way, she loves me too."

He reached out and took her hand from her lap, as touched

by her trust as by this insight into her semi-motherless past. "I did not know my mother at all. She died shortly after my birth. I would give anything to have known her."

"Then you understand why I will never cast her off, as my stepmothers frequently urged me to do."

"It would not be in your nature. Or mine. But Delly..." Her eyes lit up at his use of her name, and his heart melted all over again. "You will let me help you? You and your mother?"

"Of course," she said breathlessly, and then the curtain went up on a brightly lit stage and he released her hand to watch the display of juggling and then dancing that comprised the first part of the evening.

# Chapter Eleven

F ROM THE WINGS of the stage, hidden in the gloom, Elise
Manners searched the rows of boxes, looking for the face that
was her entire reason for being here.

She had seduced one of the hotel footmen last week, just so
that he would point Mr. and Mrs. Harris out to her. Their faces
were indelibly etched on her memory, but she saw them in none
of the small rows of boxes. Nor were they in the pit, although she
never expected them to be.

They must be coming later, just to see the play. According to
the footman, Mr. Harris had confided to him that he had a long-
term crush on Helena Hampshire, ever since seeing her in a play
in Paris. Silly old goat. He should see her up close without her
stage makeup.

Elise backed away from the wings. It looked as if she would
have to perform the play after all, and complete her task either
after the first act or during the curtain call. She would modestly
wave the others onto the stage ahead of her, and she would be
gone before anybody realized what had happened.

On her way back to the dressing room, she all but ran into
Stephens, the hotel footman.

"What the devil are you doing here?" she said, glancing
around her in case Reggie Miller should see her with this other
useful fool.

"Just keeping you informed as you asked," Stephens said petulantly. "They're not coming."

"What are you talking about? And keep your voice down!"

"The Harrises. They're still at the hotel. He's already gone down to the gaming club. She's retiring early."

She stared at him in mounting fury. How could this be? Everything was set up... And now she was stuck here every damned night until her targets appeared. *Damnation!*

"Five minutes, Miss Manners!" came the call.

Grimly, she began to think her employer was an idiot. This was a ridiculously elaborate charade for a very simple task that she could achieve anywhere in the town—any town!—with one hand tied behind her back.

On impulse, she whisked herself back to her previous observation point, and, from the pile of ropes used for changing background scenery in a previous production, she removed her pistol.

It was not large, but it its accuracy was lethal up to a certain distance. Which was, of course, the beauty of this little theatre. She could easily fire from the edge of the stage, right across the tiny auditorium to any of the boxes above, and still hit her mark.

Hiding the pistol in her skirts, she hurried back to the dressing room, mingling with the dancers running off stage. There would be a short interval now, but she was already dressed for the first act of the play. She had not been able to win herself a private dressing room—bloody Nell had seen to that—but it was easy to slip the pistol into her coat.

After the performance, she could easily visit the hotel and finish the deed. Thanks to Stephens, she knew which was the Harrises' suite. And that Mrs. Harris would be alone while her husband played the tables of the gaming club.

Then she could get out of here and let bloody Nell have back this stupid role that seemed to mean so much to her.

And Elise, finally, would be paid.

At the first interval, Denzil escorted Delilah to the Lamptons' box, where they were introduced to several other Blackhaven residents, all of whom seemed curious but delighted to make their acquaintance. One of them had met both Aubrey Vale and Elaine at the pump room.

Their courtesy and friendliness certainly contrasted soothingly with the blatant rudeness of Mrs. Match, and it soothed Denzil somewhat. He had been worried that she faced such incivility all the time. But Delilah was outwardly so calm and self-possessed that he could read nothing beyond her amiable pleasure in new acquaintance.

When the little box grew too crowded—Dr. Lampton's social appearances were clearly rare enough to be sought after—Denzil and Delilah squeezed their way out and returned to their own seats. Kicking his heels in the narrow passage outside was a very dandified young man, who straightened as they approached. With surprise, Denzil recognized young Mr. Match, whom he had glimpsed in his mother's box, clearly on escort duty.

Hoping the youth had come to apologize for his parent's lapse in manners, Denzil greeted him with calm civility.

"I'm sorry we were not here to greet you," he added, "but you had better hurry back now or you'll miss the start of the play."

"Oh, I didn't mean to stop," Match assured him. "Just bearing a message from my mother. She invites you to join her in our box—next but one to yours, if you didn't notice—at the next interval." His eyes drifted from Denzil to Delilah and gleamed with open admiration. The way they raked her from head to foot, however, was anything but respectful.

"We are already committed," Denzil snapped, which at least drew Match's attention away from Delilah. "Please thank your mother for her kindness. You will excuse us." He pulled back the curtain and handed Delilah into the box.

To his amazement, Match leaned confidingly closer to him. There was wine on his breath, a slightly unfocused look about his eyes now they weren't leering at Delilah.

"Tell you the truth, my lord," Match said in what he probably imagined was a discreet tone, "the invitation is to *you*. Got m'sister present, you see. But she's prepared to overlook your..." His eyes flickered past the open curtain to Delilah, sitting down at the front of the box. "Your indiscretion," he finished.

Denzil stared at him until the boy began to look rather like an alarmed rabbit. "It is certain that I have not overlooked yours or Mrs. Match's," he said freezingly. "Goodnight." He stepped inside and let the curtain fall before Match's face.

"Puppy!" he uttered with some restraint as he took his place beside Delilah.

Her smile was unexpectedly warm. "I rather like puppies. He is foolishly foxed and, besides, merely the messenger."

"His mother must be addled."

"No. His mother wants you for her daughter. I should be flattered she considers me competition. She is merely trying to discredit me in your eyes."

"She discredits herself."

To his surprise, Delilah smiled again, and this time it was she who took his hand and briefly pressed his fingers, as though to comfort him, when it was she who had been insulted.

"You really are an amazing woman," he said softly, and rejoiced in the responsive warmth of her eyes and her glowing cheeks.

The audience abruptly quietened down, and he realized the curtain had risen on the play.

It was an entertaining play, a mild comedy of manners, and Reginald Miller was very good. His leading lady, Elise Manners, looked lovely and simpered a lot. But when Helena Hampshire finally appeared in the final scene of the first act, the stage came suddenly alive.

Mrs. Hampshire played the heroine's long-suffering mother, but she did so with such comedic genius that she brought the house down in gales of laughter that did nothing to detract from the touching pathos of the character. Beside Denzil, Delilah was smiling broadly, laughing silently to herself.

"Oh, brava, Nell, brava!" she murmured, clapping furiously as the curtain came down. Her eyes were sparkling with delight. "She acted everyone else off the stage! One in the eye for anyone who *dares* say she is past her heyday."

"I don't think anyone at all is saying that," Denzil said, regarding the small but vocal audience who were still clapping and cheering.

"She can play anything, make you believe anything," Delilah said with pride. "It's nothing to do with her age, just sheer talent."

Denzil regarded her. "Precisely."

Her gaze flew up to his face, an oddly arrested expression in her eyes.

"Life is not over at fifty, is it?" he said softly. "And certainly not at thirty. There are more dances to be enjoyed, Delly."

Her lips parted, glistening in the candlelight. It was all he could do not to kiss them there and then. She had never looked more beautiful, more *his*. His heart swelled.

He swallowed, reminding himself where he was. He pushed back his chair. "Let me fetch you some refreshment."

DELILAH FELT ENVELOPED in the doubly warm glow of her mother's success and Lord Linfield's understanding. In truth, the whole evening felt magical and wonderful, and she was totally enchanted by him.

*"There are more dances to be enjoyed, Delly."*

The timbre of his voice made her shiver with pleasure even as the words struck a chord deep within her. Was her last dance really not over? Was it truly to be with him? She had never looked for such happiness, not now... Not ever, probably. No one had ever affected her as he did. She felt as if she had lost her iron grip on her life and was tumbling out of control—and it was lovely, not even remotely frightening, because she knew he would catch her. He defended her, protected her, saw her, and still...loved her?

*Does he love me?* Could *he?*

Dazed, she moved to the chair at the back of the box, afraid of betraying her emotion to casual passing glances.

A snort, a scuffle, and some male *giggling* sounded in the passage behind the curtain.

"Ma'am, are you alone in there?" The speaker sounded like a young man, trying for seriousness in a fit of mirth. "Would you care for some company?"

Delilah saw no need to answer that, but the curtain twitched aside and a young man she might have seen once with Aubrey smiled at her in what he probably imagined was an alluring manner. In fact, he looked fatuous and foxed.

"I would not," Delilah said, and turned her shoulder to the curtain, which she heard swish back into place.

"Oh, don't be so tame, Frobisher," came another male voice, and this time, the curtain pulled right back and three large young men—including the first speaker, presumably Frobisher, and Mr. Match—invaded the box.

They seemed so delighted with their boldness that they were no more frightening to Delilah than Aubrey in his cups. Though she hoped Aubrey had better manners.

"Won't you invite us to sit down?" Match said insolently.

"No. I invite you to leave."

The third man, who appeared more reckless than the others, took a step nearer. "You don't seem the type to be overcome with shyness."

"Not shyness, merely distaste. Begone before I inform your mothers of your ill manners."

Frobisher tugged uneasily at his friend's arm. "Come on," he mumbled. "She ain't interested."

"Neither is my mother," Match said with some amusement. "She'd never get near enough the old lady to inform her of anything"

"I won't need to," Delilah pointed out. "I expect she can see you. Good evening, gentlemen."

While Frobisher stepped back in fresh alarm, the third man dropped to a crouch beside her chair and, before she could prevent it, seized her hand. His eyes gleamed with lust and belief in the irresistible nature of his charms. For the first time since the initial giggle, she felt truly uneasy. She wished she had not removed her glove.

She tugged to free her hand but wasn't entirely surprised when his grip merely tightened.

"You really are rather lovely," he said admiringly, kissing her hand with wet lips and insolent tongue. "Damned if I won't invite you to supper."

"Perhaps you could accommodate us, too," Match said. "We come as a set, don't you know."

"Which is precisely how you'll go," said a somewhat grimmer, masculine voice, and abruptly Match and Frobisher vanished from her view. In their place stood Lord Linfield, coldly, haughtily angry.

Amidst her surge of relief, Delilah was now frightened for him against three feral youths. She searched wildly for a way to defuse the situation.

The third man blinked rapidly, his jaw slackening with astonishment before he began to flush with embarrassment to be discovered on his knees.

"Have I interrupted a proposal of marriage?" Linfield drawled, amused contempt dominating his expression. "Or are you just too drunk to stay on your feet? Allow me to assist."

Reaching down, he hauled Delilah's chief tormentor upright by his coat front and pushed him inexorably beyond the curtain.

Delilah jumped to her feet, ready to intervene, for Linfield stepped beyond the curtain too. As it fell back into place, she reached for it, then, through a chink, she saw the vignette on the other side and paused.

Linfield's manner had changed. All amusement had vanished from his face and voice—presumably it had only ever been there for her benefit. The three young men stood before him ill at ease, yet defiant, brash, and belligerent.

Linfield's lips curled. His scornful gaze lashed them. "Clearly," he said in soft, chilling tones, "you were not beaten enough at school to teach you manners. Don't make me remedy the oversight."

"Now, look here...!" the third man began to bluster. Encountering Linfield's gaze, his one raised eyebrow, the youth fell into confused silence, his throat working.

"I suggest you learn to be gentlemen, very, *very* quickly. Such behavior is not tolerated in the circles you apparently aspire to. Trust me, I shall see that it is not."

"Who the devil are you to issue such orders over a—"

"Be quiet!" Match said savagely, dragging his friend back by the arm. "He's Lord Linfield, friend of my parents', and probably yours, too."

Linfield's expression did not change. "A note of apology will be delivered to Miss Vale, care of my sister Miss Talbot, at the hotel, first thing tomorrow morning. It will be signed by all of you, and it had better be gracious. Try to pretend you are gentlemen."

The third man scowled. "Sir, that is the second time you have impugned—"

"Make sure there is not a third," Linfield said without raising his voice.

Perhaps it was the sheer force of his personality, which during the whole scene had been considerable. There was far, far more to Lord Linfield than the clever, charming gentleman he presented to Society. Or perhaps people moving in the passageway reminded the trio how easily their transgression could be made public, and in what light it would show them. Either way, they melted from view.

Linfield reached for something on the table beside the curtain, and Delilah fell hastily back into her chair. He entered with a glass of wine in either hand.

"Mannerless cubs," he observed, so mildly that she knew he was trying to lessen whatever fear she had felt at such treatment. "I believe there will be no repeat."

"I believe you are right," she said, accepting a glass. "And I daresay other women are all the safer for your intervention."

He met her gaze, and she thought a glow of pride or admiration softened his eyes. "How awful were they?"

Delilah thought about it. "Just egging each other on toward dangerous. They imagined they were entitled, and for that, I believe Mrs. Match must bear some blame." She tried to smile. "You may find our friendship difficult to maintain."

Linfield smiled, genuinely amused by the concept, which was rather touching. "In Blackhaven? She has less than no influence. Even in London, she is merely one matchmaking mama among many and has considerably less influence than an annoying fly. To friendship." He raised his glass. "And the considerable talents of Helena Hampshire."

She drank happily to that. Then, lowering her glass, she said as lightly as she could manage, "Thank you. I am glad you were there."

"I would not have them upset you for the world."

She thought about it. "I don't believe I am upset. Though I was beginning to be." She shook her head quickly. She didn't want to think about disrespectful drunks. They detracted from this special evening, and the increasingly special man by her side.

The curtain rose for the second act.

THERE WAS NO doubt that Helena Hampshire won all the plaudits. Delilah was delighted for her, though she did wonder if her mother's triumph would affect her desire to see her daughter. The adoration of the audience and the approval of her peers had always meant far more.

"I suspect she will have no time for us," Delilah said to Linfield as Nell finally left the stage and the audience kept cheering, making enough noise for several times their numbers. "We should probably just go."

Lord Linfield's eyebrows flew up. "Do you really believe that?"

Confused, Delilah blinked at him. But yes, she did believe it. Nell sought her out when she was unhappy or needed something. Only, she could not say such a thing. It demeaned Nell as well as Delilah.

Linfield smiled. "Come. I would like to pay my homage."

After that, there was little she could do except lead him downstairs before the crowds emerged. A mere wave of Nell's note got them past the porter and behind the stage. Nell had her own somewhat cramped dressing room, and her dresser admitted them.

Still in her stage makeup, sharing a glass of champagne with her husband, Nell rushed to them in delight.

"Delilah! Lah-Lah, how wonderful!" She seized both Delilah's hands and kissed the air above her cheek. "And who is this gentleman?"

"Lord Linfield. My lord, Mrs. Hampshire, and Mr. Miller, her husband."

"Charmed, ma'am," Linfield said, bowing over her hand. "I have to congratulate you on a splendid performance. Utterly delightful."

Beneath her makeup, Nell actually blushed, her smile widening impossibly.

"Is she not?" Reggie also beamed from ear to ear, and Delilah could not doubt his pride in her, his genuine pleasure in her triumph. "I am so glad you were here tonight," he added to Delilah. "I must just go and congratulate the rest of the company. You certainly gave them something to aim for, Nell!"

Nell laughed, though as soon as the door closed behind her husband, she winked at Delilah. "Gave Elsie Manners something impossible to aim for. Don't think she'll be stepping into my shoes anytime soon, not on stage or otherwise. Whatever you said to him, my sweet, it worked wonders."

Delilah, very aware of Linfield's presence, shrugged uncomfortably. "I think it was you rather than me. But you were wonderful, Nell, and I'm very glad for you. All is well now?"

Linfield backed away. "Allow me to leave you for a few moments. I'll go and find Mr. Miller, if I may..."

Delilah knew he was being tactful, giving her privacy with her mother. She actually ached with love for him.

"Well," Nell remarked as the door closed softly behind him. "A lord, eh? Isn't Linfield one of the Talbots?"

"It is certainly his family name," Delilah said, surprised that her mother should know such things. "He is a diplomat, and was granted a barony for his work in Vienna, I understand."

"Ah, of course, now I remember." Nell spun around, sat before the mirror, and picked up the cloth to remove her makeup. Then she bounced to her feet again. "Actually, he'd no need to work for his living. Heir to massive lands and considerable fortune. The family was against it, but he insisted."

"How do you know all this?" Delilah asked dubiously.

Nell laughed and winked. "I once knew his uncle very well, if you understand me. Charming man and very handsome, though I have to admit your Linfield might have the edge. What is he doing here with you, Lah-Lah?"

"He merely escorted me to the theatre. My family all happened to have previous engagements." That was, mostly, true.

"Nothing *mere* about him," Nell said shrewdly.

Hastily, Delilah changed the subject. "And you, Mother? Apart from your undoubted triumph on stage, are you truly happier?"

Nell sniffed. "Well, he still hangs around her too much, but I truly believe he is actually coaching her. He insisted she take the role, which, frankly, she is not up to, so he has to justify his choice. On the other hand, he doesn't come home late anymore, and I believe he realizes where his bread is buttered."

Unexpected laughter caught in Delilah's throat. "You are rather wonderful, Mother."

Nell looked both surprised and delighted, preening slightly. "Do you think so, darling? Was I really good tonight?"

"Utterly stole the show. You know you did."

Nell laughed, but more than that, there was relief and genuine joy in her expression. She really *had* wanted Delilah's approval. Perhaps she always had, as Delilah secretly wanted hers.

Nell sat down again and, while removing her greasepaint, launched into a critique of her own performance and everyone else's. "As for Elise Manners," she said, "she really shouldn't be on the stage at all. Reggie was carrying her the whole time. Never judge a book by its cover, I always say, and I doubt he will again. He was very good, though, wasn't he? One would never have believed his true age…"

Nell, having applied subtler paint to her face, was ready to meet her adoring public.

"You won't want to be seen with me," she said bluntly. "I'll send your gentleman back to you and you can leave discreetly." At the door, she turned and smiled directly into Delilah's eyes. "Bless you for coming, my dear. You've no idea how much it means to me."

To her horror, Delilah felt the prickle of tears. She had to blink several times, swallow, and pace around the room to dispel the rush of silly emotion.

# Chapter Twelve

B Y THE TIME Linfield sauntered back into the room, Delilah
had herself better in hand and was ready to leave.

"There are always hackneys for hire at the hotel," he said as
they walked out onto the damp street. At least it was no longer
raining. "And it's only a step."

She accepted his proffered arm. "I have left my things with
your sister."

"A fine excuse to call on you tomorrow. Will Sir Julius be at
home?"

She glanced at him, her heart skipping a beat. Why would he
want to see Julius, unless...?

*No, no, this is too quick, and I am too foolish, imagining...* He
would have some other business with Julius that had nothing to
do with her. In fact, if his family were as prominent and wealthy
as Nell believed, then anything but friendship between them was
surely doomed.

"What did you do while I was with my mother?" she asked as
calmly as she could. "Worship at the feet of Elise Manners?"

"No, I was merely introduced to her in passing as she rushed
off to change. The general opinion seems to be that her nose has
been put thoroughly out of joint by your mother's superb
performance. Do you know Reginald Miller's understudy?
Hemmel?"

Delilah shook her head. "I don't know any of them. Why?"

"Interesting young fellow. He is new to the company, has a faint accent that is not English."

She laughed. "You would hold that against him?"

"Not in itself," Linfield said as they turned into the high street. "I need to explain my suspicions to you, along with many other things."

Delilah tried to laugh at herself. This hardly sounded like a proposal of marriage, or even courtship, yet still her heart beat with hope, almost painfully.

"The hotel is busy tonight," she said with a shade of desperation, aware of swarms of people filing through the front doors several yards ahead.

"Gaming club night," Linfield said. "Perhaps to your brother Aubrey's taste?"

Delilah smiled. "He pursues the disreputable," she allowed, "but gaming is more suited to my sister Felicia. There are plenty of cabs, so I'm sure one of them will be happy to take me to Black—" She broke off as he halted abruptly, staring across the street. "What is it?"

"Someone is there, opposite the hotel, skulking in that alley."

"Does it matter?"

"I don't..."

Delilah saw the figure he meant, deep in the shadows, wrapped in a large, hooded cloak from which one arm emerged, pointing across the road at the hotel. Odd but hardly threatening—until she realized he was not pointing, but holding something with a narrow barrel, aiming above the waiting horses, carriages, and coachmen toward an upper window.

A gunman!

"Wait there. Do not move," Linfield commanded, and took off, sprinting across the road, directly at the gunman.

Appalled, Delilah saw the moment the shadowy figure became aware of Linfield. The pistol swung swiftly, pointing directly at him instead.

*Oh, dear God, no!* Without conscious intent, Delilah charged across the road, dodging a horse and cart, even knowing there was nothing she could do.

Linfield did not slow for a moment. In an instant, he would be dead.

The hugeness of that was overwhelming, unthinkable.

And then the pistol was lowered and the gunman vanished into the darkness of the alley. Still Linfield did not hesitate, but plunged after him. At least he moved sideways, presenting a smaller target, and kept close to the wall, but even as Delilah hurried after him, he pressed on.

The alley opened into another running along the backs of the shops. Linfield paused, glancing in all directions, but this alley was better lit, and his quarry clearly invisible, for his shoulders slumped in frustration.

Then he spun around, as if suddenly aware of her footsteps behind him. His fists raised to defend himself, then fell to his side.

"Delilah! You shouldn't be here!" He sounded so appalled that her heart would have shriveled, except that his arms closed around her in a sudden hug that set off a furious confusion of emotions. It lasted only a moment before he grasped her hand, drawing her back down the narrow passage to the high street.

"What is going on?" Delilah demanded. "Who *was* that? Were they...?"

"I don't know," Linfield said ruefully. "I'll explain on the way to Black Hill. First I have to leave a message."

The hotel doorman admitted them at once, and Linfield marched straight to the small coffee room on the right. Here, under Delilah's bewildered observation from the doorway, he snatched up a pen and scribbled a note in a matter of seconds. He strode out again and up to a watchful, waiting footman, whose duties were to keep the more disreputable gamers away from the hotel's staying guests.

"Deliver this at once to Mrs. Harris," he commanded, passing the note and a discreet coin into the footman's hands. "And I mean at once."

"Certainly, my lord," the footman said obediently, already scurrying off to the stairs.

Delilah, totally bewildered, allowed herself to be led out again and up to the first waiting carriage for hire. Linfield almost threw the destination at the driver as he opened the carriage door.

"Wait!" Delilah exclaimed, torn between frustration and amusement. "You cannot leave me without explaining all that!"

"I have no intention of leaving you," Linfield said, handing her into the coach. Her heart fluttered, silencing her, and he stepped inside after her, seating himself not on the back-facing bench, but beside her.

The coachman whipped up his horse, and they set off along the high street. Linfield sat forward, his arm across the back of the seat behind her as he gazed down at her. The flickering glow from passing streetlamps played across his face, shadowing the deep hollows of his handsome face. She could not look away from his warm, urgent gaze.

His hand closed over hers on her lap.

"Delly, could you ever consider marrying me?"

ELISE WAS FURIOUS as she let herself into the company's lodging house. Everyone else was out celebrating, no doubt lauding bloody Nell, just because the old has-been still had a spark of genius—and guile. There had been few signs at rehearsals that she meant to play the role with quite that degree of poignant humor. And everyone else would be delighted to see Elise's nose out of joint.

As if Elise cared.

She lit the stump of a candle from the lamp in the hall and hurried upstairs. The trouble was, she *did* care. Which meant it was past time she left this ridiculous masquerade. This evening had been a total fiasco in every way.

She threw open her bedchamber door, kicked it closed, and lit the lamp on the nearest table. The flame flared, illuminating the man who sat in her sagging armchair.

Unforgivably, it took her by surprise. But her reactions were still quick. Her fingers closed around the pistol in the pocket of her cloak. She could shoot him through the layers of wool if necessary, though it would make a hideous noise.

"Who the devil are you?" she asked casually.

"Your employer," said the intruder in German, "and so far, I am not impressed. You failed to shoot her at the theatre."

"She wasn't *at* the damned theatre," Elise retorted in the same language, casting her employer a long, curious look. Why had he thrown off the veil of secrecy between them? Was he about to betray her? Or merely lead the authorities to her through his sheer stupidity? "So I went to the hotel. I saw her almost at once, at the window, bathed in light. It was a perfect shot."

"Then she's dead?" The voice had changed to one of eagerness, almost euphoria, hoarse with delight.

Elise curled her lip, unsure whether she despised herself or her employer more. She did not like his face—heavy with self-indulgence, weak around the mouth and chin. More like the poor fools she was used to killing than those who usually employed her.

"No," she drawled. "I was seen and had to bolt. So frustrating."

Her visitor jumped to his feet. "Seen? *Seen?* By whom?"

"Oh, some fellow from the audience tonight. He came backstage, no doubt to worship at the feet of the great Helena Hampshire. Very aristocratic, deigning to be interested in the stage." She frowned suddenly. "Actually, now I think of it, *she* was with him."

His eyebrows flew up. "Who was? Helena?"

Elise waved her left hand dismissively. Her right she kept firmly around the pistol. "Of course not. Though this woman has something to do with her. She visited Nell before, and I'm pretty sure she tried to warn Reggie off me. And she was there tonight, with this man who saw me take aim at Mrs. Harris's window. What has this Harris woman ever done to you?"

"Your business is to kill her, not research her life. Go back to the man. Did he see your face?"

"Of course not. I was hooded, and most of me was in shadow. Besides which, you may have noticed I am in disguise. He will believe I am a man. I lost him easily enough."

"Maybe," came the grim response. "But *who is he?*"

She shrugged, more to annoy her employer than because she didn't care. "I was introduced to him, though I had other matters on my mind at the time. Lord Something-or-other. Linton? Linhouse? No, it was Lord Linfield. The cast were positively preening before him, and that was only the male contingent. Why? Do you want me to seduce—"

Her sarcasm was lost on her employer, who interrupted her with sudden force. "*Linfield!* Linfield? Are you sure?"

She raised one haughty eyebrow. "I believe I said so. Lord Linfield."

"But this is disastrous!" He pulled agitatedly at his lower lip. No wonder it was so droopy and sulky if he wrenched it around like that all the time. "He knows me. And he knows Mrs. Harris."

"Then you had better scarper back to the safety of whatever rock you emerged from. Why did you even come here? It makes a nonsense of all your elaborate secrecy and establishes a direct connection between us."

"I had faith in you," he said bitterly, "and wanted to be here to celebrate. I was wrong on both counts. But my alibi is strong. Everyone will know I was in York."

"Except Lord Linfield, if he sees you." She smiled. "Or Mrs. Harris. Go away, my employer. You are in my way, and therefore your own."

"Don't speak to me that way," he snapped. "Remember who holds the purse strings."

"Remember who holds the pistol," she replied.

"Is that a threat?"

"It is a warning."

His slightly protruding eyes narrowed, but with an effort, he chose not to pursue it. Wise. She could now identify him as easily as he could her. "Your escape from the theatre was planned. This effort at the hotel tonight was a foolish mistake. Anything could have happened. You didn't even fire a shot and were almost caught!"

To her annoyance, he sat back down again. "Linfield, eh? It means the British government knows she is here. She must have told them, and they sent Linfield to smooth her way. This does not matter."

"And the Vale woman?"

His eyes flew up to hers. "Vale?"

"Yes, the woman with Lord Linfield."

"Vale? *Delilah* Vale?"

"Perhaps. Yes. She was only introduced to me this evening as Miss Vale, but I'm—"

"By Linfield?"

"No, by Reggie Miller, and I'm sure he called her Delilah when she first came here. Why does she matter? Who is she?"

He gave a short, frightened bark of laughter. "My alibi! And she is Linfield's ally…"

"Who *is* this Linfield? Why is he so important? Just because he knows you?"

"That. And in Vienna, at the congress… He was known as a gatherer of intelligence."

Her eyebrows flew up in disbelief. "A spy?"

"Of course not," he said impatiently. "Though he certainly used the information of such people. In his own way, it made him as formidable as Metternich himself. Why do you think his government ennobled him?"

"I didn't know they had. So now you want me to murder this woman while your alibi and a formidable gatherer of intelligence looks on? I think I'll need more money."

"What you need is more success," he said savagely. "And then we will talk more about fees. We will keep the same plan. And I will find a way to get the Harris woman to the theatre!"

*"DELLY, COULD YOU ever consider marrying me?"*

Delilah seemed to have stopped breathing. But then, the whole world had receded, leaving only herself and Linfield, smiling down at her, melting her heart, her whole being.

"M-marry you?" she stammered. "Me?"

The carriage swayed and lurched, throwing her against him. He reached up to cup her cheek with his bare hand. "If you could bear it."

Instinctively, she twisted her fingers in his hold, to clasp his hand. *"Bear* it? But you... I... We are not s—"

"Not suited?" he said incredulously. "My dear girl, were ever two people *better* suited? I have waited my whole life to meet you. It is not even mere compatibility—it is love. On my part. And there have been moments when I was sure you felt the same. Tell me I am wrong if you must, but I won't stop trying."

"Love?" she said. "Oh God, when did I turn into such an incoherent ninnyhammer?"

"Words are not always important," he said, and swooped on her mouth like a starving man, kissing her until she was breathless and gasping and utterly won. But then, she had been won long ago.

"There," he muttered against her lips. "Now do you believe me? Will you answer me?"

She smiled as she kissed him back, pouring all her happiness, all her longing and wonder, from her mouth to his.

He groaned. "Marry me soon, Delilah. Please!"

She laughed softly, clutching his shoulders, pressing her cheek to his, kissing the soft lock of hair that fell beneath her lips. Everything was suddenly too intense, too charged, the emotion overwhelming her. She grasped for humor, for something more cerebral to leaven the mixture while she grew used to the fierce love bubbling away beneath.

"Who was that man with the gun?" she asked. "And who was he shooting at?"

Laughter shook him. His eyes were alight with it. "You see? Excellently well suited. Although the matter isn't really funny at all." He drew back a little, but kept his arm around her shoulders and dropped a kiss on her hair. "This is in confidence, Delly. You mustn't even tell your family until it's over—not because I don't trust them, but because words slip out unintentionally, overheard or repeated, and this truly is a matter of life and death, and the stability of a large piece of Europe. Vienna taught us the necessity of balance and negotiation to keep a lasting peace."

"What has that to do with—"

"Mrs. Harris was almost the victim of assassination. Harris is not her name. She is the Princess of Hazburg, here in Blackhaven with her husband to meet privately with her half-brother, who was deposed by the Hazburg people in the wake of Bonaparte's defeat in 1814, in favor of Princess Irena. Irena is by far the better ruler, endorsed by elections and the approval of the congress. However, her brother has remained a thorn in her side, fomenting discontent from abroad. Irena's aim now is to reconcile their differences and allow him to come home rather than remain in exile, a magnet, if you will, for political opponents and malcontents."

"Ah! So that is the real reason you are in Blackhaven? You are helping her?"

"I have been asked by my superiors to smooth her way if I can. I really did want Elaine to spend some time at a spa, though my suggestion of Blackhaven was influenced by the princess's wish to come here to meet Prince Karl, her brother."

Delilah nodded, smiling just a little shyly. "I'm glad you did. For any number of reasons."

"Oh, so am I." He swooped, kissing her lips again, so lingeringly that she eventually tugged at his head.

"So, someone disapproves of this reconciliation?" she said breathlessly. "Enough to assassinate her? How is that even possible here?"

"In England? It's not so long since our own prime minster was assassinated."

"True. So do you have any idea who the culprit is?"

"The assassin, I think, is somehow associated with the theatre. But he is merely the tool. The true perpetrator I believe to be Prince Karl."

Delilah sat up. "Her own brother?"

"A man more inclined to self-aggrandizement and tyranny than democracy. A destabilizing influence who would sell his country out to Prussia and start a civil war to do so. His Majesty's government will not allow that. And so, we have been watching Karl, who has been in the country for some time, living incognito and spinning his little webs."

Something had changed in Linfield as he spoke. The warmth had vanished from his eyes. No wonder. His words were bleak and ugly. And although she was so determined to know, Delilah resented the change in mood. Linfield was unreadable again, the diplomat, the statesman.

"Can we deport him?" she asked.

"And leave him free to cause more mayhem in Europe? No, he must be discredited, shown to his own people in his true colors, and his own government allowed to deal with him."

Delilah stared at him. "You are using the princess as *bait*? Risking her life?"

"At her own insistence. Although part of her still believes Karl is genuine and wants to reconcile with her, I believe tonight disproves that theory. It is also interesting that the assassin knew she would not be at the theatre but at the hotel."

"Why?"

"Because I only talked her out of going to the theatre earlier today."

"Why would he even think she would be at the theatre?" Delilah wondered. "And what makes you so sure the theatre is involved at all?"

Linfield hesitated. There was an oddly rueful glint in his eyes. Almost involuntarily, it seemed, his thumb moved against her palm in a soft, absent caress that made her shiver.

"Information," he said at last, "provided by Karl himself. Some of his correspondence has been intercepted. He is a lazy prince and, when working alone, needs someone to translate everything to German. Or his German into English or other languages."

"What, he entrusts his evil plans to the eyes of a random translator?" she said in disbelief. "Rather than his own trusted people?"

"In this he cannot trust his own people. He has to act in secret. Besides, the random translator would not know. Not his identity, or even what he was discussing. There is no cipher involved, as such—merely, one learns to recognize the vague terms. *The housewife*, for example, is his name his sister. The assassin is *my friend*. *The town* is Blackhaven. Dates and times are left as they are but attached to pointless and nonexistent events. Dull stuff that no translator would ever suspect. Especially not when sent by the assumed name."

Dull stuff that would seem trivial to a translator… Somehow, she knew then. But she asked anyway, because of the enormity, because in this world of hope and happiness she had just entered, it could not possibly be true. "The assumed name which is…?"

His eyes remained steady on hers. He didn't answer. He didn't need to.

"Mr. Charles," she whispered. "Karl. Dear God, and I have been so pleased with myself! What have I done?"

"Nothing," he said urgently. "Nothing at all. In fact, you

THE SPINSTER'S LAST DANCE

helped enormously. Without you, I would have let the princess go to the theatre and she could even now be dead."

She could. And maybe one day that would weigh with Delilah. For now... Nobody had ever called Delilah slow. Which was funny, because of course she had been. Pathetically, laughably slow. Yet now, when she would have given anything to live in ignorance for one more minute, she *knew*.

Even at the beginning, at the ball, he had been flatteringly interested in her chosen work. She remembered his calling so unexpectedly at Black Hill, strolling about the morning room as they talked, his gaze casually on her papers, and when he had looked at her again, his eyes had been cold. She had imagined her words about confidentiality had offended him, but it had never been that, only suspicion, disapproval. He had not been concerned for her the night of the Black Hill dinner party, when she had discovered him in the morning room. He had been examining her work, *spying*... Was that not beneath him?

Even her illusion of their intimacy at the cave the day of the storm was shattered. His stunning kisses on the beach, the sweetness of the carriage ride home—all deceit to win her confidence. The odd, pointless introduction to "Mrs. Harris" at the garden party—a test.

Lies. All lies she had never even guessed at.

"My translations never reached Mr. Charles," she said, her voice oddly calm and dispassionate. "You took the packet the night you came to dinner."

"I did."

"And I never saw. I never even thought it." Desolation was swamping her, and she could not let it. She had to live the rest of her life, and that meant at least a thread of pride. She freed her hand, shifting along the seat out of the reach of his arm. "What is it you want me to do? Mistranslate something for him to bring him here and make another attempt upon her life where the authorities can catch him?"

"No," he said, "although it is an idea we could consider. I

want—"

"You must let me know what you want, my lord. By letter or messenger is best. I have other work, of course, but be assured I will give yours priority."

"Delilah, don't."

"No? Well, the choice is yours."

"Stop it. This changes nothing."

It was so funny, she actually laughed, because of course it changed everything. *Everything.* Happiness was draining off her like bathwater…on a winter's day when it was cold and dark and her heart was empty.

"I may have been slow, my lord," she said, her voice small and hard, "but I am not stupid. If you wish my help—in fact, even if you don't—you will stop the pretense right now and speak to me in a businesslike manner. I deserve that much courtesy."

"Delly—"

"Stop it! That is the name my family uses, the people who love me. You may address me as Miss Vale or not at all. Is that clear?"

"You think I was pretending to love you?" he said incredulously. He was so good at this that she could almost have believed him. "I hid part of the truth before I knew you, that is all. I never lied. My love…" He reached for her, and she threw herself onto the opposite bench.

"Do not touch me. Do not *presume.*"

To her eternal humiliation, her voice cracked. She looked deliberately away from him, out of the window, seeing nothing but unrelieved darkness, no sea, no trees, no moon through the clouds spattering rain across the glass of the window. Or perhaps the blur was in her eyes.

"Delilah, I love you." His voice was hollow, curiously helpless.

She wanted to laugh, or at least yawn, but her throat was too tight.

"I should have told you before. I've been trying for days."

Incapable of speech, she waved one hand for silence, praying it looked like contempt and fearing it merely added to the impression of a hurt, gullible fool. She needed to be away from him. Would this horrendous journey never end?

"You love me," he said softly.

She shook her head.

He leaned forward, but at least he did not touch her. "Your kisses say otherwise. So do mine."

She did not even trouble to shake her head this time. Somewhere in her misery, as the carriage lumbered through the night, she was aware of his gaze never leaving her face. At least he did not speak. She could hold herself together, she thought, so long as the silence held.

He granted her that much courtesy, at least until, with utter relief, she saw the gates of Black Hill approach. Reaching up, she knocked on the carriage roof, loudly enough to hurt her knuckles.

"I shall walk from here," she announced, her voice blessedly steady. "Goodnight, my lord."

"Denzil," he said.

She ignored that, rising even before the carriage had fully stopped. Only then did he spring up himself and open the door, letting down the steps and alighting to hand her down.

"Let me at least walk with you to the house," he said low.

She affected not to see his hand. There was no point in even pretending not to be hurt by him. He knew. He had always known.

"Goodnight, my lord," she said distantly, and began to walk.

"I'll call tomorrow."

She did not—could not—look back. "I shall not be at home tomorrow, but feel free to write your instructions." She strode through the half-open gates, listening desperately for the sounds of his departure. They were a long time coming, which was a whole new agony. She did not hear him return to the carriage, but she did hear the coachman speaking to his horse, turning it to return to Blackhaven with Lord Linfield, the only man she had ever loved or ever would.

He had never loved her. He had not even trusted her. It was an illusion, a lie. He had used her gullibility to get close to her, suspecting her of collusion with Karl, and then using her to gain access to the theatre company to investigate.

*So much for my last dance.*

Ahead, the house was blurred. The whole world was blurred.

# Chapter Thirteen

DENZIL FROWNED OUT of the carriage window, churning with guilt and worry and the sheer enormity of this catastrophe—so trivial in the perspective of the world's problems, and yet the need to make it right overwhelmed him.

His fingers drummed relentlessly on his knee. All he could see was the moment of realization on her face, the sheer pain in her eyes that *he* had caused. If it could have helped, he would have punched himself. He would certainly have struck anyone else for hurting her so. He had always regarded himself as an honorable and considerate man. He was not used to feeling like an utter scoundrel, and it made him shift restlessly in his seat. But mostly, his concern was for her.

She had not believed he could be interested in her. She had imagined at one time that he was pursuing her sister. The chase had been sweet and rewarding for him, watching her open so gradually to the possibilities of friendship and love and passion. Tonight, he was sure he had won her. She would have married him.

And then he—the great diplomat who had rescued so many dubious, difficult, and downright dangerous situations—had made a colossal mess of his confession. She might have been too quick to jump to the conclusion that he had lied his way into her affections, but that too was his fault, something he should have foreseen because he knew only too well her self-deprecating nature. Behind all the bluntness and the prickles was a vulnerable woman, hurt all her life by those who undervalued her or misjudged her. He never had, and yet to her he was the worst of all because he had understood her, won her trust, and then destroyed it.

But by tomorrow, surely, she would have had time to reflect, to realize the truth. He might have begun their acquaintance to find out about Karl's correspondent in Blackhaven, but the rest was all pursuit of *her*.

Only how could she realize that? Half the time, *he* had not. He had stolen her documents, taken advantage of her behind her family's back, and been so unforgivably clumsy—and late—in his explanation.

*Shame on you, Talbot, for a fool and a scoundrel...*

He would do anything to take away that awful, betrayed look from her face, to undo the hurt. It was worse even than the contemplation of his own loneliness if he could not persuade her to forgive him and trust him again.

She loved him. This was not beyond his ability to fix...

In the meantime, he had his duty, although it was hard to focus on such matters when Delilah's face kept intruding.

At the hotel, he went straight to the princess's rooms and knocked in the precise rhythm they had agreed upon. Her maid opened the door and ushered him quickly into the sitting room.

The curtains were closed now, the princess seated at her desk, studying papers.

"Lord Linfield," she said at once. "I got your message. Did something happen at the theatre?"

"Not at the theatre, no." Quickly and calmly, he told her about the gunman, spotted by mere chance and chased away.

She stood up, her complexion pale. "And it was definitely my window?"

"Without doubt."

"I did look out several times." Her fingers twisted together.

"But we do not know it was my brother."

"Highness, we have so many links to him that it would be foolish to discount him."

She sank onto the sofa, rubbing tiredly at her forehead. "I suppose so. What is life for, my lord, if we cannot trust our own blood?"

*Or our own love,* he thought ruefully. "It is your brother's nature to want everything without earning it," he said gently. "It is not a personal hatred, I'm sure."

"I cannot hate him in return."

"That is to your credit, not his. Highness, I have to advise you not to go out, except by carriage and with great care, until this meeting with your brother is over. Or until we uncover his assassin."

"And so he wins by making me a virtual prisoner?" she snapped.

"You could cancel the meeting. Return to Hazburg."

She sighed. "We have already discussed the need to bring this into the open one way or another. No, we will stick to the plan. Is Friedrich safe? Does he know?"

"I'm going to speak to him now. Goodnight, princess."

"Goodnight, my lord."

He was almost at the door before her voice stayed him. "Is he here, Linfield?"

"Prince Karl? I would doubt it." Though he could do with some help to find out…

He went downstairs again and into the large hall at the back of the hotel where the gaming club was held. The tables were crowded, the patrons a vast array of types from card sharps and courtesans to aristocrats. He spotted Lord Braithwaite there, and Lord Wickenden and his brother-in-law Bernard Muir—who appeared to be in the company, interestingly enough, of Delilah's sister Felicia Maitland.

Friedrich was playing roulette and good-naturedly losing small amounts. He was not difficult to distract, and to his credit, looking both grave and anxious, he left immediately to return to his wife.

Denzil, feeling flat and oddly helpless, had nothing else to do but retire to his own room and determine to do better tomorrow.

IN THE MORNING, he hired a horse and, ignoring the threatening rain clouds, rode out to Black Hill. A one-armed man who walked with the rolling gait of a sailor ambled around from the stables and took his horse. Denzil knocked at the front door.

It was opened by the same pretty, smiling maid he remembered, who led him straight to Delilah the first time he had called. Unfortunately, she seemed to have learned from her mistake, for she asked him to wait while she found out if Miss Vale was at home.

Denzil, left kicking his heels in the hall, found his heart drumming with nervous anticipation. He had to find the right words to convince her. Surely, in the light of day, she would see his honesty, his love. He longed to convince her, to bring back her smiles, her happiness, to make her his wife, his life's beloved companion...

The maid came back. "Miss Vale is not at home, my lord. She is not expected for the rest of the day."

Denzil caught and held her eye. He recognized a polite fiction when he heard it. "It is a matter of vital importance that I see Miss Vale now."

Her eyes slid away. "I'm sorry, sir. Would you care to leave a message?"

Denzil considered brushing past her to find Delilah for himself. For her sake as much as his, he needed to convince her of the truth. But force was not the way to go.

"Yes," he said, "I'll leave a message."

"Here you are, sir." She showed him the paper and pen on

the table beneath the mirror, and he wrote simply, *Please. D.*

He folded the paper and handed it to the maid. "I'll wait," he said.

She opened her mouth to argue, then turned and hurried back the way she had come. So frustrating! He could see exactly which room Delilah was in, and yet he could not get to her without breaking every courtesy known to him.

It was not yet that time.

The maid did not take long. "Miss Vale is not at home," she said woodenly. "I have left your message for her. I'll show you out, my lord."

Denzil was not so easy to get rid of. "Perhaps Mrs. Maitland is at home? Or Sir Julius?"

"Mrs. Maitland is not yet up. Sir Julius went out early."

Denzil sighed. "Are any of the family receiving?"

"You seem to have called at a bad time, sir."

"I do, don't I?" Well, there were other ways to meet, to talk. It might be harder than he had imagined, but he would not give up.

As he left the house, the sky was promising rain. He walked around toward the stables in search of his horse, and found the twins feeding it.

"Well, *you're* at home," he remarked by way of greeting.

"We don't count yet," Leona said, stroking the horse's nose. "Won't Delilah see you?"

He met bluntness with bluntness. "No."

"What did you do?" Lawrence asked. The boy's voice was mild, but his eyes were not.

"I made a mistake."

"We made one of those recently," Leona admitted. "It doesn't feel good, even when *utter* disaster is averted."

Denzil took the horse's reins, glancing from her to her brother. Old eyes in innocent young faces. "I would very much like to avert utter disaster. I need to speak to Delilah."

"Are you asking for our help?" Lawrence asked.

Denzil considered. "I suspect I could do worse. So, yes, I am."
The twins exchanged looks.

"We don't know what you've done," Lawrence said frankly.
"Or what you *would* do."

"I would make it right." For the first time, terrifyingly, Denzil
began to doubt that he *could* make this right. "I love her," he
blurted. He did not even feel ridiculous admitting the fact to two
precocious children.

He was rewarded by identical dazzling smiles.

"Then don't push her," Leona advised.

"There will be opportunities," Lawrence added. "If she wishes to take them."

"Does she?"

"How would we know?" Leona asked innocently. "Goodbye!"

They ran off, leaving him to mount and ride drearily back to
Blackhaven. It had indeed begun to rain.

DENYING HERSELF TO Linfield when he called would probably
have been harder had she not been suffering one of the migraines
that so disoriented her from time to time. It had come upon her
just as she had sat down at her desk and pulled toward her the
pile of papers that contained her first drafts of "Mr. Charles's"
translations. Letters danced and disappeared before her eyes,
making it impossible to work.

Well, there was nothing she could do in any case. Linfield had
seen everything and understood better than she did what it all
meant. She could not help. She could not even think properly.

Although she didn't truly expect Linfield to call, she had
already decided she would not see him. Whether or not she
would have given in to the note she could not even see to read,
she did not know. But she could not allow him to observe her in

this weakened, vulnerable state. Not now. And so she had denied him.

She had even said to Betsy, "I am never at home to Lord Linfield." And that felt so sad she had almost wept. She did weep—again—when she heard him riding away.

By the time the twins bearded her, she had recovered both vision and calm, though a dull headache had begun to haunt her.

"We met Lord Linfield in the stables," Leona said cheerfully. "He seemed to think you were not at home."

"He understands the polite fictions as well as anyone else," Delilah said.

"We think he likes you," Leona said. She could not have known how much that hurt.

"His lordship would never be so impolite as to give any other impression," said Delilah.

"Why would he come if he didn't like you?" Lawrence asked.

"You had best inquire of his lordship," Delilah said unwisely.

"Good idea," Lawrence said.

*Don't!* Delilah pressed her lips together to prevent the word escaping.

"We all make mistakes," Leona said, ambling around the room, twitching at cushions and curtains.

"I know. I have made many in the last couple of weeks."

Lawrence said, "Lord Linfield claims he wants to make his mistake right."

It was much too late for that. "He can't," Delilah said, forcing lightness into her voice.

"I expect he'll be at the masquerade ball on Friday," Leona said.

"What masquerade ball?" Delilah demanded.

"At the castle. Lucy was desperate to go until she discovered her friend Tyler was the unspeakable Eddleston. He's here, by the way."

"What?" Delilah was so confused she thought her migraine must be returning. She knew, of course, that Lord Eddleston,

Lucy's betrothed, had upset her by turning up in Blackhaven without warning, but she had been so caught up in her own overwhelming relationship that she had lost the thread somewhere. Guilt niggled at her. She must pay more attention to her siblings.

For one thing, the twins needed more structure and discipline to their day. Lawrence at least should go to school, though the idea of separating him from Leona did not feel right. There must be a decent school in Blackhaven or Whalen, only a few miles along the coast. An investigation for another day.

She shooed the twins away and tried to return to her papers, only to be interrupted again by Lucy rushing into the room looking utterly enraptured.

"Delly, Delly, I'm going to be married!" she exclaimed, seizing Delilah's hands and dancing her around the room.

As Lucy's story tumbled out, Delilah could only be delighted for her. And if there was a small, hard knot in her heart for what she herself had dreamed of and lost, she refused to acknowledge it.

THE FOLLOWING DAY, fresh torture arrived in the form of Lord Linfield's sister.

Elaine had been so kind to her that Delilah could not refuse her, at least not after Betsy had assured her that Miss Talbot was alone.

She did wonder if Linfield had sent his sister—only why would he bother?

"So sorry to call without any warning," Miss Talbot greeted her, taking her hand and smiling. "I hope it's not too inconvenient."

"Of course not. I'm very glad to see you. Betsy will bring tea. Please, sit down. How are you?"

"Very well." Miss Talbot's perceptive gaze was on her face as she took a seat in the nearest armchair. "But you are looking a little under the weather, if you don't mind my saying so."

"I have been troubled a little with a minor headache," Delilah said, without mentioning that it had been yesterday. On the other hand, she could almost feel the beginnings of a new one.

"I hope Denzil is not the cause of it."

With difficulty, Delilah kept the smile on her face. "I can't imagine why you should think so."

"Because he is like a bear with a sore tooth himself. I cannot work out why, for he said your theatre outing was most enjoyable."

"And so it was," Delilah said pleasantly. "You should see the play if you can."

"Perhaps I shall take Antonia before she deserts me for your brother."

Betsy brought the tea in then, and Delilah hastily changed the subject to that of Lucy's engagement to Lord Eddleston.

"How lovely," Miss Talbot said, accepting a cup of tea from Delilah and helping herself to an iced tea cake. "Will they be married in Blackhaven?"

"I believe so. The banns will be called on Sunday—along with Julius's! But at the moment, Lucy seems more interested in the masquerade ball at the castle on Friday. She and Felicia are up to something." She did not say that she felt excluded. She knew that was just the way she was feeling—excluded from everything by unhappiness. Besides, Lucy and Felicia had some air to clear between them.

"Then you will be there, too?" Miss Talbot asked casually.

"Felicia accepted for all of us, so yes. Will I see you there?"

"Of course." Miss Talbot sipped her tea. "I hope Denzil did not offend you at the play."

Her unexpected return to the subject almost threw Delilah. "Of course not," she said, summoning amusement. "I cannot believe he offends anyone very often."

"Never without intention," Miss Talbot said. "Forgive me—I know he has something on his mind, and I am trying to find out what. I don't like to see him unhappy."

"Is he?" Delilah hoped she didn't sound as wistful as she felt. And how awful to wish anyone unhappy. She was merely grasping pathetically for any possible sign of his affection.

Miss Talbot set her cup and saucer on the table. "Allow me to be frank. My brother is a sociable man. He enjoys people, and though I shouldn't know it, let alone admit it, I know he has enjoyed the attentions of women in the past. And yet I have never seen him as he is with you."

*Suspicious? Determined on a distasteful course?* Delilah kept her gaze on her untouched tea. "You are mistaken if you believe any attachment could ever exist between your brother and me."

"I shall be very sorry if that is true."

Delilah, who had imagined she was offering comfort, could not resist a quick, surprised glance.

Miss Talbot leaned forward. "My dear Miss Vale—oh the devil, may I call you Delilah? I am Elaine. Delilah, if my brother gave offense, it was not intentional. I know he always seems to cool and suave, but that is not who he is. The man beneath is idealistic and passionate. If he overstepped, it was from an excess of feeling, not any kind of ill nature."

*Oh God, can this get any worse?* Delilah must have jerked her hand in distress, for there was tea in her saucer.

"No such thing," she managed. "You completely misunderstand."

"I'm certainly failing to understand something," said Elaine, sighing. "But since neither of you will tell me what, I cannot help."

"There is nothing to help, I assure you."

"But you will call on me soon?"

"Of course," said Delilah, crossing her toes inside her slippers. She would never call on Elaine while Linfield was in Blackhaven. Another friendship lost.

# Chapter Fourteen

B Y THE DAY of the castle masquerade ball, Delilah felt she was living on her nerves.

The effort of maintaining a normal façade before her siblings seemed to use up all her strength, even when she wasn't worrying about them. With some nostalgia, she remembered the days of their childhood, when their problems had been easy to fix with just a little effort and imagination. Now that they were all grown up, she didn't even know what their problems were most of the time, let alone how to improve things for them. And remembering her previous missteps with Antonia, perhaps this was just as well.

Even the twins were no longer really children but asserting their own independence and slipping through her fingers.

On some level, it all added to her uncertainty, her feelings of no longer being useful. Antonia would soon be mistress of Black Hill, and no matter how good-natured she was proving to be, she could not really want quite so many of Julius's siblings in the house. Delilah knew she should bring forward her plans to make her own home, or to travel in someone's employ. The trouble was, Mr. Charles had been the employer offering such a future, and he was a liar and a murderer. She did not doubt Linfield's interpretation.

Nor did she have enough money of her own. Like her siblings, she had given most of her small inheritance to help free Felicia from her late husband's debts, and she had not yet earned anything like enough to live independently.

Two new packets of translation work had reached her from Mr. Charles in York—so at least he was not in Blackhaven. She had rewrapped them and had them delivered by hand to Lord Linfield. He returned them to Black Hill in person, though she had not been at home to him. He requested that she translate everything as normal and return it to Mr. Charles.

This, however, was slow going, because all too frequently when she sat down to work, she was plagued by vision problems and headaches.

In all, the last thing she wished to do was attend a ball where she was bound to encounter not only Linfield but people like Mrs. Match, and no doubt the drunken young men who had imagined she was fair game at the theatre. She never gave in to such disrespect as a rule, but right now, she did not feel strong enough to relish the fight.

She was tired, miserable, and saw no end to it.

However, she put a good face on it, and wore a favorite ball gown of lilac silk with fresh trimmings. Felicia gave her a domino cloak and half-mask of almost the same shade, both sewn with occasional pearls.

"Well, they're glass," Felicia admitted, "but I do think they look quite effective, and the whole is splendid on you."

"Don't you want to wear them yourself?" Delilah asked.

"Oh, no, my task this evening is to blend in behind Lucy."

"What is she up to, Fliss?"

Felicia grinned. "Just fun. But trust me, you'll know her when you see her. If you ask me, it's all for Eddleston's benefit. The pair of them are mad as fruitcakes."

Delilah couldn't help laughing, which lifted her spirits somewhat. And when she glanced at herself in the mirror, she was further encouraged by the realization that a mask was just what she needed. And indeed, she looked very well. The masquerade was curiously liberating.

If Linfield even recognized her this evening, he would never know her pain.

Braithwaite Castle had made an exciting setting for the garden party a week ago. For the ball, it was magnificent. The great hall was decorated with flowers and greenery and what must have been thousands of candles, the French doors thrown open to the brightly lit terrace. Lanterns lit the paths of the formal gardens.

Delilah was dazzled. The luscious costumes, many glittering with jewels, created much more color than most such events, since even the gentlemen tended to eschew their formal black and white for outrageous costumes—or at least domino cloaks—of every possible shade.

At first, she did not recognize anyone, which surprised her, for Blackhaven was not a large town and the gentle families even fewer in number. But there were always enough visitors, it seemed, including Lady Braithwaite's own staying guests, to add bewildering variety. All the earl's sisters were present, from as far afield as the Scottish Highlands and the southwest of England.

Oh yes, Delilah could lose herself here easily enough. She need never even see Lord Linfield.

Except that she entered the ballroom with Julius, and he seemed to have some magnetic link to Antonia, who stood with Miss Talbot and the vicar. Julius's gaze found her immediately, and Delilah foolishly followed. In the same group, elegant and inadequately masked as he smiled down at his female companion, stood Lord Linfield.

Pain and pleasure jolted through her, depriving her of breath. Somehow, she drifted away before he noticed her and lost herself in the milling crowd who seemed to be having a wonderful time either recognizing each other or guessing identities.

Among others, she noticed the eccentric Launcetons, whose youngest family members had made friends with the twins. Lady Launceton's sister was the extraordinary beauty being pursued by

Aubrey and appeared to be the cause of his restlessness. She wasn't just lovely, either. She was delightfully kind and good-natured, and yet funny at the same time. Aubrey, Delilah thought, could do a great deal worse.

Not that she wished to pair off all her siblings. In fact, it was rather a lonely prospect, but life was always changing and moving on. It would for her, too.

The orchestra had struck up the first waltz when Lucy made her entrance. In eighteenth-century hoops and wig, she wore a ridiculous headdress that she could barely balance as she walked. Somehow, she managed to make it elegant, perhaps because Felicia was supporting her, but even behind the mask, she could not hide the irrepressible laughter in her sparkling eyes.

Responsive amusement caught at Delilah's breath, especially when she saw Eddleston stride toward her.

"Madam, may I have this dance?"

The light male voice startled her, vibrated all her taut nerves with that now-familiar mixture of pleasure and pain. She didn't even know if he recognized her. Slowly, hiding her own recognition, she turned to face Lord Linfield.

She had always seen how he veiled his eyes. It should have warned her. Instead, she had wanted to believe in the warmth he let her see, the softening she had imagined was something deeper, like her own. She had never been able to read him, and she certainly couldn't now. Yet still, she melted.

She might have felt helpless as she gazed up at him, but, thank God, she was not.

"Thank you for the honor, sir," she replied distantly. "But I do not dance."

"On the contrary—you dance delightfully."

Oh yes, he had known her all along. "Allow me to correct myself. I *shall* not dance."

For an instant, something changed in his eyes. She could almost have imagined it was disappointment. "Then perhaps I might persuade you to walk instead? We could find some refreshment on the way."

Part of her, the cowardly part, wanted to run from him as quickly as possible, but guilt as well as duty compelled her to say, "Of course. We have matters to discuss. How is Mrs. Harris?"

"Bouncing off the walls," he said, and her breath caught on laughter she didn't want, "in frustration at her enforced isolation."

"And her family?" Delilah asked.

"Still in York, I believe. Have you heard more from your correspondent there?"

"I have not. But then, the previous work is not yet complete."

She could have sworn he looked surprised at that, but she was not about to tell him of the increase in her migraines, which were happening sometimes twice in one day now. He plucked two glasses of champagne from the tray of a passing footman and presented one to her.

"How are you?" he asked.

She could almost imagine he truly cared for the answer. "Well. Lucy is engaged to be married."

"To the scamp with her now?"

Eddleston was indeed leading Lucy in a waltz made somewhat precarious by her enormous headdress, but the pair were clearly having a whale of a time, especially when a small dog peeked out of the headdress and leapt straight into Eddleston's arms.

Delilah was surprised into laughter. So was Linfield.

"No one in your family is dull, are they?" he said.

"No. Have you discovered the man we saw at the hotel on Monday?"

He paused, as if adjusting his thoughts back to business. "No. My best guess is the young actor who is Reginald Miller's understudy. John Hemmel. He is new to the company and has worked abroad. But nothing is known against him. At least there have been no further...incidents. The play will go on into next week."

"Will Mrs. Harris attend?"

"Not unless I know who to watch and have some means of protecting her."

"My brothers will help. Roderick is an excellent guardian. In fact, he is making a career out of it."

"I may well have to call on him, but at the moment, discretion is still too important."

"Of course," she said distantly. Clearly, he did not trust anyone who had anything to do with her.

A frown quirked his brow, and his lips parted, as if he would say more. And then his gaze moved beyond her, and though his expression did not change, she was sure somehow that something or someone had surprised him.

How odd that in some ways she knew him so well, while in others he was a complete mystery. How could she have fallen so deeply in love with someone she knew so little?

*Imagination,* she told herself.

"Excuse me," she said, and, giving in to cowardice, fled. The trouble was that the pain came with her.

DENZIL HAD JUST seen the woman who could, if she chose, solve several of his problems. He had known her in Paris as Lady Lewis, and in Vienna as Madame de Delon. On both occasions she had been a source of extremely valuable information.

And she had seen him.

She strolled around the ballroom and stepped out onto the terrace. Denzil followed.

"Even masked," he said lightly, "I would know you anywhere."

"Only if I chose to reveal myself." She sounded amused.

"Probably. Were you looking for me?"

"No. Though I've no objection to finding you."

Denzil offered her his arm, and after the faintest hesitation, she laid the tips of her fingers on his sleeve. Together, they walked down from the terrace to a garden path where they would not be overheard.

"Perhaps your business in Blackhaven is to do with Hazburg?" he suggested, hoping the government had sent her to him.

"Actually, no. I'm pursuing a Bonapartist conspiracy. Some fools just won't lie down."

"If you have the time or the inclination, a certain Mrs. Harris at the hotel, visiting from Hazburg, needs to be protected, probably from someone currently at the Blackhaven Theatre."

As always, she took it in her stride. "I can't promise you. But we'll keep our eyes open."

"I know you will. You look well." He was surprised how pleased he was to see this mysterious young woman who had only ever flitted briefly in and out of his life, distant, useful, and oddly trustworthy. She had a husband, too, somewhere, just as elusive and charming.

"So do you, my lord. I had forgotten what an exciting place Blackhaven can be."

She spoke as if she knew the town with affection, which was another surprise. He barely noticed her fingers slipping from his arm as she floated back toward the ballroom. She was clearly engaged upon another matter, but he was still glad of any help she could provide.

DELILAH HAD SEEN him follow the beautiful woman outside. She supposed the new pain was jealousy, an emotion she was not entitled to when she had dismissed him. She sat for a little beside Aubrey and Roderick, and then by Julius and Antonia. Usually, she sensed when her siblings sought her out for the calm and comfort of the familiar. Tonight, she was the seeker. When Julius and Antonia rose to dance, she watched them somewhat dreamily, mainly to stop herself looking for Linfield.

Someone slid into the seat beside her. A masked young man with something the look of a satyr. She was sure she had not seen him before, but he was smiling like a man sure of achieving his own way.

"I cannot believe my luck to find you all alone," he said.

She cast him a look of sardonic amusement but saw no need to reply.

"May I hope for this dance, madam?"

"No, sir, I thank you, but I do not dance."

"Why ever not? It is a ball, is it not?"

"My reasons are my own, sir."

"But you intrigue me."

She would have sparred with him, since he chose to waste his time with her, only a woman's stage whisper reached her from seats nearby.

"Will you look at that? She has Tranmere dangling after her now. She is shameless. At least Linfield must have extracted himself from her rapacious clutches."

Mrs. Match, with a couple of gossiping biddies. What had Delilah ever done to inspire such venom? She knew, of course. She had attracted Linfield's interest. Which was laughable. If only Mrs. Match knew it.

Delilah would have got up and walked away, only the mention of Linfield had floored her by its sheer injustice.

"Really?" said one of Mrs. Match's companions. "Who is she?"

"One of those Vales. Wrong side of the blanket, of course. Like mother, like daughter, it appears."

Delilah's lips thinned. Tranmere, however—if that truly was the name of the young man beside her—laughed.

"Wait, are you Aubrey's sister?" he asked. "What has the Match harridan got against you?"

"Nothing," Delilah said, rubbing her forehead. "She misunderstands a great deal."

"Not least of which is daring to criticize the guests of one's host. Even I wouldn't do that. Old Lady Braithwaite scares me to death. Come, dance with me to spite the old bat."

She could not help enjoying his descriptions of Mrs. Match, though she shook her head. "Thank you, but no. Don't let me keep you, sir." She cast a quick glance toward Mrs. Match and instead saw her son, and one of the others who had annoyed her at the theatre, smirking right at her.

It did not help that they would not have dared had Linfield been present. Nor that they were using Mrs. Match to pour scorn on her by way, presumably, of revenge on Linfield, whom they dared not attack.

On top of everything, it suddenly seemed too much. And as if on cue, she realized she could only see parts of Tranmere's face, like a partially completed jigsaw. *Oh damn,* she thought wearily.

"Ma'am, are you well?" Tranmere said uneasily. He rose, snatched a glass from a waiter, and thrust it at her. "Here, drink this, it will—"

"Look at her!" spat Mrs. Match. "Blind drunk!"

*Merely blind.* Delilah reached for the half-seen glass, misjudged, and knocked it out of Tranmere's hand. It shattered on the floor, causing a sudden silence around her.

"Well!" uttered one of Mrs. Match's cronies.

And Delilah, who had managed complicated social occasions for her father since she was eighteen years old, had no idea what to do. She knew people were staring at her, but she could not see her family. She could not see the glass to clear it up, and the malicious disapproval of the Matches and their companions seemed to pound into her.

*I want to go home. I should never have come.*

The blood sang in her ears.

"Move," said a brisk voice, and Tranmere vanished. "It's me, Lampton," the doctor said softly. "Take my arm and we'll find a quiet space."

She had never been more grateful for anything or anyone.

With no idea how she got there, she found herself in a quiet room, on a sofa, with Dr. Lampton, only partially seen, examining her eyes, taking her pulse, feeling around her neck.

Antonia was there. Antonia, to whom she had once been so unkind and to whom she was now pathetically grateful.

"Have these attacks become more severe?" Dr. Lampton asked.

"No. Just a little more frequent," Delilah replied.

"How much more frequent?"

"Every day, since Tuesday."

He still seemed to be looking at her.

She swallowed. "This is the second time today."

"Are you reading too much? Concentrating too hard?"

"I try to, but then this happens and I have to stop."

"You are anxious," he said bluntly. "Your neck and shoulders are stiff with it. I can give you something stronger to help you relax, but if possible, you need to remove yourself from the stress."

"Thank you, doctor." She didn't know what else to say.

"I'll fetch Julius," Antonia said, "and we'll take you home."

"No, please, there is no need," Delilah protested. "It is already passing. I should be fine now for the rest of the evening. Oh dear, I left all that glass…"

"Long gone," Dr. Lampton said. "The Braithwaite servants are excellent."

"Was everyone staring at me?" *Was Linfield?* Why did it matter?

"Hardly anyone noticed," the doctor said.

"The orchestra struck up," said Antonia. "Honestly, it's so warm in there this evening, no one will be surprised you seemed to faint."

"Someone said I was drunk," Delilah whispered, and was appalled by the threatening tears.

Dr. Lampton stood up. "That rumor will be quashed immediately. Mrs. Macy, if you would stay with Miss Vale until she is quite well and then escort her back to the ballroom, all will be well."

Famous last words.

Of course, all was not well. Before the evening was over, Lucy's Lord Eddleston had been shot and Roderick was engaged to marry Lady Helen Conway, who looked anything but pleased about it.

# Chapter Fifteen

APPARENTLY, DESPITE BEING shot, Lord Eddleston was expected to make a full and speedy recovery. Which meant that Denzil, once he had ascertained that the shooter was in custody and that the attack had nothing to do with Hazburg, could turn his full attention back to Delilah.

He had seen that queer, difficult, unfocused look in her eyes, and knew, even before the broken glass, that a migraine was upon her. Suspecting with fresh shame that he was at least partly responsible, Denzil had dragged Dr. Lampton unceremoniously out of his clearly enjoyable conversation and pointed him directly at Delilah.

The Match woman and her avid cronies were too close for his liking, as was the rakehell Tranmere.

"She needs rescuing, doctor, now," he'd all but snapped, adding before Lampton could speak, "I'll only make it worse."

Lampton, excellent fellow, had not replied, merely marched up to Delilah, ejected Tranmere, and guided her without fuss from the room. To his relief, Antonia Macy had hurried after them.

Lampton was not gone for long, but as Denzil made his way toward him, the doctor veered away toward old Lady Braithwaite, and from there, to his observant gaze, stemmed a whole flurry of activity.

As a result, when Delilah returned to the ballroom, managing somehow to look both frail and splendid, she was greeted by her host's sister, Lady Torridon, who appeared to inquire solicitously after her health, giving Delilah her own chair. Thereafter, all the leaders of Blackhaven Society—including the vicar, the squire, the doctor's wife, Lord Wickenden, whose wife was a native, and young Lady Braithwaite herself—made a point of speaking to her.

Denzil, who longed to, kept his distance. It was Elaine who told him what was going on, after the shooting of Eddleston had distracted everyone and the festivities had recommenced.

"That Match woman was telling everyone Delilah was drunk," Elaine murmured, distaste in every syllable.

"Drunk?" Denzil repeated in disbelief. "If so, it was the fastest sobering up in the history of alcohol. It was she who rushed around her family making sure they all knew about Eddleston."

"Also, Mrs. Match is spreading rumors that Delilah is Tranmere's latest," Elaine added, watching him with that sisterly understanding of which he was so wary.

Denzil snorted, which, for some reason, brought an approving expression to Elaine's countenance.

"However," she said, "it appears Blackhaven looks after its own. It has closed ranks around Delilah, and Mrs. Match is the one being left in the cold and made to look thoroughly ill-natured. Which she is."

"What the devil does the woman have against Delilah in the first place?"

Elaine sighed. "For a clever man, Denzil, you can be singularly thickheaded. She wants you for her poor little daughter, and Delilah is in her way."

For once, Denzil was silenced. He was so used to being judged on his work, most of it abroad, that he had forgotten his value on the English marriage mart. In fact, he had imagined everyone else had forgotten, too. But the Talbots had never been nobodies, and now there was the damned title to boost his attractions.

"Delilah herself said something similar," he murmured at last. "But it's silly. I barely know the woman or her daughter."

Elaine tapped his arm with her fan. "We didn't stay long enough in London for you to notice. But I did."

Denzil's smile was crooked. "Just think of the benefits of employing women in the diplomatic corp."

"Oh, we are already employed," Elaine said dryly. "We are just not paid or acknowledged." She cast a quick glance around her and lowered her voice. "Denzil, what have you done to that girl? She barely comes near me now, and she won't even look at you."

He glanced away from her penetrating eyes. "I misjudged. With anyone else, it would have mattered less. I could have repaired the mistake more easily. But she is hurt too often. And I forgot that practiced charm cannot cure everything. And now I am afraid I have lost her forever."

Elaine took his arm, walking him away from the couples forming a huge circle for the unmasking. It must be midnight. "Take heart, my dear. She loves you, you know."

And curiously, he did take heart.

DELILAH'S FAMILY MADE yet another splash across the evening at the unmasking when Major Roderick Vale announced his engagement to the earl's youngest sister, Lady Helen. Delilah looked as stunned as the rest of the family, although they all rallied around. Oddly, the earl's family looked less surprised, but although the match was hardly a brilliant one for Helen, they appeared to welcome it.

It was as he emerged from the cloakroom after supper that Denzil saw Miss Match all but cowering in an alcove at the entrance to the ballroom.

The Matches were hardly his favorite people, so despite a

surge of pity for a girl under the thumb of such a mother, he would have passed on without acknowledging he had seen her. Only, she suddenly sprang up looking frightened.

"Oh! My lord! I…" She trailed off in blushing confusion.

Denzil bowed coolly and was about to walk on when the genuine desperation in her eyes caught his attention. He could no more leave her in distress than he could an injured puppy.

Inwardly sighing, he said, "Miss Match, are you quite well?"

"Oh yes! That is, no, not really. I mean, I am not ill. But I am afraid I… Mama wishes… I need to apologize for… Oh dear, I don't even know how to…"

"I am not an ogre, Miss Match. And I don't recall any crime for which you need to apologize to me." The girl seemed in such an agony of embarrassment that genuine curiosity stirred.

"Mama is so strong and wishes always the best for us, only she misunderstands sometimes…" She gasped. "Miss Vale is your friend, I believe, and in this I know Mama is—was—wrong! She makes no difference to how you… I am a silly child to you, am I not?"

*Yes, you are.* But to say the words would be like kicking that injured puppy he had imagined earlier. "Of course not," he said kindly. "We hardly know each other, after all." He considered her, and the difference he might make through her for Delilah. "Perhaps, if you could bear it, we might dance together and talk about what is distressing you."

Her eyes widened. "It would make Mama so happy," she said naïvely.

"Oddly, that is not my chief concern."

A fugitive smile peeped out. When he offered his arm, she took it, and they entered the ballroom together.

Couples were already forming for the waltz, which at least meant they could talk while they danced. As he led Miss Match on to the floor, he could imagine her mother's expression of triumph all too easily. Deliberately, he did not look at her but at the wide-eyed, all-but-trembling girl in his arms.

"It must be overwhelming for you," he said, "to be faced so young with the wiles and ambitions of the world."

"Mama is ambitious for me," she admitted. "For both of us, but though my brother Gerald is the elder, I need to be married first because I am a female and I am *out*."

"Indeed. And naturally your mother wishes you to make a good marriage. Become a baroness, perhaps."

"She is realistic enough to know we could never snare a duke." Immediately, her face flamed. "Oh dear!"

His lips twitched. "Think nothing of it, but what on earth makes her imagine I would make you a suitable husband? Besides my being a baron, however newly minted."

"You must know you are extremely eligible, my lord."

"Not for a seventeen-year-old child. I am twice your age and spend years away from home at a time. Or is that the attraction? While I am abroad, you stay at home and spend my money?"

"Something like that," she said unhappily. "But you must understand, she is a widow, my lord, and feels she alone is responsible for us. She is trying to do her best."

"Does she know how much you hate this match of hers?"

"Oh dear! Of course I do not hate... That is, she knows you frighten me a little. But she is sure I will get over that once I know you a little better."

"Only you never will, will you? Because we are totally in-compatible."

She nodded agreement, and yet she did not look relieved, let alone pleased.

"Be assured," he said gently, "that while you are a charming and extremely pretty young lady, I will never be induced to offer for you. You are perfectly safe from me."

She stared unseeingly at his waistcoat. "But not from Mama," she whispered.

He frowned. "You mean she would punish you for failing to fix my interest? I really think you will have to explain to her that it is I who have failed to fix yours."

She gave a choked little laugh. "You are quite right. I need to find my courage. Mama is just…like a runaway horse, you know? Unstoppable."

"I assure you she is not. As she will discover if she again lifts a finger—or even utters a syllable—against Miss Vale. Can you manage to convey that to her so that she understands? Or must I do it? With rather less discretion that you could manage if you put your mind to it."

Alarm passed over her face, followed by doubt, and then by a mild but definite determination.

"I shall try," she said bravely. "I know she has been unforgivably unkind to…" She cast her gaze around the ballroom, stared for several moments, then swallowed hard and met his gaze once more. "My lord, I need to tell you…but I cannot here. People dance so close to us. Might we walk instead?"

Denzil did not mind. She was an uninspiring dancer. Although, to be fair to her, after his waltz with Delilah, he found all his dance partners wanting. He waltzed her to the edge of the dance floor, and again offered her his arm.

She seemed in a hurry now, which should have warned him, though at the time he attributed it to her need to get the words out before her courage failed her. He guided her toward the French windows, but she tugged him toward the passage and the antechamber on the right.

The door stood open, and the room was empty. She preceded him inside, breathing too quickly, and stopped by the door.

He walked past her. "Tell all," he invited her, fighting flippancy. He realized he was bored.

To his surprise, she moved and closed the door. Then she burst into tears.

DELILAH SHOULD HAVE been strong enough not to watch him.

Perhaps she wouldn't have had he not been dancing with Miss Match. And Mrs. Match's expression was one of ill-concealed triumph—too much surely for a mere dance, even a waltz, even with Lord Linfield.

So she ceased worrying about Roderick, and about poor Eddleston, and observed Linfield leading Miss Match from the floor. Delilah was not blind to the fact that the girl made the move to draw him to the passage—which was not even open to the guests, although she was sure Lucy had made use of it earlier to change out of her ridiculous costume and into something more demure.

And Mrs. Match went into immediate action. Not to follow her daughter before she could be compromised, but, presumably, to advertise that her daughter was not in the ballroom. She spoke to several women around her, who all gazed searchingly around the room.

Surely Linfield, a man of the world and quite up to snuff, was not about to be caught by that old trick? It should have been funny, even a suitable revenge, but it was neither. It was wrong. And Delilah was not about to hand anyone on a plate to the awful Mrs. Match.

She seized Antonia by the hand. "Come with me..." She was in time to glimpse the closing of the door, and dragged Antonia back again, almost running into one of Braithwaite's married sisters—the gentle Lady Maria, who had been so kind to Lucy.

"My lady," Delilah said without preamble, "is there another way into that antechamber than by the first door on the right?"

Lady Maria blinked. "Yes. Why?"

"Will you please take us there? One moment..." Delilah darted the few yards to Elaine Talbot, in discussion with Lord Wickenden. "Elaine, do me a favor and prevent anyone accompanying Mrs. Match from the ballroom."

Elaine's jaw dropped, but there was no time for explanations. Without waiting to see what, if anything, the woman would do, Delilah hurried back to Antonia and Lady Maria, who, looking intrigued, led them out of the ballroom, along a narrower passage and into another small room. She crossed the floor to a connecting door and threw it wide.

Inside were two people—Miss Match, weeping uncontrollably, and Lord Linfield, being clutched by the lapel, awkwardly patting her shoulder. His head jerked around, and the relief flooding his face was unmistakable.

"Delilah," he uttered.

Miss Match spun away from him and, seeing the newcomers, cried harder.

"Oh, let him go, you witless girl," Delilah said, marching across the room. "You'll spoil his coat, and gentlemen hate that."

Miss Match was so stunned that she obeyed. Her tears, however, were real, as was the alarm standing out in her eyes.

Delilah put an arm around her, pressing her down on the nearby sofa. "There, there," she said, just as the main door flew open and Mrs. Match marched in with Elaine at her heels. A gaggle of people tried to follow, but Elaine closed the door on them and leaned against it.

Mrs. Match strode across the floor like a termagant, then was brought up short by the sight of her weeping daughter on the sofa, being comforted by Delilah, of all people, while Lady Maria, Antonia, and Lord Linfield looked on with apparent concern.

"Oh, Mrs. Match, I'm so glad you're here," said Lady Maria. "Your daughter is upset."

One had to applaud Mrs. Match. She recovered quickly from shock. "Upset! I should think so, and I know exactly whom to blame!"

"Then you must tell me, ma'am," Maria said, "because we can extract no sense from her."

Mrs. Match pointed to Linfield with apparent loathing. "That man! He was seen luring her from the ballroom!"

"Luring?" Antonia said, amused. "She walked in here of her own free will."

Mrs. Match bridled. "And I suppose she closed the door!" she said with heavy sarcasm.

"Actually, yes," Antonia replied with aplomb, "but only because she saw we were here to chaperone her. Only then she burst into tears, and we are at a loss to understand why."

"She seemed eager," Lord Linfield remarked, "to apologize to Miss Vale for something."

Miss Match had stopped crying by now and was blinking blearily from Linfield to Delilah and then to her mother. And there was no doubt at all as to who frightened her the most.

"That woman?" Mrs. Match said, her voice positively throbbing with emotion. "Unhand my daughter, ma'am. You are not fit—"

"And yet Miss Vale was here to comfort her in her distress," Linfield said mildly. "Er... Where were you?"

"I am here now." Forcefully, Mrs. Match dropped onto the sofa and snatched her daughter from Delilah's hold. "And just as well! My lord, I trust you are going to do right by my daughter?"

"What a coincidence," Linfield drawled. Delilah had never seen him look so disdainful. "I was about to say the same to you."

She glared at him. "Sir, I expect your offer of marriage before these witnesses!"

He sighed. "Don't be silly. Miss Match has no desire to marry me, nor I her."

"What is more," Lady Maria added, clearly understanding exactly what was going on, "she was chaperoned the entire time she was in this room."

Mrs. Match glared at her. "I don't believe that for an instant."

"I'm not sure," Linfield said, "that maternal anxiety excuses such a remark."

"I am certainly unused to being called a liar," Lady Maria said with unexpected hauteur. "I should rethink the accusation before you repeat it in this house or anywhere else. As for your other accusation, ma'am, you are not only mistaken but...really, what kind of mother insists on ruining her daughter when there is absolutely no need?"

Mrs. Match's eyes widened.

Lady Maria smiled kindly. "Do you wish to take your daughter home? If so, I shall have your carriage summoned immediately. Or if you prefer, I shall escort you back to the ballroom with my sister's other guests."

There was nothing for Mrs. Match to do but snap at her daughter to dry her tears, then drag her from the room while her ladyship waited patiently by the door.

"Well," said Elaine, when the door had closed behind them. She regarded her brother with tolerant amusement. "Who would have expected *you* to be caught by such a trick? And by such a chit of a girl."

To Delilah's surprise, color seeped along Linfield's cheekbones. She hadn't realized he could blush.

"I certainly did not," he admitted. "And must accept the humiliation."

"You owe Miss Vale a debt of gratitude."

"Another one," he said, suddenly meeting her gaze so that she could not look away. "Thank you once more for my salvation."

"I would do the same for anyone caught in that creature's wiles."

"Of course you would," Linfield agreed. "Oddly, I believe the daughter is her chief victim. She was waiting for me near the cloakroom with, I could swear, the need to apologize—to you as well as to me—and to explain that she did not really want to marry me, whatever her mother's ambitions. I still believe that part was genuine. She is terrified of her mother."

"Who could blame her?" Antonia murmured. "Detestable woman. God preserve us from interfering parents."

Delilah cast her a quick, sympathetic smile.

Linfield frowned. "While we were dancing, something changed. Perhaps she saw her mother and received some silent order. Whatever, I was too slow in picking it up. I truly thought she had something more damning to tell me." His gaze flickered back to Delilah. "I thought it was to do with you. I should have guessed when she was suddenly in such a hurry."

"Yes, you should have," Elaine said bluntly.

"Then she closed the door and burst into tears. I like to think I am better than most of my sex at dealing with weeping women, but she was inconsolable."

"She had to be," Elaine pointed out, "to be sure you kept your arm around her until her mother dragged all and sundry into the room to catch you in that compromising position."

"I could swear the tears were genuine," Linfield said.

Elaine and Antonia looked dubious.

"I think so, too," Delilah said. "She was obeying her mother, but she didn't like it."

"One in the eye for my self-esteem," Linfield murmured. "But I thank you, ladies, all the same."

"You're not out of the woods yet," Delilah said, rising to her feet. "Mrs. Match will not give up easily on her best chance. She will still spread the lie, and we will not have been the only people who saw you leave with the girl. Mrs. Match will not hesitate to impugn her daughter's honor if she can thereby force you to the altar."

"She can't," Linfield said.

Delilah inclined her head before she could be drawn into his humorous gaze, back into the illusion of their alliance against the world. "You will excuse me," she said, and let herself out into the passage.

Now, surely, this dreadful evening had ended and she could go home.

But before then, Cornelius called upon her to perform a very similar service for the earl's sister, Lady Alice, who was on the verge of being compromised by a haughty and slightly sinister duke. Once more, Elaine was with her. And Lord Linfield added his weight to the proceedings, adding a light, diplomatic touch that prevented any quarrel.

He was, she realized, a true gentleman. Which did not fit

with her angry vision of him as an arch liar and manipulator. The truth was never so simple.

As for Cornelius, it seemed he had a personal interest in Lady Alice. Delilah's siblings seemed to be falling in love all around her.

LUCY HAD ARRANGED to stay the night at the castle to be near Eddleston. The rest of the Vales piled out to their various carriages, squabbling over who would travel in which one, while Julius bade Antonia a tender farewell for the night.

When they parted, Delilah caught Antonia's arm. "I meant to say thank you for summoning Dr. Lampton to rescue me. But you won't tell Jul—"

"I didn't summon him. It was Lord Linfield who noticed you were unwell and sent the doctor to you. As for telling, Delly—*you* should."

Delilah was silenced by both answers.

On the journey back to Black Hill, conversation hurtled between the shooting and Roderick's betrothal, while Delilah rested her head back against the squabs and closed her eyes, wondering rather pathetically what Linfield's solicitude meant. Nothing, she was sure, and yet that he alone had noticed, and acted so quietly and swiftly, warmed her cold, empty heart.

# Chapter Sixteen

THE MORNING AFTER the ball, Delilah woke feeling different. At least, different from the last several days. She actually felt more like herself. The air of oppressive misery had lifted just a little. She did not look too closely as to why this should be, although she had the sneaking feeling it was because Linfield had sent Dr. Lampton to her last night. And even before she knew that, she had helped him extricate himself from Mrs. Match's machinations, without a second thought.

More than that, he had thought he was helping the girl. It was his nature. Had she been too harsh in her judgment of him with respect to herself? Acting from the intensity of her own hurt than from the reality between them?

She refused to dwell on that, to talk herself into a new false happiness. Instead, she broke deliberately out of the pattern of the last week. She did not dash straight to work to stop herself from thinking. Instead, after breakfast, she went to the drawing room to write letters to old friends whom she had rather neglected recently.

She also hoped Roderick might find her there and talk about his sudden engagement. News came from Lucy at the castle that Lord Eddleston had spent a peaceful night and had so far avoided fever from his wound.

When the door opened again, it was not Roderick but Aubrey

who entered, clutching a bundle of papers and looking uncharac-
teristically serious.

"Are you busy, Delly?"

"Not so busy that I wouldn't like to be distracted." She laid
down her pen. "You missed breakfast. Is everything well?"

"I don't know." He came and thrust his bundle at her.
"Would you do me a favor? Read this and tell me if it's rubbish."

Surprised, she took them from him. He nodded casually and
strolled out again as if he didn't care, only Delilah knew he did.
There was a barely suppressed air of excitement about him, a
serious sort of excitement rather than that which tended to
accompany his pursuit of fresh mischief or a new girl. Aubrey,
newly healthy after a lifetime of illness, had rather exploded into
hedonistic rakishness, but his nature was too sweet for him to
keep to such ways for very long.

With some interest, she looked through what he had given
her. It was all in his handwriting. A description of Florence caught
her eye and made her smile. Her hand crept to her cheek,
supporting her head as she read and smiled some more. Aubrey
had always had a clever and humorous turn of phrase, but she
had forgotten how well he wrote. Having been confined to bed or
the sofa for so much of his youth, he had entertained himself with
journal entries and these light, evocative descriptions of places
they had lived or visited. Sometimes he had only glimpsed them
from the windows of houses and carriages. Sometimes he had
walked or even, on rare occasions, explored and played.

Delilah was enchanted. When she had read all his vignettes,
as she thought of them, she jumped to her feet and, carrying
them with her, went in search of the author.

She found him in the kitchen, munching and getting in
Cook's way.

"Aubrey, these are brilliant!" she said at once. "What are you
going to do with them? Put them in a book?"

Aubrey flushed, his expression eager. "You think they're good
enough?"

"More than good enough, but you must write more."

"I have more. But it will be dull travel book without illustrations. I don't suppose you still have your drawings, do you?"

Delilah blinked. She had almost forgotten that she had tried to sketch some of the glorious places they had been with Papa. It had been fun, but she had always recognized the limits of her skill. She could draw accurately, but not with soul, not the way Aubrey wrote. And so she had stopped. But surely, with her accuracy and Aubrey's vivid writing...

"Come with me," she said, and they marched up to her bedchamber, where Delilah drew the box of drawings from under her bed.

Aubrey seized the box from her and raked through them, pulling out several. After a little, he grinned up at her. "This is a start. Shall we make a book?"

She helped him find a few more of the places he had described, and he dashed off again, leaving her both excited and pleased for him because he was finding a genuine purpose in life, and he truly did have a talent.

She began to put the other drawings away, congratulating herself on having not destroyed them. As she tidied, her fingers came across a screwed-up piece of paper. A smaller drawing? She smoothed it out, to find only a word.

*Please. D.*

What on earth was that? Why had she kept such a thing?

Her breath caught with sudden memory.

Last week, when Lord Linfield called and she had refused to see him, he had given Betsy a note for her. At the time, she had been too blind to read it. She had crushed it in her hand and sent Betsy to show him out while she stumbled up the back stairs to her bedchamber and peace.

Barely knowing what she did, she had tossed the note into the box with her drawings. Why, she could no longer remember. She had meant to put it in the wastepaper basket. Perhaps on some level, she had wanted to keep it, to read what he had written to her. Only she had been so churned up with misery, so confused and in physical and emotional pain…

*Please,* he had written. Just *please.*

Why should that touch her so? It made no difference to what he had done, to the lies and deceit, and…

He had bothered to come, humbly, when he hadn't needed to. He already knew she would help.

*Please.*

Somehow, the word told her he was in as much pain as she. Nothing was ever black and white. He had not known her when they met, and he had reason for suspicion. It might have been the reason he had approached her, even gone to the theatre, but it was not the reason for their friendship, for what had happened during the storm.

Her face was wet, and yet her whole being felt suddenly lighter, free of the oppression of self-doubt and anger. In its place came guilt, of course, because in the end it was she, not Linfield, who had behaved badly.

But she could make it right. He still cared enough to have helped her last night. And now she would help him.

Carefully, she tore around the note, around the single word and the letter of his signature. Discarding the excess paper, she folded the little note as small as she could. Then she reached inside her gown for the locket that had been her mother's one gift to her. Opening it, she squashed the note inside, closed it, and touched it to her cheek before hiding the locket once more inside her bodice.

She drew a deep, not-quite-steady breath, and rose to return to her work. Today, there would be no migraine, no blindness. She would go over everything Mr. Charles had ever sent her, and she would work out who the assassin was and where he could be found. She knew it would be there somewhere, if she just looked in the right way.

She was thorough, pausing frequently to think about the names and descriptions used for possible meanings. So she had not got very far before she was disturbed again by Aubrey, who demanded that she accompany him to the pump room for his daily dose of the waters while they discussed their book.

Delilah was happy enough to do so while she let things settle in her mind. At the pump room, they matched a few more sketches to descriptions, arguing out the format the book should take. Here also, she was granted a glimpse into what had suddenly inspired Aubrey to such hard work.

Miss Henrietta Gaunt entered the pump room with her sister, who was expecting a baby, and Aubrey's manner immediately changed. The papers were swiped out of sight. A hint of color tinged his pale cheeks, and his eyes could not hide his eagerness.

The lovely Miss Gaunt, however, looked nervous and anxious to escape. She and Aubrey had clearly quarreled. Just as clearly, he wished to make amends. He was serious about the girl and wanted a means to support her as well as impress her. First, of course, he needed her to speak to him, and this Henrietta's sister, Lady Launceton, accomplished by insisting Aubrey escort Henrietta home while she and Delilah called on Miss Talbot.

Delilah, her heart drumming, almost refused. But in truth, she owed Elaine a visit, and she dearly longed to see Linfield again, to look into his eyes with her refreshed perception.

Being shown into the familiar sitting room, Delilah almost collided with the Match family being shown out. The younger Matches looked mortified. Mr. Match was tugging at his cravat, though he managed a civil nod of greeting. His sister's face was crimson. Their mother, her expression furious, managed a grimace of a smile with her greeting to Lady Launceton. Delilah she cut, as usual.

"I am so sorry," Miss Match whispered as she scurried after her mother.

Lady Launceton blinked and glanced inquiringly at Delilah, who shrugged.

"Oh, thank goodness!" Elaine exclaimed. "Friendly faces! I swear if I see that dreadful woman one more time, I will not be responsible for my actions! She had the nerve to come here demanding to see my brother, and when I assured her he was out, she accused me of hiding him! I'm sure she is already spreading her vile rumors about Denzil."

"What rumors?" Lady Launceton asked.

"Oh, the pretense that Denzil compromised her poor daughter."

Lady Launceton, who had apparently known the Talbots well in Vienna, regarded her in amazement. "Linfield? Besides being a perfect gentleman, what would he want with a terrified debutante?"

"Nothing," Elaine said with satisfaction. "But I can't bear such lies to damage him at all."

"Oh, no one would believe such nonsense," Lady Launceton said comfortably. "It's her own daughter she will damage. Someone should tell her so."

"Someone already did," Elaine said. "Come, sit down and let us talk of other things. What brings you to see me this afternoon?"

"Actually, I have rather forced myself on poor Miss Vale," Lady Launceton said happily. "I want to know all about her brother Aubrey."

DENZIL HAD SPENT the afternoon with the princess, making arrangements for her to receive her brother in safety. The siblings would have their discussions in private, while Prince Friedrich and Linfield would "entertain" whatever entourage Karl brought with him.

"Just don't go anywhere with him without telling us first," Linfield insisted.

When he finally obtained Irena's agreement, he returned to the sitting room he shared with Elaine, wondering if he should ride out to Black Hill. The speed with which Delilah had come to his aid last night had given him hope, even if the incident set him in a poor light as far as common sense went.

But then, Delilah too had seemed to believe in Miss Match's basic innocence. The mother was the malicious force. What sort of a life did she imagine she was obtaining for her daughter with such machinations? A hostile, grudging marriage at best. At worst, ruin and no marriage at all, ever.

"Ah, there you are," Elaine greeted him. "You have just missed Miss Vale."

"Oh, the *devil!*"

"On the bright side, you also missed Mrs. Match, although she is still determined on her course, so you may yet have a storm to weather."

"How was Miss Vale?" he asked, totally ignoring the Match information.

"She looked a little better than last night—fielding Lizzie Launceton's questions about her brother Aubrey, who is apparently courting Henrietta."

"The world is courting Henrietta. I'm glad Delilah came to see you."

"They usually go to church," Elaine said casually. "The Vales. After all, half the service is taken up with the vicar calling the banns for various members of their family."

To the surprise of Prince Karl, Blackhaven turned out to be a devout little town. Every man and his wife went to church on Sunday.

"The vicar is young and handsome," Elise told him cynically as they stood behind the curtain of Karl's dingy room and observed the throngs in their Sunday best heading toward the church. "And he is quite the orator in an understated way, much appreciated by those who tread the boards. See? There goes bloody Nell, with her pet Reggie, looking virtuous. Actually, they're looking for hints to sharpen their techniques."

"Then you had better go, too. You must not stand out as different until the deed is done."

Elise regarded him with dislike. "These weeks have been a colossal waste of time. Your sister could be dead twice over by now and I could be in France, where a very lucrative contract awaits me. I could have been to Ireland and back and seen off a—"

"I don't wish to know the sordid details of your life and work," Karl snapped. "I pay you to complete this task properly."

"Not yet, you don't," Elise said, crossing the room to the grubby mirror by the door. She straightened her hat. "Bear in mind that if I don't see the money, my trigger finger will slip at the crucial moment."

"Again," Karl said nastily.

"You have made the business unnecessarily complicated," Elise said. "God preserve me from amateurs."

Karl stared at her. "I don't suppose God pays a great deal of attention to the prayers of members of your profession."

"Just imagine his opinion of those who employ us," Elise said serenely, and sailed out of his room with impressive grace.

Karl scowled after her. He had the uneasy feeling she was right about everything. For a moment, he regretted coming to Blackhaven early, since it meant confining himself to this disgusting room to avoid not only his sister and brother-in-law, but also Lord Linfield, whom he blamed for Irena's change of plans and the failure of the shot that should have killed her.

*I should be the ruling Prince of Hazburg by now! I should always have been the ruling Prince of Hazburg! And if I have to stare at these four walls for much longer, I shall be the mad Prince of Hazburg...*

The church bells began to ring, though it seemed the faithful of the town needed no physical summons to divine service.

The town was at church. *Linfield* would be at church, and Irena would not go out. For this hour, at least, he was free.

Seizing his hat, he all but dashed from the room, and from the building, striding toward the sea with massive relief.

He had just reached the harbor when he almost ran smack into Lord Linfield.

The man was leaning against the rail, hat in hand, gazing out to sea. Karl halted too suddenly, but Linfield never stirred. Stealthily, Karl began to walk backward.

The bells stopped ringing.

Linfield straightened, clapped his hat on his head, and strode toward the church.

Karl breathed again.

However, Linfield was a problem. Karl did not doubt his ability to get Irena to the theatre, where Karl's own presence in her box would be his alibi when Elise shot her. But Linfield was just the sort of idiot to throw himself in the way, to charge after the assassin as he had done at the hotel, and if he caught her…

Elise would not stay silent if she could buy her life with her employer's.

Which was why Karl had every intention of shooting Elise rather than paying her. But to reach that happy state, he really needed Linfield to be absent.

ALTHOUGH THE REST of the week was somewhat fraught for Delilah and the Vales, she was not troubled by migraines. Which was odd, for she spent a good deal of time going over her translations, worrying about Roderick—who was being married by common license as soon as Friday!—and about her other siblings for various reasons. But the agony of her own personal misery seemed to have lifted with her determination to do something about it. Even the fact there was no opportunity to speak to Lord Linfield after church did not depress her unduly.

Worse was the moment she realized he had called at Black

Hill and been sent away.

She was crossing the hall for tea on Wednesday when Betsy passed her with the teapot. "Oh, ma'am, that gentleman was here again."

"Lord Linfield?" Delilah said, clutching her jolting heart.

"Yes, ma'am. I told him you weren't at home. He seemed awfully disappointed."

A spurt of rage almost annihilated poor Betsy, who had done nothing except obey Delilah's orders. It was Delilah's fault for not rescinding those orders, and that made her even angrier. Clamping her lips shut to prevent the explosion, she counted to five.

"I believe I am now prepared to receive him," she managed, "should he call again."

"Very good, ma'am," Betsy said with a grin of clear approval.

"Should who call again?" Leona demanded, dancing past them both.

"The prince regent," said Delilah.

By then, of course, they were in the midst of wedding preparations for Roderick on Friday, and Julius the following Tuesday. In between weddings was to be the card party at the town's respectable inn, nominally hosted by the vicar and his wife but actually organized by Felicia and Bernard Muir, with whom she seemed to have become rather more than friends.

Roderick was rarely around in the week before his wedding, although he and Aubrey seemed to have gone into partnership to start up a local newspaper. He seemed to Delilah to be running himself ragged—far from good for his nerves, which, the whole family knew, had been badly shattered at Waterloo. He was talking now about returning to the army, and Delilah felt very strongly that he should not. Was he avoiding his bride?

Lady Helen was a very odd match for him. She was much younger, and from a noble family far above the Vales in rank. Delilah feared the pair were making a great mistake. They looked more anxious than overjoyed whenever she saw them, either together or apart, but Roderick was adamant the marriage was their choice.

And perhaps it was. Cornelius, it seemed, had a particular fondness for Helen's only unmarried sister, Lady Alice.

Everyone's mind was on love and marriage—except Delilah's, which was full of dull documents, itineraries, and lists she had made from her translations of people, places, and times. Something began to niggle at the back of her mind, something that was not right. And then on Thursday afternoon, a new document arrived that made no sense at all. Unless...

She sprang to her feet, ready to dash off to Blackhaven and Linfield—only this was Roderick's last night at home. Helen's brother the earl had gifted them a charming little house in town, with views of the sea and a pleasant garden, and after tomorrow's wedding, it would be his new home. She could not break up the warmth, the mingled sadness and happiness, of their last night together as a family in the family home.

Their healing idyll was over. Everyone was moving on and life was changing. Everyone felt it, the twins most of all. No doubt they had a hand in whatever machinations had brought Rod and Helen together, yet now they sat very close to Delilah, their constant in life since their father's death.

Perhaps Lord Linfield would be at the wedding and she could speak to him then. One more night could make no difference when the princess was confined to the hotel.

# Chapter Seventeen

SINCE THE MASQUERADE ball at the castle, Marjorie Match had grown to loathe leaving the inn where the family put up. When she accompanied her mother, she had to listen to Mama's embarrassing half-truths and innuendos about Lord Linfield, and her cheeks burned with embarrassment at what people must think of her. When she slipped out alone or with Gerald, she imagined everyone was staring at her because she was compromised and ruined. Or might be. No one had cut her yet, not even Lady Maria, who had lied to stop Mama forcing Lord Linfield's hand in marriage.

In truth, the real lie was her own and Mama's. And that upset her more than anything.

Dragged for a walk with her mother on Friday, she tried to keep her shoulders straight and a smile on her lips, when her instinct was to cringe. Especially when they passed the church and discovered a crowd waiting outside.

Many of the crowd were ordinary townspeople and country folk, though a few were more gently born, including visitors to the town to whom Mama inevitably gravitated.

"Good day, Mrs. Colinton," she greeted one of her favorite gossips. "What on earth is everyone waiting for?"

"Lady Helen Conway, of course. She is being married to Major Vale as we speak. Such a beautiful bride. I caught sight of her entering the church with her brother the earl and her sisters..."

"I own that I am surprised his lordship countenanced such a match," Mama remarked. "So condescending."

"Oh, the Vales are a very old and respected family, I believe."

"But somewhat ramshackle," Mama responded in a stage whisper. "I suppose they will all be there, the base-born mingling with respectable, decent people."

"Hush, Mama," Marjorie begged in an agony of embarrassment, for she had seen some of the stunned, outraged, and contemptuous glances thrown at them.

Mama sniffed. "Well, I am more careful myself, but then, I have always been a high stickler, as you know, Mrs. Colinton..."

The church door was thrown open and Mr. Grant emerged, smiling as he stood aside and turned to allow the newly married pair to emerge.

Major Vale was one of those tall, commanding men who overwhelmed Marjorie. Fortunately, he never noticed her, so she was able to admire him from a distance, so handsome and distinguished in his military uniform, his lovely young wife on his arm, looking dazed and serene.

"What a beautiful couple," she blurted.

Mama patted her arm. "It will be your turn soon. It all seems rather rushed to me. Lady Helen is not even out."

Marjorie tried not to cringe. Really, had Mama no idea of the reverence surrounding the earl's family? But of course, to her, they were mere throwaway remarks. Her real target, Lord Linfield, strolled out of the church after the families of the bride and groom, his sister on his arm.

"You see my problem, Mrs. Colinton? The association of the Braithwaites—such a noble and respected family—with such a man as this *Linfield*. Especially after what he has done."

Marjorie seized a breath and, greatly daring, blurted, "The Talbots are also a very old and respected family. I have always found Lord Linfield a perfect gentleman."

Her pinched flesh under her mother's cruel fingers promised that she would pay for that. But Mama was never easily defeated.

"Oh, my poor child," she declared sadly. "So innocent and deluded! So wronged! You do not recognize the wiles of a man of the world. But be assured he will do right by you. I shall see to it."

Marjorie, her face burning to the ears, wanted the ground to rise up and swallow her. Or perhaps her mother.

DESPITE THE HASTE of the wedding, Lady Helen's family provided a magnificent breakfast, with many distinguished guests from among their own family and friends as well as Roderick's. Delilah, who had initially been terrified of encountering Linfield among the guests, was now highly relieved to see him there. Only too aware of his tall, distinguished figure, she had to remind herself of necessary discretion to avoid rushing at him.

In the end, she went to Elaine first, and felt his gaze on her, burning her skin. Longing rose, fierce and wonderful, and yet it took courage to meet his gaze.

He had veiled his eyes. And yet there was warmth and hope in the faint curve of his expressive mouth. She gave a quick smile, hoping it did not look as nervous as she felt. And to her immense relief, he moved toward her and bowed.

"Miss Vale, a pleasure to meet you on such a happy occasion."

"Likewise, my lord." She moved a little away to an empty space on the floor and came straight to the point. "He is here."

He blinked. "Who?"

"Karl. Another document for translation was delivered yesterday, only it did not come from York."

"How do you know?" he asked at once.

"Because although it was collected from the inn with the other post for Black Hill, it was too uncrushed, too pristine, to have come across the country in sacks of mail. I think it was added in Blackhaven. And besides, it is in German from Mr. Charles, instructing his servant to close the house."

"Is it, by God?" he said softly. "And why would he put such an instruction in writing if he were still there? And, moreover, send it by you? In fact, I cannot understand your receiving such a document at all."

"That's the thing," she said, trying to keep hold of her excitement. "Many of these documents, especially the later ones, are pointless. What if they are only sent from York to prove his presence there? The crime should have been committed last Monday, only you prevented the princess attending the theatre and pursued the assassin. Karl could have been here all along, while this servant in York kept sending me increasingly pointless documents—until this final one, which I probably was not meant to receive at all. The servant made a mistake, just because he was used to sending me drivel, and perhaps there is a genuine language problem between him and Karl. But the important thing is, Karl is probably in Blackhaven."

"He is not expected officially until Monday," Linfield said slowly. "He is certainly not at the hotel. More to the point, what the devil has he been doing here all this time?"

"He could not resist being here to savor his moment of victory. Perhaps his servant would have been ordered to travel here from York, when Karl would take his place, loudly mourning his sister. We'll never know that part. But if he is still here, surely he still means to carry out his murder by alternative means."

"I don't like this. I don't like this at all."

"No… But at least he seems to be…inept."

A breath of surprised laughter escaped him. "The silver lining to our cloud. If it were not Major Vale's wedding, I would ask him to keep watch on various members of the theatre company, especially Mr. Hemmel."

"Well, they are not planning a wedding journey. They will remain in Blackhaven, and besides, Roderick has a partner,

Captain Skelton—who, in fact, is staying at the inn."

"Indeed? I shall have a word with him if I can. Thank you for this, Delilah."

Her name on his lips once more caused a delighted little frisson. Although it was so much less than she desired, it was more than she had expected.

He glanced around then returned his suddenly intense gaze to her face. "I did not doubt you, you know, not after our first meeting."

"It was I who doubted you," she admitted, her heart hammering.

He reached toward her. "Delilah—"

"Breakfast is served!" announced the stately butler, and everyone began milling upstairs to the formal dining room.

Once more, she was separated from Linfield, just when they might have reached some kind of reconciliation or at least understanding. She ached for that. Especially when she glimpsed Roderick in an unguarded moment, watching his new wife, and realized that whatever the reasons behind the haste of the wedding or the bride's tension, there was no lack of love on Roderick's part, at least.

As for Helen, she was so young to be taking on a man like Roderick, damaged by war...

"She is right for him," Lucy murmured in Delilah's ear. "Just what he needs. And she adores him."

"I'm glad," Delilah managed, suddenly choked with emotion. It never entered her head to doubt Lucy, who had the rare gift of understanding people almost as soon as she met them.

Lucy gave her an affectionate nudge and flitted off to be sure that her betrothed, his arm romantically in a sling, had everything he needed.

FOR SOME REASON, Felicia set huge store by her charity card party the following evening. Delilah suspected it had something to do with the charming Bernard Muir—until Julius told her, "Waller Harlaw will be there."

He sounded so uneasy that Delilah focused her attention with a frown.

"Who on earth is Waller Harlaw?" she asked.

"Everyone regarded him as Nick Maitland's friend, though, trust me, he was anything but. Most of the debts we settled after Nick's death were debts of honor to Harlaw. He is the chief reason we had to sell Felicia's house and use most of our inheritance money."

Delilah stared at him. "Does Felicia know?"

"She has always known. My worry is, she thinks to take revenge in some kind of retaliatory card game."

"That is madness! She will lose whatever she has left!"

"She's no fool, Delly. And we can't stop her. All I ask of you is that you keep an eye on her."

And then, at dinner, Felicia told them what she meant to do.

THE LIKELY PRESENCE of Delilah at the charity card party ensured that Denzil would look in. And the event's hosting by the vicar and his wife meant that he was happy to escort Elaine and Mrs. Macy there too.

For such an apparently relaxed and good-natured event, raising money for the local hospital and other charities, there was an air of excitement and expectation. He could see it in Delilah, when they played at the same table and when they were at opposite sides of the room. She barely seemed to notice the presence of young Mr. Match, though Denzil spotted him right away.

In fact, he kept a close eye on the boy, for several of his disreputable friends were present, too, including Lord Tranmere. None of them approached Delilah, who played only at the lower-stakes tables, although Match certainly watched her, a puzzled expression on his face, as though trying to equate the graceful, ladylike Miss Vale with the creature his mother was trying to discredit for her own ends. He must have wondered why those above reproach, like Mrs. Grant the vicar's wife, Lady Braithwaite, and Mrs. Winslow treated her with such friendliness and respect. Hopefully, he would learn from the experience.

Denzil was not a great gambler by nature. He played to be sociable and enjoyed the fun surrounding games in good company. So he played both high and low stakes, winning a little and losing slightly more, paying his dues to charity, until he realized more and more people were being drawn to a single game of piquet between Delilah's sister Felicia and one Waller Harlaw, whom Linfield vaguely recalled from the Season in London. And Felicia was wiping the floor with him. All her siblings were watching closely.

Beside Denzil, Aubrey Vale murmured in excitement, almost as if he were unaware of it, "She's got you."

And she had. A large pile of notes, coins, and vowels lay at her elegant elbow. Bernard Muir, who had helped organize the event, stood at her side, his eyes blazing, and yet watching not Felicia but Harlaw. She had won everything from him except his townhouse, which was his current stake. And then Bernard's hand shot out and he discovered the card hidden in Harlaw's sleeve.

It was masterful—the villain responsible for Felicia's poverty revealed as a cheat. The Vale brothers moved discreetly to the exits while Harlaw desperately tried to pretend he was not cheating, that Felicia was, that a mere woman could not have beaten him by any other means, an accusation laughed to scorn by the Vales.

Sir George, Denzil recalled, had been terribly proud of one of his little girls who could beat any of his adult male colleagues or guests at the embassy...

And there was no doubting the pride of her siblings as Harlaw was removed. Oddly, it made him feel an outsider. Quite suddenly, he longed to be part of the Vales' large, chaotic family, standing firmly at Delilah's side. For they were part of her.

He stepped back, letting everyone else in to congratulate Felicia. He saw Delilah's hand grip her sister's shoulder for an instant, and the quick smile of mingled triumph and gratitude as Felicia glanced up at her.

"I have missed all the excitement, no?" said a familiar voice in Denzil's ear.

He whirled around to face Prince Friedrich, his blood running cold. "Please tell me you have not brought Mrs. Harris here."

"Of course I have not," Friedrich said indignantly. "She rests and reads, ready to face her brother on Monday. I escape only for a few moments."

"I'm sorry," Denzil said. "Of course, this must be as hard on you as on her."

"Harder, for I don't even believe in the outcome. She would never be safe with K—her brother back in the country."

"She knows your view?"

Friedrich sighed. "And still she hopes. Now, I play."

As the prince sat down at a card table, rubbing his hands together, Denzil's eye was caught by Delilah, sitting alone and very still in a shadowy corner. Concern and sheer yearning to be with her sent him across the room to sit beside her.

"What is it?" he asked quietly.

She blinked, her head snapping around as though she hadn't seen his approach. Color seeped into her face. Her eyes were full, and she blinked rapidly, hastily dashing the back of her hand against her cheek.

"Lord Linfield," she managed.

"Has someone upset you?" he asked.

"Oh, no. I'm just so proud of Felicia, and you know, she did it for us? Nick left her in so much debt—most of it to that Harlaw creature—that we all contributed what we could, and now she insists on paying us back, and there was no need..."

"Perhaps there was to her."

A faint noise escaped her, part sob, part laughter. "You are right, of course. And she has won back her self-respect. I didn't realize how badly it was missing until this evening. I-I'm sorry, you have caught me at a bad time. I shall be more coherent in just a—"

She jumped to her feet, but he caught her hand.

"Please. Stay a moment."

Her eyes refocused on him, not in fear or outrage, but otherwise impossible to read. "Please," she repeated incomprehensibly, and sank back down.

He released her hand reluctantly. "Are we friends, Delilah?"

"We seem to be," she said, so low that he had to bend nearer to hear her.

"Then you forgive me?"

She swallowed. "I'm not sure there is much to forgive. It is I who—"

"Miss Vale."

Denzil glared at Mr. Match with something approaching fury. The young man, however, was gazing only at Delilah. He bowed stiffly.

"Mr. Match," she said, her expression smoothing while Denzil's fists itched.

"I owe you a profound apology," he said with unexpected seriousness.

"I believe you already made it, sir."

"Under threat and grudgingly. I apologize for that, too. I was laboring under a totally false impression, but nothing excuses my behavior." He tugged once at his cravat. "You must know that my mother has spoken unfairly against you. I will do what I can to mitigate...to stop her."

Delilah looked as stunned as Denzil felt. A moment longer, Match stood there, as though waiting for the retaliation to fall on his head and knowing he deserved whatever anger or opprobrium they chose to heap upon him.

"That is a very gracious apology, Mr. Match," she said, clearly surprising him in return. "I appreciate it and I accept it. Excuse me."

She rose and hurried away. Denzil would have followed her, except that Match dropped into her vacated chair.

"We owe you apologies, too. I think it's time I exerted my status as head of the family and took my mother and sister home."

"I think it is," Denzil agreed.

Match cast him a quick look. "In a feeble effort to make up for my undoubted sins... I should tell you some sinister character is hanging about the inn asking about you."

Denzil's eyebrows flew up. "About me? What sinister character? Is he still there?"

"Let's go and see," Match said at once.

Denzil was no fool. From experience, he was suspicious of sudden volte-faces and would not have been surprised if some ambush awaited him outside the inn. But in fact, apart from the Vale twins lurking just outside the front door and a couple embracing in the shadows, no one else was there.

"He must have gone," Match said, clearly disappointed.

"When did you see him?"

"Just before I spoke to you and Miss Vale. I was outside— working up my courage, if you want the truth—and this fellow came up to me, asking if you were at the inn. He called you by name."

"What did he look like? Sound like?"

"Smallish, slight, hat pulled low, cloak gathered close. Very quietly spoken, but normal enough."

"English?"

"So far as I could tell."

"A gentleman? Or someone of the lower orders?"

Match frowned, thinking about it. "Not sure, to be honest. A gentleman, I think. Is it important? Is *he* important?"

"I think he might be," Denzil said grimly, already turning to go back to the inn and collect his hat.

Smallish, slight, and cloaked sounded very like a description of the gunman he had chased down the alley opposite the hotel. And it was late enough that the play should be over. After a quick word in Friedrich's ear, he bolted around to the hotel to be sure the princess was safe and that no one who shouldn't be was lurking nearby.

Then he ran to the alehouse near the theatre where, he had already established, the cast and stagehands often drank after the performance. Reginald Miller was there. So, Denzil was disappointed to see, was his understudy, Hemmel, with no cloak about his slight person. Had he got rid of it? Or was Denzil completely wrong and it was someone else entirely?

As he strode back to the inn in order to escort Elaine home—and hopefully resume his interrupted conversation with Delilah—he wondered why the assassin should be looking for him. Afraid of his interference protecting the princess? Or was the assassin now after him too?

The back of his neck prickled. But he was as sure as he could be that no one followed him.

When he returned to the inn, Delilah had gone home.

# Chapter Eighteen

P ART OF THE reason Delilah had suddenly felt so emotional
about Felicia's triumph was due to the knowledge that a
month ago, the money Felicia won back would have made a huge
difference to Delilah. The possibility of an independent home, or
the ability to travel and be useful, had been all she wanted. Now,
her world was confused by love and longing, and it no longer
mattered at all whom she lived with, and where, if it was not with
Linfield.

He was not at church the following day, although Delilah's
disappointment was quickly lost in pleasure for Felicia as the
banns were called for marriage between her and Bernard Muir. If
anyone deserved the happiness of a love match, it was Felicia.

And, oddly enough, it was Felicia who unwittingly set her on
a different track in her increasingly urgent endeavors to learn the
identity of the assassin.

In the upstairs hallway, Delilah almost collided with the
chambermaid, who was about to return the day's fresh laundry to
Felicia's bedchamber.

"I think you have Lawrence's breeches there by mistake,"
Delilah said with a quick smile, and would have passed on except
that the maid blurted, "I got them from Mrs. Maitland's room,
ma'am, so I thought I should put them back there."

"You're probably right," Delilah said after a short pause. "No doubt she is practicing some amateur dramatics with the twins."

She did not believe that for an instant. Felicia had been playing for huge stakes last night, stakes none of the Vales could afford. Where had she got such money from if she had not been gambling in unrespectable places that ladies were not permitted?

It was a dangerous game, dressing up as a man, but she did not put it past Felicia. Thank God she had Bernard now to look after her.

*How would she look as a man?* Delilah wondered.

And then she stopped suddenly on the stairs and sat down.

What would *anyone* look like as a man? The would-be assassin of the Princess of Hazburg was not necessarily a man. Anyone, surely, with practice, could point a pistol and shoot. What if it was a woman who had disguised herself as a man outside the hotel the night she and Linfield had pursued the assassin? Or her...

She sprang up again, rushing down the rest of the stairs to look at her wretched translations with a fresh eye.

She had little time, of course, because Cornelius came home at the end of the day engaged to Lady Alice Conway, and confessing to being the fashionable poet Simon Sacheverill. And the following day was Julius and Antonia's wedding.

Never a dull moment.

The wedding was a very happy affair. And when Lord Linfield sought Delilah out, she could not have been gladder. And yet she felt awkward, unable to say what she wished, or even to explain her most recent thoughts about the assassin.

All she managed to ask was, "Has Mrs. Harris's brother arrived?"

"He has. All sweetness and light."

"Are you not afraid to leave her?"

"Yes," he said. "But nothing will happen to her while he is in the room with her. He has asked her to attend the theatre with him tomorrow. I believe it is the last night of Mrs. Hampshire's play."

"She will be delighted to hear it so described," Delilah said wryly. "And yes, after tomorrow, they move on to Carlisle and York, and then to London. Will the princess attend?"

"Again, I believe nothing will happen to her while he is with her. But I shall be there just in case. I still have no idea whom I should be looking for."

Delilah opened her mouth, but since she had no definite answers either, she closed it again and turned awkwardly away. She felt as if she were failing at everything, that he could no longer possibly be interested in someone so dull and inept. What value was she to a diplomat like him?

The following day, the Vales did their best to give Julius and Antonia some privacy at Black Hill. Delilah shut herself in her own room, the translations spread around her, looking for patterns, for words, for mistakes and slips…

And suddenly, she saw it.

The breath left her body, for she knew now who the assassin was.

Seizing her bonnet and her cloak, she ran downstairs, calling to the servants to have the carriage sent around immediately. She needed to tell Linfield at once, for tomorrow, even tonight, would be too late.

BY WEDNESDAY, DENZIL was so bored that he was afraid of being lulled into a false sense of security. He had spent most of the last three days in one of the rooms off the princess's sitting room. Here, he, along with Friederich and Karl's blank-faced attendant, made conversation, drank tea, and ate, while in the sitting room, the brother and sister discussed, negotiated, and quarreled. On one occasion, the princess retreated to her bedchamber and would not come out again, even for her husband, until Karl had left.

Friedrich sighed with relief, but by the following day, the siblings were talking once more. Until Karl stormed out. After that, things settled down, and it truly began to look as if they had found a way forward. Even Friedrich wondered aloud if he had been wrong about Karl.

Denzil might have wondered the same thing had it not seemed to him that Karl was merely going through the motions. When temper did not get the better of him, he really might not have given a curse for what his sister offered or what he himself demanded. They did not matter to him because he still meant to have everything. That was what chilled Denzil's blood and kept him alert.

During the afternoon, when tea was brought in, it came with a note addressed to Denzil. It was not in the princess's hand, but he read it anyway.

*My lord,*

*Forgive the incivility of a summons, but some very disturbing information has come to light that I believe only you, as Miss Vale's friend, can help me with. Please, therefore, come to me as soon as you receive this. I shall await you at the back door of the theatre, to be sure we are private.*

*Gratefully yours,*
*H. Hampshire.*

Delilah's mother... Had she learned something vital about the assassin? Was Delilah herself in some kind of danger?

He rose at once, catching Friedrich's eye. "Excuse me, gentlemen. I should not be longer than half an hour."

He strode around to the theatre, retaining enough sense to make sure no one followed him.

The stage door was at the side of the building, but the note had distinctly said the back door. To be certain, he tried the front and stage doors first, and found them both locked, before picking his way around to the back of the theatre.

It was a mess, a mixture of ancient and broken scenery and assorted rubbish that must have been collecting for years. He had the impression his were the first human feet to find their way around here for a decade. He could not speak for the rats.

There was a padlocked iron door into the back of the building. As he approached it, his neck prickled. But the yard was empty, and the padlock had been unchained. The door was ajar, unbolted from the inside, though he could not see beyond it into the darkness.

He paused, hoping against hope that Delilah was not here, then he knocked softly.

Getting no response, he said, "Mrs. Hampshire? It's Linfield."

Still nothing.

He pushed open the door and at last saw a light at the end of what seemed to be a narrow passage. "Mrs. Hampshire."

"Come in, my lord," said a breathless female voice.

Seeing the outline of a woman, he stepped inside.

"Close the door," she begged.

Reluctantly, he turned to obey. The sudden movement behind gave him an instant's warning, but not enough. He had only half spun before something crashed into his head and he seemed to explode with pain. He fell to his knees, peering into the darkness, then into the blurred, candlelit face of...not Helena Hampshire, but Elise Manners.

He tried to speak, to focus on making his body work. But there was only darkness.

DELILAH KNOCKED MOST peremptorily on Elaine's door, and brushed past the maid as soon as she opened it.

"Elaine, where is he?" she demanded. She was at a loss to account for the urgency that had flared during her journey into town, but she could no longer hold it back.

Elaine laid down her book in surprise. "Delilah! Are you looking for Denzil? He is with Mrs. Harris."

"Of course he is. Which room is hers?"

Elaine regarded her uneasily. "You can't go in there. You will not be allowed through the door. Neither will I."

"But this is urgent! It is the danger he always feared, and I know who it is! I have to tell him before it is too late!

Elaine bit her lip and made a decision. "Perhaps we can send in a note. I'll just tell him to come out for a moment."

As she spoke, she was already scribbling on a piece of paper, which she shook in her hand to dry as she sailed across the room to the door and led the way across the hall and down the passage.

She knocked on the door at the end of the passage. It opened surprisingly quickly, but only a crack, to reveal part of a severe maidservant, and behind her, a very large footman.

"Mrs. Harris is not at home," the maid said in heavily accented English.

"I am aware," Elaine said pleasantly. "And we have no wish to disturb her. Be so good as to give this note to Lord Linfield, who I believe is with Mr. Harris."

Although the maid glared in a suspicious manner, she snatched the note and closed the door.

"Well," Elaine said, amused, "we are unlikely to suffer illusions as to our own importance."

"What if he doesn't come?" Delilah said uneasily.

"He will come," Elaine assured her. "He always does, because I so rarely disturb him."

It seemed she was right, for in less than a minute, the door opened again—only it was not Lord Linfield but the round, amiable "Mr. Harris" who appeared and stepped into the passage, closing the door behind him.

"Miss Talbot," he said, beaming. "And…Miss Vale, is it not? How very pleasant to see you again. I am afraid Lord Linfield is not here."

"Not here?" Elaine repeated, frowning. Delilah's reasonless

unease began to grow again.

"No, he received a note and left immediately, saying he would be back in half an hour. Although"—the prince picked up his fob watch and regarded it—"that was an hour ago now."

"Who was the note from?" Delilah demanded. "Where did he go?" She swallowed. "If you please, sir."

He gazed at her with some alarm. "He did not say. Nor did he leave the note, but he would not have left at that point had it not been important."

"Did you not glimpse it at all? Read any words by accident?" Delilah pursued.

"No, I was too far away," he said apologetically. He hesitated, then added, "I thought it was a woman's hand."

"My brother does not pursue women while on duty," Elaine said frigidly.

"Of course not," the prince agreed. He scratched his chin. "I cannot leave right now, but give me half an hour or so and I will help you find him if necessary."

Elaine curtseyed, reminding Delilah to do the same. The prince bowed and vanished back inside.

"So we wait another half-hour," Elaine said restlessly. "I don't like this, Delilah."

"Neither do I." Delilah took a deep breath as they walked back along the passage. "Is there a woman who would dare summon him at such a time? A woman for whom he would drop everything and go?"

Elaine looked at her, and Delilah retained enough sense to keep her face neutral.

"Apart from you, you mean?" Elaine said.

Heat burned Delilah's face, although there was an odd, painful pleasure in hearing the words, too.

"We have not always understood each other very well," she said with difficulty. She stopped dead. "I think I know where he has gone. Wait here in case I am wrong, in case Lord Linfield comes back. Otherwise, accept all the search parties Mr. Harris offers. And begin with the theatre."

Before Elaine could speak, Delilah was running down the staircase.

Outside the hotel, she all but ran into the twins, looking somewhat scruffy and disreputable.

"What are you two doing in town?" she asked, feeling harassed.

"Looking for you. We've sorted everyone else out," said Lawrence.

Delilah let that go for now. "I think...I think you need to summon your brothers to the theatre."

"For the play?" Leona called after her.

"If necessary," Delilah said, already hurrying away toward the theatre. She didn't want the twins anywhere near it until she could be sure of their safety. But Linfield...

*Oh God, don't let him be dead.*

DENZIL CAME TO himself with a horribly sore head—which, however, was nothing to the dizzying agony he felt when he tried to move. He could not suppress his groan. Memory flooded back, bringing with it anger at his own stupidity.

He had walked straight into a trap because he was afraid for Delilah, or, at best, for her mother. And what use was he to either of them now?

"Ah, you're awake," said a light voice with some reproach. "You were meant to sleep a little longer."

He opened his eyes reluctantly. Elise Manners stood before him in pretty bonnet and old cloak, examining him with cool dispassion. She had hit him with some strength and moved with great speed. Not an opponent to disrespect with false ideas of the gentler sex.

"I had better tell you now, so you might save your energy for survival, that you can shout all you like and no one will hear you."

He could not see a whole lot by the light of the single candle that burned nearby, and there was no window, but the large, filthy room was curiously decorated, as if there were cushions on the walls and ceiling.

Like a padded cell where they put violent lunatics so they did not injure themselves. And so other inmates were not upset by the screams...

"It's an old rehearsal room," Elise explained, "fitted out by the theatre's first eccentric manager, to keep his new plays secret from those both inside and outside the building. Extremely clever and painstakingly carried out. And yet it's been left to rot. No one uses it now. Most people don't even know of it."

"Except you," Denzil pointed out. "Um, not that I am unflattered, but why did you summon me here? Just to hit me over the head?"

"Be grateful," she said wryly. "My employer wants you dead."

"And here I thought he wanted the princess dead."

"He thinks you're in the way. In which, of course, he is quite right, but there are less elaborate and considerably less risky ways to go to work, if only he would see them. He has a tendency to overcomplicate everything, usually in an effort to wriggle out of any connection to the crime. I don't suppose you like working with fools either."

"No," he admitted. "But if you are so clever—and I am, of course, prepared to take your word for it—why would you risk your life to kill another clever woman at the behest of a fool?"

She sighed. "A good question, my lord. He is not a *complete* fool, and a girl has to earn her living as best she can. I'm sure you noticed I am not a great stage actress. I am, however, an excellent assassin. The acting helps a little, to gain the confidence of necessary people."

"Like Reginald Miller?"

"Of course."

He stirred, finding he could move now with only minor pain. He heaved himself slowly to a sitting position. It was difficult with his hands tied behind his back and his feet tied at the ankles. The girl opposite watched him carefully from her stool.

"You'll forgive me if I am not much comforted by your explanations," he said. "Nor by the fact that you showed yourself to me at all. You must mean to kill me at some point. If you can."

She smiled. "Oh, I can. I choose not to, or you would already be dead."

"Why? If your employer ordered it?"

"It is not part of our agreement, and he certainly does not mean to pay for extra bodies. In fact, it's my belief he doesn't mean to pay me at all. Apart from the deposit I insisted on to be engaged in the first place."

"Then don't kill the princess either."

"Oh, one has to keep one's reputation," she said vaguely. "Though it means I shall have to escape doubly quick. He could, after all, shoot me in front of a whole theatre audience and be justified because I killed his sister."

"Then don't. I will see you are paid to spare her."

She smiled—an oddly appealing smile, considering her vile profession. "Don't be silly. You'd have me caught, imprisoned, or dead before you got to the bank. Just be grateful to escape with your own life." She rose to her feet. "And now, you must excuse me. I have a play to perform."

"Wait. I'll die here anyway if no one can hear me and no one knows where I am."

She took a familiar note from her pocket and waved it at him. "I took it from your coat. If they find it in the dressing room, they'll know where to search for you."

"You've thought of everything."

"I usually do."

"You would not consider a career change? I know of people who could use your skills."

"Perhaps they already do," she taunted him. "You would never be informed. Goodbye, my lord. You have at least made this tedious task more interesting."

She sauntered off to the passage, and he heard the slamming of the thick iron door. At once, he staggered to his feet, jumping his way after her in an effort to open the door before she could padlock it.

With his back to the door, he got his fingers around the handle and pulled violently. Nothing happened. She had already locked the door and gone.

With some difficulty, he jumped back the way he had come, ignoring the harsh throbbing of his head. There were no obvious sharp or even rough surfaces to cut or fray his bonds.

And even if he could be free of the ropes, he could not get out…

Or could he? Was there another exit? A way into this cellar from the theatre? The candle could burn out before he found it. And the candle was the only way to break his bonds. He heaved himself over to it, sat on the stool beside it and turned his back to thrust his wrists toward the flame. This was not going to be *comfortable*.

IT WAS TOO early for the front of the theatre to be open. Delilah wondered whether to run to her mother's lodgings. After all, he could be there—only, surely Elise Manners would not risk meeting him in front of the company? Impossible to know what she would risk. On impulse, Delilah tried the stage door and found it opened at once.

"Is Mrs. Hampshire here already?" she asked the porter, who obviously recognized her.

"Yes, ma'am, she's in her dressing room, but she don't like to be disturbed before the performance. After is much better."

"I know," Delilah said, slipping past him. "I won't keep her."

In fact, she had no intention of going near her mother at this point, unless she really needed her.

If he had come here, where would he be? Surely Elise could not have killed him here? How would she hide the noise, the body? Almost sobbing with fear, Delilah walked smartly toward the dressing rooms. Nell's was shut. So was the men's, although a faint murmur could be heard behind it. The door to the women's shared dressing room was ajar.

Warily, Delilah crept up to it.

"Think you'll get the next leading role?" someone asked, sympathy barely covering the spite in her voice.

"No."

Delilah's stomach lurched. Surely that was Elise's voice? Pressed against the wall, she peered through the crack in the door. Elise, half in costume, was flouncing across the room, her back to Delilah.

"Don't know if I'll stay with this company," Elise said. "Don't you get weary of constantly playing second fiddle to old Nell?"

"She ain't that old," someone argued. "And you must admit she's better than...us."

Delilah darted past, unsure now where she was going. Elise was preparing for the performance, so where was Linfield? Surely nowhere he could be discovered before the play began? Before the princess arrived?

She found herself behind the deserted stage, among the painted scenery and the furniture used for the play. It all looked a chaotic guddle, though she supposed there was method in it understood by the stagehands.

She moved across the backstage area, behind all the curtains, scuffing her feet across the floor because the light was poor here and she wanted to feel for trapdoors, even while she ran her fingers along the walls.

There were steps up to the theatre foyer from the street. So there must be space below. A basement, a cellar? Back and forth she walked, tapping her foot on the floor, her knuckles on the wall, searching for any hollow sound. She tripped over a thin, scrunched-up rug that must have been meant to muffle the patter of feet approaching the stage. She probably scuffed it up in her last pass across the floor.

On impulse, she bent and pulled the rug aside. Her fingers found the shape of a door in the floor, and a ring to pull it.

Excitement surged, although she knew there must be several secret ways onto the stage for various complicated performances. Only this was on the other side from the dressing rooms, and it was some distance from the stage.

Moving off the door, she lifted the ring and pulled.

Nothing happened. Tightening her grip, she tugged harder, and the door lifted just a little. It must be wretchedly heavy! Bracing herself, she crouched, exerted all her strength, and pulled open the door. It rose smoothly and silently, as though its hinges had recently been oiled, even though below it smelt musty, as if no one had been down there for years.

It was also pitch dark. And the underside of the trapdoor was unexpectedly soft, thickly cushioned. *Bizarre.*

From the other side of the stage, she could hear more of the company arriving, calling to each other, the odd burst of laughter. Delilah rose to her feet, stumbling to where she had seen candles, flint, and tinder box. Having lit one candle, she stuffed the flint and tinder in her reticule, in case the candle went out, and made her way back to the trapdoor. Now she could see there were stairs leading downward.

Her heart was thudding with fear as to what she would find. Elise could have an accomplice, waiting below to attack her...

Delilah listened but heard nothing. She had to go down there, if only to be sure Linfield was not trapped, hurt, or worse... She put her foot on the first step and began to descend. After another brief hesitation, she pulled the trapdoor closed behind her in case someone else fell in. Only then did she realize how well the underside of the door blended into the rest of the ceiling. It was all padded, presumably to muffle sound. So were the walls, and the door she found at the foot of the stairs. It opened when she pushed it.

The candle flame flickered because her hand was shaking. Forcing herself, she walked forward from a dingy passage into a large room. One step inside. Two. And then hands seized her.

She cried out and dropped the candle, plunging the world into darkness. She lashed out blindly, struggling in her attacker's hold.

# Chapter Nineteen

A S SOON AS the knock sounded at her door, Elaine flew past her maid and wrenched it open. She could not disguise her disappointment that it was not Denzil who stood there, only Mr. Harris, alias Prince Friedrich.

"Your pardon, ma'am," he said, "but has his lordship returned?"

"Not here."

"Nor to our rooms. You have received no word?"

"None. Will you help me look for him?"

"Of course. I will just—"

"Good afternoon, Miss Talbot," a cheerful voice said from the passage, quickly followed by the figure of a very young, ill-dressed man. Because he was alone, it took Elaine a moment to recognize the Vale twin, Lawrence.

"Oh goodness! Lawrence, how unexpected. What—"

"Delilah said we should go to the theatre. Leona's gone to fetch Rod and Julius and whoever else is at home. In fact, we can probably get the mad Russian along with Aubrey, if we play our cards right."

"Lawrence, what do you know of my brother?" Elaine asked urgently.

Lawrence shrugged. "Only that Delilah has the matter in hand. She always does, you know."

Elaine tried to make allowances and discount the admiration of a devoted little brother, but somehow, when she looked at him, she believed him. "And the... Mrs. Harris?" Elaine said. "I don't think she should go to the theatre at all now that this has happened."

"You are probably right," Friedrich said unhappily. "But she will not hear of it. She insists on going. Don't worry, I shall keep my brother-in-law close."

"GET *OFF* ME!" Delilah cried, as fingers like steel closed around her wrists. "I have a gun!"

Her words certainly seemed to cause her attacker to change his grip. Her wrists were released so suddenly that she would fallen backward with her own momentum had he not seized her and held her hard against him.

By contrast, his voice was curiously soft and muffled as he murmured, "Delly! Oh, my sweet Delly, how are you here?"

The voice washed over her in painful, wonderful relief. "Denzil, is it you? Is it really you? I cannot—" She seized his face between her hands, recognizing the contours, the scent of him, even in the darkness. "Oh, thank God!" Sheer relief flooded her. She scarcely knew what she was doing as she pressed demented kisses to his cravat and chin and jaw, the only bits she could reach until his head swooped down in the darkness and his mouth landed on her cheek and then her lips.

She sobbed with utter gladness as she kissed him back, salty tears streaming down her face and lips.

"You love me," he whispered in wonder. "You still love me a little."

"Oh God, I love you more than *life*. I could not bear it if she'd killed you. I am so sorry, Denzil, I only just realized..."

The rest of her words were lost in another frantic kiss, after which he drew back enough to say unsteadily, "You only just realized that you love me to distraction?"

"Oh no, I always knew *that*," she said. "About Elise. It's there in the documents. The assassin never has a pronoun in the original German documents, except once, and it's *sie*. Not as in *they*, but *she*. Elise joined the company only recently and would never have got the role if Reggie hadn't insisted. The clues were always there. Oh, and Denzil, it's to be at the interval after the first act. That was in there, too, disguised as an order for refreshment. The princess must not come—"

"On the contrary, she must, or we'll never catch them."

"But there will still be nothing to tie the shooting to Karl, only to Elise."

"Karl means to kill Elise, pretending he is defending Irena. Then she can never accuse him."

"How can you know that?"

"She told me. She still means to kill Irena, and to elude capture after. I wouldn't put either past her."

Delilah stared at him. Impossible to make out his features, his expression. "You almost sound as if you like her."

"I almost do, since she was instructed to kill me and didn't. But how did you get here? Please tell me Elise did not shove you in here, too?"

"Oh, no. I found a trapdoor from the theatre. Once I knew the assassin was Elise, I came to tell you, and we discovered you had left the talks in response to a note. You always knew the assassin was part of the theatre, so I suspected you had either come here or found the actors' lodgings. Elise was here early... How did she catch you?"

"I'll tell you when we're out of here. Can you find the way out again?"

"It will be hard in the darkness. You made me drop my candle. Let's find it."

Searching for his hand, she seized him by the wrist and heard his hiss of pain. She released him at once.

"What is it? Are you hurt?" she demanded, frightened again.

"Devil a bit. Ah." He bent and picked up a candle. "Unfortunately, we can't light it."

"Yes, we can. Is there a table?"

He led her a few steps through the darkness and stood the candle up on the table. "Mine burned out, but at least it destroyed the rope around my wrists first."

She heard the smile in his voice as he heard the flint striking. In a moment, she had the candle lit and was able to see his poor, burned wrists and hands.

"That must hurt…" she said in distress.

"Not as much as my head, though I deserve that for carelessness." He held up the candle and, hand in hand, they walked forward.

At the padded door, he stopped. "Delilah? Will you marry me, now?"

"I'll marry you any time you like," she said unsteadily. "I'm sorry I was so foolish. I was just so hurt because I thought you liked me, and then it seemed you had just been using my attraction for your own ends."

"I was. To make you love me and marry me. I made a mess of it." For a moment, he buried his lips in her hair. "Come on, let's get out of here."

"We'll have to be quiet. Elise is in the theatre."

"Well, we don't want her to know I'm free. It's almost six of the clock. We have an hour before the play begins, and we need to make good use of it…"

ELISE DID NOT shine in the first act. Not that she cared. The play had become a chore she could not wait to shake off. She was more than happy to walk off to very mild applause, because she would never again step onto the damned stage. Besides, it gave her a reason to sulk and hold back from the others.

No one spared her a glance as they hurried off to their dressing rooms for their short break.

*Go home, boys and girls, the play is finished!* Smiling to herself, she went to the familiar pile of ropes and plunged her hand in until it closed around the little pistol she had left there an hour ago. She had seen the princess from the stage, in the box where she should have been two weeks ago. Now she was there, Elise's employer beside her. Not too close, of course. He would not want to be shot by mistake if her aim were off.

Her aim was never off. The pistol felt light and lethal in her fingers as she strode into the wings. She already knew exactly where to stand. She had worked it out before the first night of the play, which seemed a lifetime ago now.

Without fuss, she raised the pistol and aimed it straight at Princess Irena. She looked like a nice woman. Pity.

She pulled the trigger. And heard only a faint click. *What the...?* In sudden, unprecedented panic, she squeezed the trigger again, and still it did not fire.

The blood drained dizzyingly from her face.

Someone had found the pistol and removed the ball. She was discovered.

She spun away just as someone screamed in the auditorium, "Assassin! Stand back!" Karl, of course.

Damn, she would *not* be shot in the back! She turned to face him, saw his pistol level with her head.

And then, beside him, she saw Lord Linfield. *Impossible!* He smiled.

Karl's gun did not fire either. He threw it down in rage, and Elise laughed. Linfield had saved the princess and saved her too.

But who the devil had saved Linfield?

She could not wait to find out. She bolted behind the stage, heading straight for the stage door because the other actors had no clue that anything was wrong. She should have a clear line from where she stood to freedom, only as she jumped forward, she collided with a large, tall man, so hard that all the breath was knocked out of her body.

Both her arms were seized.

Of course. Linfield had planned ahead, cut off her escape routes.

One of her captors wore an eye patch. The other was young and gloriously handsome.

"Oh, please, sir, let me go!" she begged the younger man piteously. "I am so frightened...!"

"Stow it," growled the one-eyed man. "Perhaps it's time you gave us the name of your employer."

It went against the grain. She did, after all, have a code of honor.

But this was an emergency, and the fool was already responsible for too much fiddling about when they should have been killing and safely out of this wretched town.

"Oh, I'll give you *everything*. Names, times, and motives," she said amiably. She smiled. "If you let me go afterward."

THE THEATRE WAS in uproar. Prince Friedrich had pushed his wife behind his sheltering body. Only the very observant, like Denzil, would have noticed that Friederich shielded her not only from the stage but from her brother, who now threw his pistol to the ground in rage.

Denzil dragged his gaze from the vanishing assassin to Karl.

"I unloaded it," he explained.

"You imbecile!" Karl roared. "Now the assassin will get away! Call the Watch! Arrest that man!"

"Actually," said the tall, military figure of Major Roderick Vale from the doorway of the box, "I am afraid it is you who must come with us."

"I? I am trying to defend my sister, while this dolt—"

"Unloaded both guns," Cornelius Vale said. "He saved your sister while you tried to shoot the only witness to your crimes. This way, sir. I believe Prince Friedrich will look after his wife."

"How can he, how can anyone, with that madwoman still free?" Karl screamed.

"Oh, I doubt she's free," Major Vale said. "Our brothers should have her in custody, and I imagine she is doing a good deal of talking." He grasped Karl's arm and hauled him outside, where Cornelius caught his swinging fist and raised it behind his back.

"Thank you, gentlemen," said Denzil as the Vales hauled Karl away protesting in outrage.

"Are we really sure it was Karl?" the princess asked in a small voice.

"Quite sure," Denzil said gently. "The assassin confessed everything to me, and I'm sure is doing so again to whomever will listen. Besides, we have documentary proof. There is absolutely no other reason for the existence of these documents. Miss Vale discovered the final meaning," he added as Delilah and Elaine came in from the box next door. "If you will just excuse me, I'll nip downstairs and make sure all is well."

Elaine and Lady Launceton came in to sit with the princess. Delilah's hand crept into Denzil's, and he smiled as they hurried along the passage to the stairs. Most people were in a huge hurry to leave the theatre. Others were avidly asking questions and demanding to know what had happened. Denzil and Delilah weaved between them, down the staircase and through the foyer toward the backstage area.

Elise was sitting in the porter's little box, hemmed in by Julius and Aubrey Vale. She might have been making conversation at a tea party, apart from the stunned expressions on the faces of Delilah's brothers.

Catching sight of Linfield, she stopped talking.

Delilah squeezed his hand, and he found her care inexpressibly sweet. In fact, the whole afternoon of humiliation and pain had been more than worth it just to feel her passionate kisses on his lips. Her words of love had cocooned him in warmth and a fierce determination to be worthy. The woman in the porter's box was a very different prospect. She chilled his blood, and yet, oddly, he imagined he understood her.

"I suppose I have you to thank for unloading my pistol," she greeted him without noticeable ire.

"No, that was me," Delilah said, drawing the assassin's attention in a way Denzil didn't quite like. "There seemed to be nowhere to conceal such a thing in your costume, so I knew it had to be hidden close to where you would leave the stage and to the place from which you could best take aim at the princess's box."

Elise's eyebrows flew up. "Really? Quite the clever-clogs, are you not? Wait, though I know you too, don't I? You're bloody Nell's friend, the translator. I should have known you were trouble, letting me go through the motions to show my intent to the world, but drawing my claws, as it were. Who exactly are you?"

"Our sister," Sir Julius growled with a pride that brought the color to Delilah's face. She did not realize how her own family valued her.

"And my betrothed," Denzil said, which earned him sudden, searching looks from the Vale brothers.

Elise glanced from one to the other, a faint smile on her lips. "I suppose I owe you for unloading Karl's pistol, too. Not that he can hit a barn at twenty paces, but think of the carnage. I haven't decided yet whether I prefer death or imprisonment."

"Fortunately, that isn't up to you," Denzil said pleasantly.

Elise sighed. "Very well. Tell me. How did you get out from the cellar in time?"

"My betrothed rescued me," Denzil said.

Elise blinked, then laughed. "How wonderful! Captured and freed by women. And you don't even mind, do you?"

"Not the freeing part," Denzil said. He glanced at the outer stage door, where a tall man in black stood, clearly waiting for her. The man looked oddly familiar, but then, a good many events in Blackhaven recently had commanded the services of the magistrate and constables.

"He burned his hands freeing himself from your ropes," Delilah said, her voice tight with indignation.

"Dear me," Elise drawled, though her gaze flickered to the bandages just visible at Denzil's cuffs. "I shouldn't have left the candle. A lesson in carelessness. Oh no."

Nell and Reggie came bolting into the passage from the dressing room area. "Lah-Lah!" Nell exclaimed, embracing her daughter with unprecedented affection. "What on earth have you been about? That woman…" Catching sight of Elise, she slowly pushed Delilah to one side and looked her rival up and down. She sniffed. "I take it back. You are not a bad actress after all. Come, Reggie, let us go home."

"My dear," Reggie said willingly and tenderly, bowing her toward the man in black, who flattened himself against the outer door to let them pass. Elise watched them, a cynical smile on her lips.

"Is she ready for gaol?" the man at the door asked impatiently.

"Yes," said Denzil.

"No," said Elise. "Another matter in which I seem to have lost a say." She walked out of the box between the Vale brothers, and the man at the door grasped her by the arm.

"You do have guards with the carriage?" Denzil said uneasily.

"Oh yes," said the man in black, and took her away.

"Something familiar about that fellow," Aubrey said, frowning.

"That's what I thought," Denzil agreed. His stomach suddenly jolted. "Louis Delon! Anna's husband." He bolted for the door.

Behind him, Aubrey said, stunned, "I only met the fellow yesterday! How did I not see…"

The carriage was vanishing up the street. But through the back window Denzil could see Elise's uneasy face and Anna Delon's smiling one. Anger, outrage, and finally humor passed through him as Delilah's hand grasped his once more.

"Won't she go to prison after all?" Delilah asked.

"Not a conventional one. I think she might have changed sides, if Anna has saved a soul."

"Who is she?"

"That is a long story."

"She's Lord Tamar's sister," Aubrey said unexpectedly. "And she does turn up in the oddest places."

"She doesn't have Prince Karl in there too, does she?" Denzil asked uneasily.

"No," Delilah said, nodding to the left, where the unmistakable figure of Mr. Winslow, the magistrate, and his genuine constables were forcing the struggling Karl into a carriage.

"Thank goodness," Denzil said mildly. "He will stand trial under Hazburg law."

Absently, he caressed Delilah's palm with his thumb.

On his other side, Sir Julius said, "Did I hear you make an offer for my sister, Linfield?"

"I trust it meets with your approval," Denzil said.

"If it meets with Delilah's," Julius said evenly.

Delilah, blushing and beautiful in the lamplight, smiled and nodded.

"Then you may call upon me tomorrow," Sir Julius said.

It was generous, and suddenly not enough. "I would like to take Delilah for a walk on the beach. We have had a difficult day with much to discuss. I will escort her safely home."

Sir Julius's eyes narrowed. Aubrey, who had just engaged himself to Henrietta Gaunt, the most beautiful girl in Blackhaven or anywhere else, nudged his brother and received a scowl, quickly followed by a breath of laughter.

"Delly?" Sir Julius demanded.

"I would like a walk on the beach of all things," Delilah said, meeting her eldest brother's gaze squarely.

Sir Julius shrugged. His rather hard face softened. "Then bless you, my children," he said, and Delilah laughed, hurrying toward the shore with her hand firmly in Denzil's.

# Chapter Twenty

M ARJORIE MATCH FELT greatly daring as she escaped the inn alone. Mama and Gerald were quarreling again. At least, Mama was quarreling. Gerald, white faced and unaccustomedly stiff, would neither rise to her furious arguments nor give in. They were leaving Blackhaven for their country house, where their paternal grandmother was already in residence.

Grandmama, of course, was the one person Mama was afraid of. Marjorie didn't blame her. Grandmama was terrifying, but at least she would prevent any more schemes such as the pursuit of Lord Linfield.

Shuddering, Marjorie hurried toward the shore, drawn to the sea and the peace of nature. How wonderful to be alone and quiet and—

"Ouch!" said an aggrieved voice as she jumped down onto the sand and grasped something bony to steady herself.

Snatching back her hand with a gasp, she peered with some displeasure at the young man sitting on the sand who'd interrupted her solitude. He was rubbing his shoulder and scowling up at her.

"Miss Match?" he said, belatedly starting to rise. "You're not alone, are you?"

"Yes," she said defiantly, recognizing Gerald's friend Lord Tranmere. "But please, ignore me. Forget you have seen me."

She walked on hastily, her feet sinking into the soft sand with each step. After a moment, he appeared again beside her.

"Dash it all, I can't ignore you," he said. "I'm trying to be a gentleman again."

"Again?" she said, diverted in spite of herself. "Weren't you always a gentleman?"

"By birth, not by recent behavior. I've been told off."

"So have I," Marjorie admitted with some sympathy. "Your mother?"

His smile was twisted. "No. Friend of mine. I don't suppose you've ever had cause to really look at yourself and realize you despise what you see."

"Oh, yes," she said fervently.

He looked startled. "Really?"

"I give in to everyone. Do and say things I know in my heart are wrong because I'm too feeble to refuse."

"Your mother?"

"Mostly. Gerald has suddenly decided to stand up to her, which is good, I think, only the quarrels are hideous, and now I will have Mama on one side and Grandmama on the other and know I will please neither of them."

"That sounds rough," Tranmere said with unexpected sympathy.

She cast him another fleeting glance. "Yes... What will you do? Now that you are a gentleman again."

"Oh, go back to my family, I suppose, learn to be a responsible landowner and stop raking about the country upsetting everyone. Think I might have led Gerald a bit astray. Among other people. Glad he's finding his feet."

"You will, too. I hope it makes you happier."

He frowned. "You think I'm unhappy?"

"Aren't you?"

He closed his mouth. After a moment, he said, "You know, you're not just a pretty face, Miss Match."

"I'm not pretty at all," she said ruefully. "That is the problem.

I will never recover my family's fortunes."

"Not pretty?" Tranmere repeated, his frown deepening. "Of course you are! You're why I took Gerald up in the first place. Mind you, I got distracted. Not a very constant person. Did you like Linfield then?"

Unexpected delight that he thought her pretty warred with shame that he should know about the Linfield machinations. But then, Mama had scarcely kept them secret.

"Of course I like him," she said in a small voice. "He is so kind and clever and…terrifying."

"Terrifying?" Tranmere positively scowled. "What the devil did he do to you?"

"Nothing! That's the trouble. He says things I don't understand, and then I have no idea how to answer him or interest him. And although he is so handsome, he is really quite old, like one's father or the vicar, or *God…*"

Tranmere began to laugh, which for some reason made her feel better "Tell you what, Marjorie Match, why don't we be allies, you and me? I'll call on you in the country, and perhaps you and Gerald will call on my grandparents and me? We can teach other backbone, and you can make sure I'm making progress as a gentleman. What do you say? Friends?"

Marjorie had never really had a friend before. She had certainly never imagined one like the rakish Tranmere. But she wasn't afraid of him. In fact, she felt rather comfortable with him, and she liked the way his eyes smiled. And it seemed they understood each other.

She smiled. "Friends," she agreed, and took his proffered arm, only to yank him suddenly to a standstill. "Look," she breathed.

They had walked almost to the harbor, and there, coming down the harbor steps hand in hand, were none other than Lord Linfield and Miss Delilah Vale.

Marjorie found she was smiling. Tranmere turned her gently, and they began to walk back the way they had come.

IT WAS A pleasant evening, with no rain in the air, just a little salt spray on the breeze. The tide, on its way out, had left a few pools in the sand to negotiate in the dark, but Delilah didn't care. The gentle rushing of the waves was booth soothing and exciting, and the man at her side, his ungloved fingers gripping hers, filled her with such intense and sweet emotions that she never wanted these moments to end.

Perhaps everything was heightened by her earlier, frantic anxiety for him, and by the dangers of the evening at the theatre. She didn't know. She was just sure she needed this time with him, easing the hurt of the last couple of weeks, absorbing her new wonder and happiness.

They spoke at first of the evening's events and the couple who had absconded with Elise.

"They are a little shadowy," Denzil explained. "I first came upon them in Vienna, where they supplied me with information vital to the continuance of the congress. Though I admit I didn't know of her connection to Lord Tamar and Braithwaite... I suspect more than one government employs them, but I have known them to work only toward peace. They have an odd sympathy for the common man, and for women in adversity, which may explain their interest in Elise."

"I should think adversity would come off worst against that particular woman," Delilah observed.

"Now, perhaps. But don't you wonder how she came to be like this? And while her crimes are undeniable, she does have her own code of honor, even if you and I don't quite recognize it. I suspect Anna and Louis have found her both savable and useful. It may not excuse what she has done, but her contribution to the good of the world might well be greater with them than in prison. Or hanged."

"You have a very pragmatic view of the world."

"Not really. I have just learned the value of flexibility. In some cases. In others, I assure you, I am a positively high stickler."

She smiled at the change in tone. "Name your high stickles."

"Fidelity in love and marriage. Devotion to you, always."

His words seemed to flutter in her heart. She rested her head against his arm. "I do love you, Denzil," she whispered. "I never thought I was capable of this kind of love. I never even imagined it, to be honest. Not for me."

"I think you were too prickly to let it in. I won't deny there are better, more charming men than me who would have loved to win you. But on some profound level, I am yours and you are mine."

"I am…" She lifted her face, and he paused to kiss her.

It began gently, but there was far too much raw emotion between them for it to stay that way for long.

"Take me to the cave," she said suddenly against his lips. "Where we sheltered from the storm."

"I wanted you so much that day…"

"As I wanted you."

Her heart thundered with anticipation, for he knew she had just offered herself to him. It was in the tension of his stride, the sensual caress of his arm at her waist. He could not stop touching her, and she gloried in it.

The few courting couples from the town thinned to none on the empty beach. They carried no lantern, but the stars and the moon seemed to be on their side, shining in a cloudless sky to show them the way. Perhaps it was madness to climb the rocks in the dark, in her evening gown, but when her skirt tore, he made her laugh by promising to buy her another gown just like it.

"We can keep this one for special occasions," he whispered, lifting her into the cave and arranging her beneath him.

It seemed the most natural thing in the world to kiss him at once, and she did, with longing and passion. Somehow, he got his coat off and spread beneath her—along with her cloak, it gave her some protection from the hardness of the cave floor. And then she lost track of their garments, focused only on the pleasure of his caresses and the wonder of his arousal. She rejoiced in his heavy, ragged breath, the voluptuous touch of his open mouth on her skin, utterly lost in the physical delights that had melted inseparably into her love.

She gave herself with eager joy, and he took her in the same overwhelming spirit. Yet he hung by a thread to tenderness and care until the last savage, beautiful moment, when their ecstasy became one.

"Did I hurt you?" he whispered when he could speak again, and when she was capable of hearing more than the thundering of her own heart.

She shook her head, boneless with pleasure and wonder, and hung on to him tighter in case he moved. The rumpled clothes, tangled about their limbs, did not disturb her, but she would not lose the delight of his hot, damp skin beneath her fingers, the beat of his heart against hers, slowing gradually.

"The next time," he promised, "it will be in comfort, and I will make it last."

"Last?" she said, uncomprehending, overcome still by the strange, intimate beauty of what they had done.

He smiled, burying his mouth in hers once more. "Oh, yes..."

He turned her so that they could lie together in greater comfort. The locket that had been hidden under the bodice of her gown swung against his hand, and he caught it.

"This is pretty. Why do you hide it?"

"My mother gave me it." She knew he would understand that, and he did, for he kissed the locket and then her fingers.

After a moment, she took the locket from him and pressed the catch to open it. The folded paper she had put there sprang free. She pushed it into his hands.

"What is it?" he asked, for there was not nearly enough light in the cave to read it.

"Your first love letter. It just says, *Please*. I had a migraine when Betsy gave me it. I was blind and couldn't read it. When I did…somehow it changed everything. Like a puzzle falling into place, only I couldn't work out how to fix what I had done."

He stroked her hair. "You did. We both did. And there will be no more such misunderstandings."

"No," she whispered, pressing her cheek to his. "There won't."

They talked a little more then, of love and the future.

"What shall we do?" he asked. "Shall I seek out a post in London, or would you consider traveling with me?"

"I would love to travel with you," she said honestly, and knew from his smile that this was his preference too. "What of Elaine?"

"I think Elaine craves the stability of a permanent home," he said. "This last year has been hard on her health. I would see her settled in comfort in whatever place she desires, whether our own lands, London, or even Blackhaven. She will be happy to do so, now that you are my wife."

"I am not that quite yet."

"You are, in any way that matters. We have made our vows."

She liked that so much that she hugged him. After a moment, she repeated, *"Our own lands.* How wealthy are you, my lord?"

"Hideously. It's useful. But I am a landowner by accident, not by nature. I employ excellent stewards and follow my own inclination to serve in the Foreign Office. But we shall never be poor, and you will always have a home, with or without me."

She didn't want to think about being without him. "I will try to be a good wife and help you as I did my father. I shall do better without my prickles, as you call them."

He kissed her again. "You are perfect as you are, my Delly."

And that was so sweet to hear it was some time before they rose, replacing and straightening each other's clothes. Then they climbed down from the cave and walked happily on to Black Hill in the moonlight. And to Delilah, the whole world was perfect.

THEY WERE MARRIED four weeks later at what was meant to have been a quiet ceremony, for Delilah's bags were already packed to travel to London, where Denzil would report to his superiors and receive instructions for his next posting.

But their families and their circle of friends in Blackhaven proved to be too large. The quiet wedding breakfast at Black Hill inevitably expanded into a party, and when Roderick sat down at the pianoforte and began to play a lively waltz, the twins called loudly for the bride and groom.

Delilah and Denzil happened to be at opposite sides of the drawing room at the time, but the crowd between them rapidly moved aside so that they suddenly faced each other over the expanse of empty floor.

Roderick played a louder, more peremptory introduction to his waltz, making everyone laugh.

Denzil, equal to any social occasion, strolled elegantly across the room and bowed to his blushing bride. Smiling, he held out one hand. "Madam, may I have the honor? Will you dance?"

Tears and laughter mingled, trying to choke her. But there was only one thing she could do. And she wanted to with all her heart. She took his hand.

"Yes, sir, I will dance"

And she did.

# Epilogue

*Four years later*

L EONA VALE HUMMED to herself as she moved between the henhouses, collecting eggs for breakfast.

*Today is the day. Delilah is coming home!*

It was the first time in ages that they would all be together again at Black Hill—though, of course, their numbers had swelled with husbands and wives and children. Lucy and her Eddleston had arrived yesterday. Felicia and Bernard, Cornelius and Alice, Roderick and Helen, and Aubrey and Henrietta were all coming over in the afternoon and would stay for dinner. Antonia was even hosting a ball next week, and everyone who was anyone in Blackhaven would be there, from the Earl and Countess of Braithwaite to the visiting Lord and Lady Launceton and their family.

Before then, Leona would have to find a way to tell Lawrence her secret. Separation had been hard when he first went to university, but actually, it was good to stand on their own feet rather than on each other's. There was still an unbreakable bond, and she would not change that for the world. But now there was a change of emphasis, a possibility that it would not always be the most important bond in her life. Or his. And that was good, too. If it did not hurt Lawrence.

*Delilah is coming home…*

Delilah had always held a special place in their hearts, part mother, part sister, all friend. And she had found her soulmate in Lord Linfield. At least, Leona hoped that was true. It had been when she last saw Delilah more than a year ago, but…

"They're coming!" Lawrence yelled out of his bedroom window. "I can see the carriage!"

Leona bolted into the kitchen, depositing the eggs, unbroken more by luck than by care, and ran through to the front of the house, all but clashing with Lawrence in the doorway. Laughing, they exploded together through the front door.

In front of them, the formal garden now looked brilliant, alive with color and beauty, thanks to Antonia's eye and art.

Cornelius was riding hard across the fields toward them, his baby in one arm.

Julius and Antonia appeared beside Leona.

"I think that's Rod and Aubrey riding behind the carriages," Julius said, grinning. "They must have seen them arrive through the town." He moved forward for a better look. These days, his limp was almost gone, his injured leg troubling him only in very wet weather. And this summer, unlike the summer of 1816 that had seen so many of them married, was idyllically warm and sunny. "Yes, and Felicia's there, too!"

Leona laughed with sheer joy, desperate for Delilah to be there and yet afraid suddenly that she would be different. She lived such an exciting life, traveling the world with Linfield, the king's special ambassador, mixing with the most powerful of princes, politicians, and generals. Surely that would change anyone, just a little…

The carriage arrived at the gallop, and it had barely stopped before Delilah tumbled out, her arms already reaching for the twins in a massive, rare but wonderful Delly-hug, before she embraced Julius and Antonia, and Leona was left to gaze at her niece and nephew clutching their father's hands.

Denzil extricated himself from his children's clutches to shake

Julius's hand.

"You're twins," remarked George Talbot, beginning to smile.

"So are you," Lawrence said, gravely offering his hand while Leona gazed at little Delia.

"Hurray!" Delia said, laughing and seizing Leona by the hand.

Lawrence had dragged forward their stepbrother, Antonia's son, now a strapping lad of ten. "This is Edward. He's not a twin, but he's great fun despite that. Are you hungry? Our cook's making a *huge* breakfast…"

An hour later, the siblings were all together in the drawing room. Leona and Lawrence sat on the floor, their backs against Delilah's knees. She didn't object and no one told them off, even though they were nineteen and grown up. Edward had taken the Talbot twins—so known to distinguish them from the original Vale twins, the Eddleston twins, and the Aubrey twins—to explore the house, supervised by Antonia and Lord Linfield, and hindered no doubt by Julius's own lively offspring. Laughter drifted with thuds from various places, making Leona smile.

"And breathe," Felicia said. "While you can! Once all the children are here, it will be utterly hectic."

"Like our own childhood," said Aubrey. "How did our father transport us all over Europe—in wartime—without going insane?"

"Love, of course," Lucy said.

"And Delilah," Roderick said, raising his coffee cup to her. She looked surprised, and blushed. "Though Jules and I were older, she always took responsibility for the younger ones."

"She did," Julius agreed. "While I ran off to sea."

"You came back," Cornelius said. "We had a good childhood. I like to think our own children do, too, however unconventional we might be."

Delilah smiled, looking about her at the drawing room, which had changed little except in the small, comfortable ways that Antonia had initiated to make this home—for Leona and Lawrence as well as their own children.

"It's good to be home," Delilah said. "Do you ever look back on that summer in 1816 and think it was magical?"

"That wasn't magic, that was the twins," Aubrey said. "Interfering little—"

"Worked for you, didn't it?" Lawrence retorted.

"It did," Aubrey admitted. "Worked for all of us. In fact, I'll admit I'm dashed glad you manipulated and deceived us all into going to the ball that night. We all got married on the strength of it!"

"Except the twins," Delilah pointed out, ruffling their heads. "You're the only two of us left unmarried. Which of you will be the first?"

"Leona," said Lawrence promptly. He held her surprised gaze, and she realized he already knew her secret, that it wasn't a secret at all. Neither should it be. And he didn't mind. He didn't mind at all. His lips quirked, and she read his happiness for her. Everything really would be fine.

"We are lucky," Leona said, her voice only slightly husky. "So very lucky..."

"We are," Julius agreed. "Welcome home, my family."

# About the Author

Mary Lancaster lives in Scotland with her husband, three mostly grown-up kids and a small, crazy dog.

Her first literary love was historical fiction, a genre which she relishes mixing up with romance and adventure in her own writing. Her most recent books are light, fun Regency romances written for Dragonblade Publishing: *The Imperial Season* series set at the Congress of Vienna; and the popular *Blackhaven Brides* series, which is set in a fashionable English spa town frequented by the great and the bad of Regency society.

Connect with Mary on-line – she loves to hear from readers:

Email Mary:
Mary@MaryLancaster.com

Website:
www.MaryLancaster.com

Newsletter sign-up:
http://eepurl.com/b4Xoif

Facebook:
facebook.com/mary.lancaster.1656

Facebook Author Page:
facebook.com/MaryLancasterNovelist

Twitter:
@MaryLancNovels

Amazon Author Page:
amazon.com/Mary-Lancaster/e/B00DJ5IACI

Bookbub:
bookbub.com/profile/mary-lancaster